THE
MURDER
HOUR

BOOKS BY ALICE CASTLE

A Beth Haldane Mystery

The Murder Mystery

The Murder Museum

The Murder Question

The Murder Plot

The Murder Walk

The Murder Club

THE MURDER HOUR

ALICE CASTLE

bookouture

Published by Bookouture in 2022

An imprint of Storyfire Ltd.
Carmelite House
50 Victoria Embankment
London EC4Y 0DZ

www.bookouture.com

ISBN: 978-1-80314-496-2
eBook ISBN: 978-1-80314-495-5

To Ella and Connie, with love

ONE

Beth Haldane stood at the ornate front door, her tiny frame hunched against the mean November wind. She was certainly getting ample opportunity to examine this house's 'stunning original features', she thought, as she eyed the letterbox crossly. There was a dusty oval of stained glass but that was way above her head. She pushed the letterbox open instead and peered into the hall. It was dark and quiet. Too quiet, surely?

She rang the doorbell for the third time. She could hear the peal dying away somewhere inside. The estate agent had been even more fulsome than usual when describing the glories of this Edwardian gem and, fair enough, it was quite a chunk of a place. But she'd like to look at the inside as well as the outside. Where on earth was the blessed man?

The whole idea of looking at houses in Sydenham, Norwood and other areas outside the sanctified SE21 postcode was wearing pretty thin already, and she was only in week two of her search. Cancelled appointments, agents running late, mix-ups over rendezvous... this no-show was just the latest in a run of disasters which was more than enough to convince her it was all a terrible mistake. As if the very notion of leaving Dulwich wasn't giving her palpitations on its own.

She checked her phone yet again, in case a message had popped up with another lame excuse. Nope. Nothing at all. She dialled the office number quickly. A harassed-sounding woman picked up the call. Sounded like Beth had caught her just before she left. She explained the situation quickly. There was a lot of blathering and tutting at the other end of the phone, and some vague promises that the agent was bound to be along in a minute, if Beth could just be patient.

But Beth really couldn't be patient, not for a moment longer. There was steam coming out of her ears as it was. She didn't even want to see this house, not after a long day (well, several consecutive hours, at any rate) in the Wyatt's archives office, and then the prospect of having to find something to feed Jake – her increasingly finicky son – when she got home. She decided to play her trump card.

'Well, if you can't send someone out, I'll just abandon this. And no, I don't think there's another time I can manage to see the house. Not for the next three weeks or so, probably longer; a couple of months anyway,' she said.

The threat worked, as she'd known it would. The estate agent's life, as she'd discovered, was a simple one. Get people booked in, drag them around a few houses, and they'd obligingly fall for one and buy. But if you never got them over a real live threshold... well, it was game over. Everyone enjoyed browsing the online property websites, but few would actually buy until they'd seen a place in the flesh, as it were.

'I'll be there myself in five minutes,' said the woman, resigned to her fate and no doubt cursing her missing colleague.

Beth looked around. Having got her way so successfully, she was now rather regretting having forced things along. She could just have gone home and spared herself the bother. But that would have meant facing the enormous disappointment of her large and gorgeous boyfriend, Detective Inspector Harry York of the Metropolitan Police. He was the one pushing the move, on the perfectly sensible grounds that their current place was much too small.

And while Beth, as usual, was in more than two minds about it all, she definitely didn't want to face one of those more-in-sorrow-than-in-anger looks Harry put on. These worked brilliantly with his entire team at the Camberwell Police Station; with Jake; with her ancient Labrador, Colin; with her semi-feral black and white cat, Magpie; and, if the truth were told, with Beth too. She harrumphed a little and resigned herself to her fate.

She ambled over to the low garden wall at the front of the property, brushed it fruitlessly with her hand, then realised it was a bit pointless; her scruffy jeans had definitely seen worse. Perching uneasily, she felt the chill of the bricks beginning to seep into her nether regions. She hoped the woman had been telling the truth about the 'five minutes', and that it wasn't one of those elastic estate agent lies, like 'immaculate décor' for 1980s' time-warp kitchens, or 'some scope to improve' for tumbledown shacks. She felt she'd already seen it all in her fortnight of house-hunting.

Certainly, the road was as quiet as she'd been promised, which was a plus. There was no one in sight. And although this small patch of front garden looked pretty neglected, the neighbours had put in some effort on their side of the little wooden fence, which was waist-high to Beth, knee-high to anyone else.

Those were the good points. On the negative side, now she craned up to look at the house itself, it was pretty scary-looking. It was definitely redbrick and solid, as the details had promised, and a 'magnificent architectural example', though of what no one had quite said. To Beth's mind, it was a bit too gothic. And, from this angle, perhaps even a tad like a south-east London version of the Bates Motel. The stained-glass porthole in the front door, which Beth hadn't been able to reach despite all her efforts, appeared to have been expressly designed to keep light out rather than do anything to entice it in. And the sitting room windows, which she now got up and wandered over to inspect, had a supercilious look about their high arches. The closed curtains stopped her getting a better view inside.

Beth squinted at her watch yet again and tutted. She went and sat back down on the cold wall. This was all getting her exactly nowhere. Harry would not be pleased. Like a rufty-tufty sheepdog in a navy-blue peacoat, he was showing distinct signs of impatience to get them all rounded up under one roof. His enthusiasm was flattering, she acknowledged with a little shiver of surprised gladness, but he wouldn't be at all happy if she trailed back to Pickwick Road and admitted that she'd had no luck this evening.

Besides, the issue of space in her weeny house was now becoming pressing. What had been ample accommodation for a tiny single mum and her equally little boy was now struggling to contain them all. The trouble was that Harry, as well as being so tall Beth couldn't swear she'd ever clapped eyes on the top of his head, seemed to come complete with every Golden Age detective novel ever published. The downstairs of the house was now stacked with box after box of these tomes, which he appeared to be hopelessly addicted to. This was something that he had not thought fit even to whisper about before their discussion on living arrangements. Not that Beth actually remembered inviting him to move in. It had been more of a gradual, irresistible takeover.

Beth sighed. If the agent didn't show up, Harry would be giving her that sideways glance again. And seeing the property only from the outside wasn't going to cut it. He was going to want a full run-down of the place's merits. He'd picked it out himself during their last cruise through the Rightmove website.

She had to admit that looking at property was curiously addictive, though she remained, in her secret heart of hearts, pretty unconvinced that leaving Dulwich was any kind of solution to their problems. She now got alerts on her phone when anything came in that suited their price bracket. Every time, she surprised herself by opening them up with all the enthusiasm of a child with a new Christmas present.

This particular place had really appealed to Harry. Maybe because it was a very tall, solid and rather forbidding house, she now thought a little sourly. Or maybe because it was very close to the station, near a clutch of bus stops, even a stone's throw from a Tesco Metro. Beth had to concede these were all excellent things. Yet her beloved Pickwick Road, where they currently lived, was also beautifully close to North Dulwich Station, there were bus stops aplenty at the top of the road and they were absurdly close to two food shops. Mind you, they weren't exactly *useful* shops. They were both delicatessens, which were super-handy if you'd run out of buffalo mozzarella at £15 a ball, or had a massive smoked paprika emergency, but were not nearly so great if you actually needed bog-standard cheddar and change from a fiver. But she wasn't going to dwell on that in any discussions with Harry.

Oh, what was she supposed to do now? She got up again, feeling numb, and shifted from foot to foot, wrapping her thin jacket around herself in an attempt to keep warm. Should she carry on waiting, and risk hypothermia? Or maybe she should just cut her losses, and go home to face the music and Jake's empty stomach.

She had wandered back to the front door and was just lifting the brass flap over the letterbox again, having another squint into the dark hall to see if she'd missed anything, when a hand tapped her sharply on the shoulder. Beth jumped at least a foot.

'You must be Beth,' trilled a tall girl – unnecessarily tall, as far as Beth was concerned. She had finally turned up. 'Lovely to meet you. Sorry we're a tiny bit behind schedule, it's been *crazy*,' she added. 'And I have simply no idea what's happened to Richard.'

Beth instantly bristled. It was hardly an apology. 'We' weren't behind schedule; this girl's estate agency was just plain disorganised. She was pretty sure the market hadn't gone wild in the short time that had elapsed between her making the appointment and this late hour. But never mind. The girl was here at last, and they could finally get on.

'Good to meet you,' she said, extending a hand.

The girl looking back at her was so typical of Dulwich, Beth could only imagine that one of the reasons she was late was because she'd simply been unable to find Sydenham on the map. Although she wasn't quite wearing the regulation white jeans – they were now entering the autumn months when these could finally be put away – she was wearing a posh cashmere version of the Breton-striped sweater that was the other staple garment of the Dulwich Yummy. She had accessorised it with large diamond earrings, a private school accent and a beautifully cut navy trench coat – the sort that popped up in the 'capsule wardrobe' articles that Beth hopelessly failed to emulate. The girl now flicked her eyes very slightly up and down Beth's own random assembly of clothes and readjusted her smile. A series of noughts seemed to be vanishing off her estimation of Beth's net worth. If a sale wasn't likely to be made, she needn't try so hard.

'Well, let's just press on, shall we, Bel?' The woman turned, suddenly business-like and as keen as Beth to get this over with. She fished out a huge bunch of keys and set about finding the right one.

'*Beth*, that's my name, actually,' Beth said as firmly as she could. She was, after all, the customer here, and felt she could insist on a bit of respect.

'Absolutely,' the girl said brightly but vaguely, hardly even listening, all her attention on rooting through her keys. 'Ah, gotcha,' she said with a smile, holding up the right one to Beth. But as she steadied her hand on the doorknob before fitting the key into the lock, it turned smoothly. And the door fell open.

They looked at each other – Beth puzzled; the girl astonished.

'Oh,' the girl said slowly. 'Just think, you've been waiting outside all this time and it was actually unlocked.'

Thanks for rubbing that in, thought Beth, but a deep frown had appeared on the estate agent's face.

'That really shouldn't be happening,' she went on. 'All our properties are very carefully secured. Usually...'

They both peered into the darkened hallway. As Beth had suspected, the stained-glass porthole did nothing at all to add any light to the mix. She couldn't see much, only that the floor was littered with junk mail; the standard pizza leaflets and catalogues of clothes even Beth recognised as strange and frumpy, modelled by women whose expressions conveyed intense delight.

She looked quickly over her shoulder, but the street was still deserted. No one else was mad enough to be standing outside in this biting chill, or even to be walking briskly past.

The two women now exchanged another glance. There was suddenly a bit more fellow feeling between them. Whatever their obvious differences, they had both once upon a time been little girls listening to cautionary tales about the big bad wolf. But Beth was, by now, accustomed to being bold. Yes, it was a bit creepy that the door was open, but it was very cold on the doorstep. And pointless. She had other stuff she needed to be doing. The sooner she ticked this chore off her list, the sooner she could get on to the rest. It didn't sound that enticing, and it wasn't, but it was the way forward.

She took another look at the estate agent and then stepped over the threshold. Immediately something about the echoey feeling inside made Beth sure the place was deserted. She breathed a bit more easily.

The estate agent walked in behind her and reached automatically for the light switch. It clicked, but nothing happened. Was the electricity off? Exactly how long had this place been empty, anyway? Beth tried to remember the precise wording beneath the pictures on the website. Had there been any of those unspoken clues? 'Needs love and attention', for example, which could generally be decoded as meaning 'a wreck abandoned for years'. There had certainly been nothing she'd picked up on as meaning the previous owners had decamped, which would once have been very unusual in London. For years, vendors had been tied up in great long camel trains of buyers, and one slip would cause umpteen sales to fall through. But everything had changed recently. Working from home meant you didn't have to be tied into the mad London property market any more, and there had been quite an exodus from the city.

This creepy place certainly seemed to be chain-free and empty. Beth looked round with a shiver.

The estate agent now stepped forward in the gloom, suddenly more intrepid even than Beth. Then Beth realised the girl probably just knew the layout of the place. Doubtless she'd been here before – probably many times, judging by the deserted air which suggested the place had languished on the market for ages.

Beth fumbled with her phone, finally getting it onto torch mode, and followed the agent. What about the front door, though? They couldn't really leave it swinging open, could they? It was an invitation to anyone passing on the street. Looking out, she didn't see anyone in either direction – the neighbourhood really seemed to be every bit as quiet as promised – but you never knew. She pulled the door so that it was almost shut but not quite, and looked around as best she could with the phone's puny beam. All was silent, dark and still. Goodness knew what the estate agent girl was up to, but now she was nowhere to be seen. Where on earth had she disappeared to?

What was the best thing to do? If it was all going to be in total darkness, Beth really wouldn't be able to get any idea of what it was like and whether it would be a viable option for her little family. At the moment it all just seemed a bit spooky, and she felt uneasy. Not the best vibe to be getting from a potential future home.

She could still give up on the place. Drive back home, as quickly as she could. She was tempted, but Harry... The downward tug of his mouth would say it all. No, she might as well have a look while she was here. Maybe a bulb had just blown in the hall. If the other lights were working, then she'd be able to get a proper look at the place. At least then she could cross it firmly off Harry's list.

There was a door to the left of the hall and Beth opened it slowly, cautiously. It didn't seem quite right to be wandering around on her own, but the estate agent might as well have dropped off the face of the earth.

This must be the sitting room she had been trying to see into from the outside. It had a musty smell. The light here went on at the first time of trying, thank goodness. Beth's shoulders dropped immediately, making her realise how tense she'd been.

She was dazzled for a second after the gloom, but then soon took in some lovely coving, a pretty ceiling rose and reasonable décor. There were square sooty marks on the walls where pictures had been removed, but the pink paint, though not something Beth would have chosen herself, was welcoming. The windows looked less sinister from this side, shrouded in thick velvet curtains in a slightly darker shade of wilted rhubarb.

The room was furnished with a shabby but comfortable-looking sofa and a matching pair of easy chairs, but it was very clear from the feeling of dusty disuse that the original owners were long gone. The telly that the three-piece suite had no doubt been positioned around was conspicuous by its absence, leaving the chairs looking like a group of worshippers in search of a deity.

Still, it was a perfectly nice room, and Beth's own equally beaten-up sofa would fit right in. She could even picture Magpie and Colin fighting over who got prime position on it when her back was turned. Maybe she'd go crazy and upgrade their settee a bit, if and when they did get a new house. But how long would it look smart with the pets draped all over it? Much as she loved them, they didn't help with her attempts to be house-proud. Beth determinedly shut her eyes to the fact that other people with multiple dogs and cats seemed to manage.

She sauntered out through the dark hall, which seemed less oppressive now she knew that some of the lights were working. At the end must be the kitchen. But just before it, there was another door. She pushed at it. It was a small room, which in her grandmother's day would probably have been called the 'back parlour' and reserved strictly for formal entertaining. It had about it a lingering smell of best behaviour.

There was no furniture, but Beth knew what she'd put here, if she moved in – several hundred mouldering whodunits. And her own not-insubstantial library of books. In these days of Kindles, both she and Harry were unfashionably dependent on old-school tomes. She still found something comforting in handling a real live book that, so far, a device could not replace. Although the sheer volume of Harry's collection was a very strong argument in favour of digitalisation.

Beth stepped out of the room and jumped another mile,

almost colliding with the estate agent. She'd been silently hunched over her phone in the shadows of the passageway. Beth was surprised. Would she be getting really important work messages, so late at night? But there was no reason to suppose they were official texts, she realised. Maybe the girl just had a very active social life.

She sniffed, and wondered how exactly to say, 'Ah, *there* you are,' without sounding even more disapproving than she felt, but the estate agent forestalled her.

'Ah, there you are,' the girl said, quite unabashed, as though she'd been searching high and low for Beth, which both knew was not the case. 'Been enjoying a little look around?'

Beth wasn't sure how to reply. Surely the whole purpose of her visit was to look around? But she hadn't been enjoying it that much.

'Sort of,' she was reduced to muttering. But she needn't have worried. Transparently not listening, the girl poked away at her phone for a few seconds more before snapping effortlessly back into work mode.

'So, here we have such a useful reception room. Perfect as a little study or maybe a playroom for the children,' she said, gesturing back to the room Beth had just left.

'Hmm,' Beth replied, thinking some response was called for.

'And really excellent, of course, for homework, or maybe as a dining or hobby room...' the girl continued, clearly hoping to strike lucky and hit on whatever Beth had set her heart on.

It must be so hard being an estate agent, Beth thought. Could you really persuade people to buy something as big as a house on impulse? Surely the purchaser had to feel some sort of visceral connection to the house, to make such a huge commitment? It definitely wasn't happening for her yet.

She gave a last look around the room, smiled politely, and made it clear that she wanted to get on with the tour by stepping further down the hall. The estate agent followed, then deftly overtook her so she was shepherding Beth along to the end of the passageway. This must be the kitchen – the last room on the ground floor but, as far as Beth was concerned, the most important one.

A door glazed with that weird bubbly glass that had been such a thing in the 1970s swung open, and Beth automatically reached again for the light switch. There was a rather anxious pause as an ancient neon strip in the centre of the ceiling decided whether or not to bother showing up for work. Finally, it erupted into life with an angry buzz and threw its unforgiving glare over a bashed wooden table and chairs, an old fridge which was taller than Beth, a grimy-looking cooker and a low, wide window facing over what must be the back garden but was now just an oblong of blackness.

Beth dreaded to think how awful she must look in this harsh, all-seeing white glow. Even the estate agent, with her Dulwich gloss, suddenly looked tired and unkempt under its forensic beam. If Beth did buy this house, the first thing she'd do would be to rip out the neon and put some much subtler lighting in.

'And now here we have the true heart of the home,' the estate agent was burbling. 'A lovely eat-in kitchen, as you can see, with plenty of room for all the family.'

Beth looked at her sharply. The girl had no idea how many there were in Beth's family. There could have been twenty Haldanes, for all she knew. If there had been, they certainly wouldn't have squeezed in all that easily. It wasn't an enormous kitchen, by any means. Mind you, it was fine, and definitely more than adequate for three. Maybe she'd even get round to more entertaining if they lived here. Beth shuddered slightly and tried to take in the room's proportions while the estate agent wittered on, making hugely enthusiastic noises about the perfectly ordinary sink and draining board, and even the blinds, which in Beth's view were horrible.

The smell of bygone casseroles lingered in the air, probably trapped in the fabric of those nasty blinds. Someone had had quite a thing about roast dinners. But these familiar English smells were mingled with something sharper, more recent, that Beth couldn't quite put her finger on. She supposed it was nothing that a vat or two of bleach wouldn't put right. With that, and an equally large vat of paint, new windows, units, flooring and appliances, it might all be quite nice.

It was dark and very silent here at the back of the house, far from the street, which was not exactly jumping anyway. Beth was used to more footfall, living as close to the centre of Dulwich Village as she did. Her road was hardly a thoroughfare – it was a little loop which ran behind the main street – but there was always a comforting sense that people were coming and going nearby. People that she knew.

All her neighbours were friends by now. Lots of their children had babysat Jake, and everyone knew Colin and Magpie. Everyone had known and mourned James, and they all now accepted Harry, too. It was going to be hard to move, to build up all that goodwill again somewhere new, particularly as Beth wasn't a chatting-over-the-garden-fence sort of person. She'd become embedded by osmosis, without really trying. Could she face a couple of decades – at least – of feeling like a newbie before she eventually settled down somewhere like here?

Suddenly there was a rumble and then a hum from the corner of the room, and Beth jumped yet again. She seemed to be going for her personal best record tonight. But it was only the venerable fridge cranking through some well-worn cooling cycle. The estate agent raised an eyebrow at her and Beth's face flamed; she knew she was being silly. She needed to get a grip, and not leap out of her skin at the faintest sound. But an empty house could do that.

And, even though there were two of them here in the

kitchen, she had the feeling that the rest of the silent house was breathing, listening, watching. For something. But for what?

She forced herself to think dispassionately about the place as a potential new home. The whole downstairs area had a similar layout to Beth's own house, though it lacked the quaint angles that gave Pickwick Road homes their quirky charm. On the other hand, it had a spaciousness which she had to admit could compensate for that. The ceilings were so high that looking up almost gave her vertigo. Harry would definitely have enough headroom here, and he would enjoy the sense of space. His books would also look great in that small sitting room. But could she see herself here?

She squeezed her eyes shut, thinking back to this morning's breakfast. She, Harry and Jake had been jammed in, as usual, around the table that was slightly too large and meant that to access the fridge, you had to sidestep like someone making their way across a precipice. Of course, this was easier for some of them than for others. Nothing Harry did was dainty, and he complained often and loudly of the bruises he collected on the way from one end of the kitchen to the other. There would certainly be more elbow room in this place.

Their table would have room to breathe here. And you'd be able to push a chair out without risking kneecapping someone else or denting the wall. These fitted cupboards weren't inspiring, but they might be able to do something clever like change the doors or give them a coat of paint. Oh, who was she kidding? She'd had two tins of B&Q's finest magnolia cluttering up her hall for more than a year, waiting for her to dip a brush in and spruce up the hall, and it still hadn't happened. She was realistic enough to know that now, the moment might never come.

And Harry didn't seem any more enthused about painting and decorating than she did. He'd been passing the tins by for almost as long as she had. Not for the first time, she thought wistfully of all those women whose other halves were constantly surprising them by fashioning shelves out of off-cuts or mending stuff with one hand tied behind their back. Although Harry certainly had his plus points, a domestic god he wasn't. Any more than she was a domestic goddess. And after all the upheaval of a move, would either of them seriously be in any state for DIY? No, they'd have to get someone in, and that would be pricey. Oh, well. Time enough to worry about that when and if they ever took the plunge.

Meanwhile, her eyes skimmed the kitchen. What-ifs cost nothing, and she was quite enjoying projecting herself and her loved ones into this new arena. It was harmless enough, wasn't it?

Wait a minute. Her eyes snagged on a door over in the far corner, near the sink. Beth looked at it hopefully. It couldn't be, could it? She'd always wanted a walk-in larder, somewhere to stow all the packets and jars that ended up infesting her kitchen counters, particularly with two slapdash males about the place who never seemed to put anything away 'in case they needed it later'. If it really was a nice big store cupboard, then all of a sudden this house did have distinct possibilities. Strange how one little thing could sway you, change your mind.

And there were advantages in not having the owners on site, she realised. It meant that, as long as the estate agent didn't put up too much of a fuss, she could snoop around to her heart's content. Normally she balked a little at having to ask if she could shove her nose into every nook and cranny. But this girl didn't look as though she'd stop her having a tiny peek. In fact, the more Beth thought about it, the more she realised the estate agent had gone into a curiously passive mode. After her initial spiel about the nasty blinds, she was now standing quietly in the middle of the kitchen, peering again at her phone like someone in a trance.

Beth stepped boldly over to the door and made to pull it

open. Just before she did, a hand came down on hers. The estate agent had come back to life.

'Let's go and have a look around upstairs, shall we?' she said, eyes wide. 'Three double bedrooms and a boxroom. I'm supposed to say four bedrooms, but really you couldn't swing a dead cat in there,' she said, in what was clearly an uncharacteristic moment of candour.

Or was it a double bluff, Beth wondered. A display of honesty that was meant to make her believe they were on the same side?

'Why would I want to swing a cat, alive or dead?' Beth asked with distaste. 'I'd rather finish looking at the kitchen.'

'Dead? Did I say dead? Ha-ha, no, that would make it Schrödinger's boxroom, wouldn't it?' The girl was getting quite carried away with her own brilliance. And, for some reason, she seemed very keen to chivvy Beth out of the kitchen, taking another look around and sniffing. 'In here, surely you'd just rip all this out, redo everything?' She looked at the tired décor disapprovingly, as though it had personally let her down quite badly.

'Um, well,' said Beth, not willing to reveal the fact that buying a place like this was going to virtually clean them out, leaving precious little budget to spare for ripping. They'd have to hang onto her magnolia paint for dear life. 'All the same, the cupboard is a fixture, isn't it? That won't change, no matter how, ah, creative we're going to be with the décor. So, I'm just going to...' she said, a little breathlessly, continuing to pull on the door handle. It seemed to be stuck.

The estate agent sighed. 'Here, let me,' she said, seeming almost as unimpressed with Beth's efforts as she was with the cupboards.

Beth let her hand drop and the woman gave the door a sharp tug, causing it to fly open at last. 'There,' she said, with slightly self-righteous satisfaction. 'Just needed a little bit of muscle.'

Trying not to feel that her biceps were being dissed, Beth nodded and inched forward to crane into the depths of the cupboard. And then, just a moment later, really wished she hadn't.

With a horrible slithering sound, something bulky toppled inside the cupboard and started to fall towards her. She jumped away by reflex, cannoning into the estate agent, who squealed indignantly.

Beth turned to apologise, hardly able to explain her jittery overreaction, but realised that she'd entirely lost her audience. The estate agent was staring, like someone transfixed, right behind her.

Beth wheeled round. Like a flag unfurling in the most casual slow motion, a hand flopped forward out of the cupboard, almost touching Beth's little pixie boots, white fingers splayed. This time, she leapt away as though she had been shot, and whacked painfully into the sink. She pressed herself back against it, but she couldn't get any further away from the thing if she tried.

The estate agent skittered across the tiled floor, too, fingers pressed to her mouth, and they cowered together.

But the horror didn't stop there. As if the pale, lifeless hand, which almost seemed to be reaching out across the floor towards them, wasn't dreadful enough, there was now another ghastly noise from the cupboard. If there was a hand, there must be a body. And it seemed to be hell-bent on joining the party.

Beth looked around frantically. Was there anywhere she could run to? To get away from this horror? But it was too late. Between the sink and the estate agent, she was cornered. As she watched, mesmerised, the head and shoulders of a man followed the hand out of the cupboard and hit the tiled floor with a nasty crack.

Beth winced reflexively, but it didn't take her long to realise that whoever this was, they were now well beyond feeling pain. Meanwhile, the momentum caused by the sudden opening of the cupboard made the body slide a little way across the shiny floor, towards her. Then it came to a dead stop.

She had a horrible feeling that the owner of the house had just turned up.

TWO

Beth sat on the wall outside the house in Sydenham, her hands wrapped around a Styrofoam cup of coffee. Normally, she would have worried just a tad about the effect on the planet from yet another disposable cup. But at the moment she was many carbon footprints away from caring, and very grateful for the warmth and a cloying sweetness that otherwise would have had her turning up her small nose. Harry's arm, clamped round her shoulder, didn't hurt either. The rest of his attention, though, was definitely elsewhere, tersely directing SOCOs into the house, barking instructions at his hapless sidekick Narinda Khan, and generally acting as though someone had committed this murder with the sole intention of pissing him off.

'Boss, what do you want us to do with the back-garden containment?' came a nervous enquiry from a lad who looked much too young to be even asking for a Playmobil policeman set, let alone let alone wearing the uniform and doing the job.

'Blithering idiots,' Harry muttered, perfectly audibly.

The little policeman looked as though he might burst into tears, and Beth, despite her frozen state, felt for him.

'I'll have to go. This bunch has no idea which way is up,'

Harry said to Beth, getting off the wall. Immediately, he was all business, though he did press a tiny kiss into the side of her ponytail before stomping off along the plastic sheeting now covering the hallway.

Beth felt fleetingly sorry for whoever it was who'd committed the major blunder. The baby policeman was just collateral damage. Someone, somewhere, had fucked up royally. She knew exactly how it felt to be in their shoes, and it wasn't fun. She shivered, alone, and wondered what to do next. The estate agent had already been led off, shaking and crying, to make a full statement at the police station. At least Beth's exalted status as girlfriend of the Senior Investigating Officer meant she could avoid that duty until the morning.

She put the cup down on the bit of the wall that Harry had just vacated, and held her hand up. It quivered like a leaf in the strong November wind. She tried the other one. Even worse. At least both were a lot less pale than that ghastly white claw she'd just seen. She shuddered. Maybe she wasn't quite up to driving home yet. Harry had said Jake was adamant that he'd be fine on his own for a bit. Beth didn't like to leave him too long, but nor did she want to crash the car on the short journey back. She needed to get herself under control.

She looked speculatively towards the still-open front door of the house. With light now blazing from the scene-of-crime rigs and a hum of activity within, it was bustling with life. Unlike the poor old householder, of course – or whoever he was. Don't think about that. Don't think about it, Beth told herself sternly. But what could she do as a distraction?

Almost without thinking, she found she was on her feet and wandering back into the house. The person with the clipboard, who was supposed to be taking the names of everyone coming and going, was in the kitchen being yelled at by Harry, she could hear him loud and very clear. That just gave her time to pop into the sitting room again and have another look around.

Why not? It was warmer than shivering her fringe off outside and, to be honest, this was actually the best house she'd looked at so far. And wouldn't a recent death like this one take absolutely thousands off the price?

Oh my God, thought Beth, that's really sick. Maybe I'm getting a bit numb to death and destruction these days. She couldn't help gazing about, though, even as the thought struck her. That coving was really nice. The rose colour scheme wasn't her thing at all, but if they painted it a soft yellow? And maybe even bought a new sofa...

No, there was no point even considering this house. Beth would never be able to get over the horror of the kitchen. That moment, with that *hand*, must have taken years off her life. She didn't want to replay it in her head every time she reached into the cupboard for a tin of beans. And with Jake's refusal to try anything fancy, that was going to be an almost daily occurrence. Unless they followed the last piece of advice the estate agent had given her before turning into a gibbering wreck, and just removed the whole kitchen, including the cupboard, and started from scratch? Would that be enough to banish the memories of that pale, splayed starfish of a thing, slithering out into the neon light? Beth shuddered.

More to the point, didn't she really owe a debt to the poor person who'd been crushed into that cupboard with all the casual contempt that Beth treated her own bags for life? She really ought to be thinking about him, instead of measuring up rooms in her head and thinking about new curtains. She'd assumed the poor man was the owner. But he'd looked very young, in the split second she'd seen his purplish face before rapidly averting her gaze. Much younger than her. Maybe early twenties? Could he really have afforded a huge place like this, at such an age? Beth tutted at herself. It was impossible to think about people's houses without an element of judgement. You could take the girl out of Dulwich, but you couldn't take

Dulwich out of the girl, it seemed. There were loads of reasons why someone in their twenties might already be a householder.

But there was another possibility entirely. Beth absently perched on the arm of one of the dusty old easy chairs and thought. Maybe he'd just been in the wrong place at the wrong time? Had he only gone to the house in the first place in order to get it ready to show to her? The tetchy girl estate agent had shown up to replace someone, after all. Was he the original estate agent? Wasn't it then, by one remove, actually Beth's fault he was dead? The awful thing was that she couldn't even remember his name. They'd had a couple of quick conversations, but all the estate agents, male or female, sounded very similar. Chirpy, upbeat, deeply insincere. And in his case, unreliable, she'd thought, given the fact he hadn't been there to meet her at all. But maybe he'd been unavoidably detained... in the cupboard?

Beth really didn't want to take on any more guilt. Like most single working mothers, she was already racked by enough doubts and fears to keep even the busiest psychoanalyst in Dulwich going for years. Yet there was something inescapably sad about the death of this person and the way he'd been shoved so unceremoniously into that larder, to moulder away with the dried-up cleaning cloths. If Beth hadn't been so nosy, he'd still be there now, a horrible moving-in present for someone else.

She thought about it, even as she had a look at the really rather fine fireplace. One corner of her mind was musing on the moulded marble surround, the rest was acknowledging something even more weighty. It looked as though the universe, yet again, was foisting a corpse on her. And more or less telling her it was her duty to set about solving the puzzle of why it had ended up where it had.

Beth sighed. She had come to some decisions. She walked to the doorway, took a quick glance in both directions and tiptoed towards the stairs. Her feet rustled terribly on the forensic sheeting. With one hand on the banister, she paused, just to see if anyone would stop her. She could still hear Harry thundering away in the kitchen, but there was no one else in sight. They must all be inside the cupboard.

She suppressed an entirely inappropriate smile and climbed the first couple of stairs. They creaked ominously, and she paused again, expecting someone to pop up and forbid her access to the upper floor. But there was no one. Emboldened, she sneaked up the rest of the flight as silently as she could, and took stock on the landing. All the doors were open; it looked as though the place had already been searched.

She stuck her head through the first doorway. There were two SOCOs inside, wearing overalls that made them look like Primark spacemen. They were flicking away with brushes and fingerprint powder, but in a curiously desultory way. Beth waved. They both waved back, seeming glad of the distraction.

'How's things, Beth?' said one. She realised it was an officer she'd bumped into at one of her other crime scenes.

I really must get a new hobby, she thought, as she exchanged a bit of chit-chat.

'Erm, just having a look around, if that's OK?' Beth asked.

'Sure, anything that's OK with the big boss is fine with us.' The two SOCOs smiled.

Beth grinned without saying a word. That didn't count as lying, right?

Next door there was a stained mattress on a bed, dingy curtains hanging droopily, fitted wardrobes with doors that didn't quite close – it was all deeply depressing. Beth was about to turn and check out the family bathroom, which she guessed would be equally grim, when she saw something on the far side of the bed, nearest the window. It was hidden from the doorway, but there was a little huddle of belongings here. A couple of sweatshirts, a tangle of underwear, jeans. Some copies of the freebie newspaper *Metro*, which infested all the London stations. Even a couple of old Costa coffee cups.

Had someone been living here? She looked around reflexively, then stirred the heap with the tip of her boot. Under the sweatshirts was a laptop, the latest Mac model, if she wasn't mistaken. It was very pricey – she knew, because she'd idly browsed them online recently, in case she won the lottery she never got round to entering. How odd to see it lying here, abandoned.

But wait, could it belong to the body downstairs? And how, actually, had he been dressed? Beth really didn't want to have to cast her mind back. The memory came distressingly adorned with sound effects: the unearthly slithering in the cupboard; the crack of the head against tiles. But what had the corpse been wearing? If he had been the estate agent, she would have expected a smart shirt, maybe a tie, possibly one of those ill-fitting suits the breed seemed strangely drawn to. If he had been the house owner, something more casual.

She squeezed her eyes closed, concentrating as hard as she could. It was no good, she wasn't getting any details. The best she could do was dark clothing – but then, who didn't wear that? She looked down at herself. Dark jumper, dark jeans, dark boots. On a dark night, she'd disappear completely, which was rather the idea. Could these items on the floor belong to the body downstairs? And what did that mean he was doing here? Surely the real owner of the house wouldn't have kept his stuff in a sad little puddle, as though he were only there for a night. It was all very odd.

She abandoned the idea of looking at the bathroom or even the other bedroom. All she wanted to do now was leave. But before she went, she stuck her head round the door where the SOCOs were still busy.

'There's a pile of stuff in the next room you might want to see,' she said, raising her eyebrows.

'On it, thanks!' The officers raised their hands, again seeming pleased to be distracted. It was such painstaking work, and so much of it must be fruitless.

Beth decided to leave them all to it. There were so many aspects of an investigation that the police covered more efficiently than she ever could. All that dedicated work sifting through information that she didn't have access to. She was in awe at the way Harry's team got their heads down and tackled a mass of data that made even her ironing pile look as tiny as one of the nascent pimples on Jake's nose.

Having this bit of time to wander around had clarified something for her. There was just no way she could buy a house where someone had so recently met such a violent end. And better yet, she realised with a spark of joy that was unbecoming with a corpse downstairs, this whole business had probably given her a free pass out of ever looking at another property again.

She knew Harry was feeling dreadful. He'd more or less forced her out into the night to look at the place that was now no doubt going to be known as the Sydenham House of Death, if she knew anything about the ghoulish ways of the local journalists. But she had also realised that, although she'd never met the luckless estate agent/owner in life, their meeting once he was so thoroughly dead was a turning point for her. Maybe he would have been killed even if she hadn't wanted to view the house this evening. Maybe his time was up for some other reason. But she was sure of one thing. She had to find out what had happened. She owed him that much.

THREE

Beth was taking shelter in Jane's Café in Dulwich Village. Nowadays, Jake liked to walk himself to school. Sometimes, she tried to keep up with his lengthening strides as he loped from their home to the glorious gates of Wyatt's, but usually she just let him get on with it. She remembered how appallingly embarrassing parents had been when she was his age – although, of course, her parents actually *had* been embarrassing, and she wasn't. But still.

This morning, though, with the horrific events of last night so fresh in her mind, she'd insisted they walk together. Yet when it had come to it, she had left him at the entrance to find his way to his classroom, and she had done an abrupt U-turn herself. She hadn't felt quite ready to tackle her in-tray in the archives office. When did she ever? a small voice asked, but she shushed it.

A quick phone call later, she was waiting for her best friend, Katie, at a table for two. Beth badly needed this comfort after last night's grisliness. And besides, she'd have to go down to Camberwell Police Station later to make an official statement. As she knew to her cost, that was always a lengthy process involving rock-hard institutional chairs and machine coffee (that actually tasted like machines), if she was very lucky. And probably some grumpy stares from her beloved. He hated it when she infringed his workspace, even if he'd commanded that she show herself. She definitely deserved a little treat to set herself up for all that.

Her shoulders were hunched as she sat in Dulwich's trendiest café and attempted to blot out the barrages of conversation coming at her from all directions. She might have had a terrible time last night, but for the rest of Dulwich it was business as usual, and that business was loud, proud and not bothered who knew every detail of it.

'So, I had to sack Greta yesterday,' shrilled a young mum on the table by the door. 'Well, I'd had enough of her moaning about how difficult it is to get settled status here. Honestly, it's not like I made the rules, is it? And how hard can it be to fill in a couple of forms, huh.' There were nods of sympathy all around. Politics, it seemed, were really playing havoc with staffing levels.

As usual, Jane's was full to the rafters. There were mummies who'd just been relieved of their charges by the lovely local schools, au pairs who hadn't yet started on their mountains of chores, and now even the odd person attempting to 'work from home' by plugging their laptops and themselves into Jane's electricity and caffeine supplies.

Beth looked at them with covert astonishment. How could they possibly concentrate with this hubbub all around? But maybe they were the sort who liked white noise. She knew that the constant carousel of chat about wildly expensive holidays, the impossibility of the last round of school entrance exams, and the die-hard rumour that Waitrose was finally going to open a branch up the road, would drive her crackers within minutes. It was fine for a coffee – sometimes – but as a working environment? Beth much preferred the deep peace of the archives office, where the only sound was Colin's occasional fruity snore.

She looked up for the umpteenth time and was finally rewarded by seeing, not yet another glamorous forty-something woman in a suede biker jacket, high-heeled boots and effortless skinnies, but the familiar and beloved blonde halo of hair and happy smile that could belong only to Katie, her perpetual ray of sunshine. Katie also looked immaculate, as every woman in Dulwich apart from Beth always did, but that wasn't the first thing you noticed about her. It was the aura of sane, steady love-liness which lit up life for her many friends.

Today, Katie just held her arms out for Beth as she reached her table, and her little friend, despite an instinctive dislike of public displays, got up and melted straight into them, horrifying herself by bursting into noisy sobs.

'I'm sorry, I'm sorry,' Beth mumbled, trying to get hold of herself as Katie hugged her tighter and told her not to be so silly.

Finally, they broke apart and Katie stepped over to the counter to get the coffees, not to mention a few paper napkins to mop up with. Beth knew her friend was giving her time to drag her dignity together, and she blessed her for it. She hunted through her ratty handbag for tissues, eventually disinterring one that didn't look as though it had been ravaged too much by life and Colin. By the time Katie was back with a tray including two massive brownies, Beth was past even the hiccupping stage, managed a watery smile, and hid the soggy tissue under her thigh.

Katie pushed the napkins over, and Beth dabbed at her eyes in as dainty a fashion as she could manage, hoping against hope that not too many people had seen her dreadful display, and that it wouldn't be all round Dulwich by lunchtime.

'Just had breakfast,' Beth said, pointing at the slabs that were nearly as big as her.

'Strictly medicinal. I'm afraid I'm going to have to insist,' said Katie blithely, plonking the plate down in front of her friend and showing no surprise at all when Beth immediately dug in. Once they'd both got through more than half of the deliciously unctuous concoctions, Katie spoke again, her words a little muffled.

'So. Want to tell me about it?'

Beth shuddered. 'Ugh. You really don't want to know. That poor man.'

'Who on earth was it? The estate agent? The house owner? Had you met him before?'

'Turns out it was the estate agent. Well, Harry hasn't actually said as much, I just listened in a bit last night when he finally got in. He was still giving people orders at three a.m. No wonder I'm knackered.'

'He must be absolutely exhausted, too. And he'll have so much to do,' said Katie.

'Hmm, he's used to it,' said Beth, then realised she was being very unfair. She'd resented her broken night, after the horror of her discovery. But poor Harry was constantly finding things that were every bit as awful, if not worse, and then spending days and weeks dealing with the consequences. Of course, it was part of his job, but Katie was right. He worked very hard and she should be more sympathetic. Beth silently resolved to do better – or at least to try.

'The awful thing is that I actually talked to the man on the phone yesterday, and he was as perky as anything. A bit too perky, if you know what I mean; one of those really bouncy estate agents,' Beth said with a grimace.

Katie nodded sympathetically. She'd bought a holiday home earlier in the year, and although she was dealing with sums of money that tended to make estate agents hushed and deferential instead of annoyingly uppity, Beth remembered even she had had a terse word or two to say about them at the time.

'It was one of those viewings that takes ages to arrange,' Beth went on. 'I rang him initially, then he had to speak to the vendors. He promised to get back to me in minutes, then I didn't hear for so long that I more or less forgot all about it. Harry had to remind me about it; he was really keen on this one. Then the bloke suggested various daytime viewings I couldn't manage because of work...'

Katie choked a little on her cappuccino, but forbore to say anything. They both knew that Beth's schedule at Wyatt's was as elastic as a bungee-jumping cord – when she wanted it to be.

'...Then, finally, just when I thought it was all completely hopeless, we settled on last night. And, well, here we are. Or rather – here *I* am. And he... well.' Again, Beth shuddered. 'Here he isn't.'

'How awful. It must have been such a shock. And what are the chances? I mean seriously, Beth, it's like you have a radar.' Katie's eyebrows were steepled.

'It wasn't *me* this time, though,' Beth said, sitting up a little straighter. She knew she sounded defensive, but she thought it was important to emphasise the point. 'It was the woman estate agent, the one who had to come out when my chap didn't turn up – or *couldn't* turn up, as we found out. She was the one who actually opened the cupboard. I did try, but it was stuck, and then, well, she was just that bit stronger... I looked inside but I didn't see a thing. It was so dark. Then there was this awful slithering sound... I thought it might be one of those things where the owners move and forget to take their pet snake with them. But no, it was just a dead body.'

Katie blanched and turned her head away. 'God,' she said faintly. 'How horrific for you.'

'Well, yes, but *I* didn't actually find it,' Beth insisted. 'It was horrific for *us* – me and the estate agent girl. Otherwise, it would be like me saying you'd found the body that time when we were out with the dogs on Peckham Rye...'

'Don't remind me.' Katie shook her head. 'That was definitely you.'

Beth sighed over the rim of her cup. She knew when to give

up. And it was a fair cop, there was no denying that one. 'Harry says I'm like a cadaver dog. Honestly, if I never see another dead body as long as I live, that would suit me just fine.'

'Mmm, it seems like destiny, though, doesn't it?' Katie had a worried look in her eye, but Beth spoke immediately.

'That's just what I think. It's even sort of my fault the poor man was there in the first place. I mean, if I hadn't made the appointment... And then, I do have a bit of a knack of getting in the thick of these things. Or maybe it's just my bad luck.' Beth chewed at the last morsel of brownie in a disconsolate way.

'Well, there's something going on, you have to admit that,' said Katie, head on one side. 'Either it's coincidence, or...'

Beth waited for Katie to finish, but her friend seemed stumped. Beth wasn't surprised. She couldn't say herself whether it was karma, happenstance or something more malign behind the dreadful inevitability that seemed to make her trip over corpses wherever she went. But at this point, she simply had to accept her fate. She looked over at Katie, studying her friend's unusually thoughtful blue eyes. She might as well come straight out and say it.

'Anyway, the upshot is that I feel I ought to look into it.'

Katie merely smiled gently, as though she'd been expecting something of the sort. There was resigned affection in her eyes. That was better than disapproval, but it was certainly a long way from joyful acceptance of Beth's position. Wait a minute. Was Katie perhaps feeling left out?

Beth had thought, at one point, that Katie could be her side-kick in her investigations. Well, she had thought sidekick; possibly Katie had seen herself as an equal partner. But somehow it hadn't panned out. Teddy – Katie's disreputable puppy – had really got in the way.

Now that Teddy was growing up and, while not yet a responsible member of the Dulwich doggy community, at least not an outright menace any more, Katie was surely free to lend a hand. Quickly, Beth made the offer. 'Of course, if you'd like to help me, that would be amazing. I mean, you've got time, haven't you?'

It was Katie's turn to look doubtful. 'I'll do what I can, Beth, and you know I really, really want to help you out. But it's just that, what with the yoga, and with everything that's gone on with Charlie...'

Katie's approach to her yoga empire was as flexible as her well-honed limbs – and almost as flexible as Beth's own attitude towards the Wyatt's archives. Initially, Katie had had dreams of cornering the flourishing Dulwich market in terms of fitness, and the ladies of the area had obligingly flooded her classes, wearing the finest Lycra money could buy and tirelessly lining up to do the downward dog. But during the past months, Katie had scaled back, her anxious attention fixed unwaveringly on her only son instead.

It was sad that Charlie, Jake's best friend, had had such a tough start at Wyatt's. The transition from the cosy atmosphere of the Village Primary to the Wyatt's hothouse had been challenging. And Katie had definitely found the homework burden stretched them both. Then one of the other boys in the class had started picking on him.

When it turned out the culprit was none other than Billy McKenzie – son of the dreaded Belinda, uber-mummy and boss of playgrounds right across SE21 – then poor Katie had endured a very busy first half-term, during which she'd hovered over her son's every move. Beth considered this a pointless exercise that probably hadn't helped Charlie much anyway. The boys were at the age now where they had to fend for themselves; they didn't need and certainly wouldn't want endless interfering from their parents. How would they learn to operate in the big world outside the Wyatt's gates, if every problem was ironed out for them the moment it appeared? But it was no good telling Katie that.

Beth also felt that truth and justice ought to come before other concerns – yet she knew that if Jake ever really needed her help, he would of course be top priority. Luckily for her, he seemed to be chugging along without too many problems at the moment.

Belinda had finally been dragged in for a talking-to from Dr Grover, the awe-inspiring headmaster of Wyatt's and the problem now seemed largely sorted, thank heavens. Beth wished she had been listening in on that particular meeting. Though she had some sneaking sympathy for Belinda – a highly competent woman, who'd opted to give up work and whose energy overflowed the tiny wife-and-mother basket she'd crammed it into – Beth mostly just recoiled from the self-styled Queen Bee of Dulwich. Belinda had the armour-plated confidence that went hand in hand with plenty of money and a cushy lifestyle, neither of which Beth had ever enjoyed. The woman was bossy and brash, and her life's work was an endless game of one-upmanship.

Beth couldn't stop watching, riveted, from the sidelines, but she was as unsuited to the competition as a Shetland pony in the ring with a glossy showjumper. During her more soul-searching moments, Beth wondered if some of her antipathy towards Belinda came from sheer envy. But then she'd overhear yet another of Belinda's outrageous pronouncements and putdowns, and realise that the woman was, indeed, a monster. And the last thing she'd ever want would be to resemble her in any way.

There was, though, another monster at large in south London, as of last night – as Beth unfortunately knew only too well. And finding this fiend was a lot more important than worrying about what Belinda was up to. The estate agent had been shoved in that cupboard with a contemptuousness that was as casual as it was cruel. Whoever had choked the life out of that young man (or however else he might have been killed;

Beth was a little hazy on this point, despite doing her best to eavesdrop on Harry's terse chats with his subordinates), his body had been treated as an inconvenient bit of rubbish to be pushed out of sight without a second thought.

'Maybe just talking about the, erm, latest *situation* together would help, Beth?' Katie asked anxiously, steering clear of the dreaded word murder and having a quick look around the café to see who might be hanging on their every word. 'What do you think? You should probably get it out of your system. If we discuss it, some detail might pop up that will be useful. That way, I'll still be helping, even though I can't give it as much time as I'd really like to.'

Bless Katie, ever the diplomat, thought Beth. There were a million other things she was certain her friend would rather talk about than another grim death. It was so like her to make this selfless offer.

'Are you sure?' Beth asked quickly, but couldn't resist plunging in as soon as she got a nod from that lovely blonde head. 'Well, chatting about it now, I realise how little I know about the guy. I mean, it's awful, but I can't even really remember his name. We'd never met, of course, but I had spoken to him quite a few times. I must say, I didn't love his breezy telephone manner. I've been dealing with so many estate agents, you know, trying to show willing for Harry,' she said with a slight roll of her eyes. 'I have all their names on my email, but in my head they're all just one young man in a shiny suit who wants to make me sign on the dotted line, even if he's showing me a dump. To be fair, some of them have been women – but they're all pretty similar.'

'Yeah, I remember what it's like. It's been ages since we looked in London, but with the Cornwall house there were a few like that. I think they're probably a bit less pushy out there, though.'

'Sadly, I wouldn't know.' Beth smiled.

Katie's bijou holiday cottage was the type of property that cried out to be featured on a lavish box of chocolates. Beth had spent what seemed like days admiring every step of the – in her view – totally unnecessary root-and-branch overhaul of the already pristine cottage.

'But listen, do you think the killer could have been lurking in the house when you were there? Was it something random? Or is there any chance that this whole thing wasn't an accident, that you've been targeted?'

Beth's eyes went wide. None of those were nice notions. She thought again about the house. It had seemed to be watching, waiting for the horrible discovery to be made. She hadn't got the sense that there'd been anyone else in there, while she'd gone round with the estate agent girl. Well, no one alive anyway. Mind you, nor had she had a sixth sense that there was a corpse about the place, either – until the very moment when that hand had slapped onto the floor... She shook her head slightly to clear the unwelcome vision.

'I definitely didn't get that feeling of being watched last night. You know how it is when you feel there are eyes on you, your hackles sort of rise... that didn't happen at all. But I wasn't alone in the house, as the girl from the estate agents arrived in the end and we went in together. Maybe that meant my antennae weren't working properly? She was quite distracted herself, just kept on looking at her phone... I don't know. But the house definitely had a deserted feeling, as though there was no one there apart from us, and hadn't been for ages. Which turned out to be completely wrong. There was someone there. He just wasn't alive any more.'

Until Katie had mentioned the possibility, it hadn't even occurred to Beth that she might have been the intended victim. But the idea was enough to get her hand shaking again, as she discovered when she tried to take a steadying sip of cappuccino. She cupped the drink in both palms instead, breathing deeply.

Both women looked down at the table. It was definitely a sobering thought. But Beth tried to rally herself.

'You know, I can't believe this was targeted at me. The person would have had to have known about my appointment; they would have had to have got there first. And let's face it, if that was the case and they'd been lurking on the premises, they could easily have killed me and the girl from the agents without too much trouble. Why kill a male estate agent instead? That must have been more difficult, I would have thought. True, the girl's wrists were stronger than mine – she pulled that door open in the kitchen – but she was skinny as anything. I don't think she'd have been much good in a fight.'

'Well, I wouldn't say that's a quality they really look for when they hire agents, is it?' remarked Katie, raising an eyebrow.

'I don't know,' Beth said lightly. 'Sometimes there can be skirmishes if two people want the same house round here. Imagine if someone like, well, Belinda, set her heart on a house and you'd already made an offer on it? It wouldn't be pretty, would it?'

They both paused briefly to imagine the scenes worthy of Armageddon which would no doubt ensue if anyone got between Mrs McKenzie and anything she had really set her heart on – from a part in a play for one of her children, to a top job for her husband.

'Thank God, that's not likely to happen,' Katie said with a shiver. 'She's already got the best house on Court Lane. And I know that, because she's always telling me.'

Beth, though not much given to physical display – this morning's sobbing aside – knew this was the moment to pat Katie's hand consolingly. 'Well, I know, and so does everyone else around here, that it's actually you who owns the most beautiful place in SE21, so there,' she said with a reassuring smile.

Though Katie had framed it as a joke, Belinda's constant

jostling must rankle, particularly after the recent discovery that the woman had stolen her interior design ideas wholesale and shamelessly created a carbon copy of her minimalist marble and copper kitchen.

Beth's smile died as her thoughts turned again to the events of last night. 'Even though I really don't think the killer was still in the house, I also can't believe the whole thing was entirely random. If the last couple of years have taught us anything, it's that stuff round here rarely is,' she said slowly.

Katie made a face and nodded. 'Maybe someone with a grudge against estate agents, then?'

'That's everyone who's ever bought a house,' Beth said, laughing out loud for the first time in what seemed like a long while. It felt good to lighten the tone a little, even if sudden death was hardly a fit subject for levity.

'Mmm. I wonder if he's anyone we knew. You didn't, erm...?'

'Recognise him?' Beth made a moue of distaste. She'd pondered this very question every time she'd woken up with a jolt in the dead of the night. That face, suffused with blood, had been a purple-red colour – the sort that would have looked natural on a whisky-soaked colonel, not a twenty-something man. The hand, though. By contrast, that had been pale as an uncooked chicken breast. And the ungainliness of the corpse had been particularly nasty. It had been as floppy as overdone spaghetti, with no trace of the sense of tidy containment that a live body maintained even when it was unconscious.

'No. I'd never seen him before,' she said slowly. 'It was supposed to have been our first meeting. Like I said, we'd spoken quite a lot on the phone, but it wasn't social chit-chat, it was just a quick "How are you?" in that way that means neither of you are really listening to the answer. And then it was all about this property or that one. I mean, well, he just talked like an estate agent. A bit annoying, frankly. Going on and on about the house when, from what I'd seen on the website, it was pretty meh. Bumptious, I'd suppose you'd say. Full of beans.' Beth looked down at her empty plate. 'Well, he's a bean-free zone now.'

'Grim,' said Katie, screwing up her face. 'I suppose Harry will have to tell the parents and so on. How awful. Can you imagine?'

The bustle of the café seemed to dim for a moment as both contemplated the horror of receiving news like that. It was surely the worst fate that could ever befall a parent. Dealing with a death of a child must be the sort of agony which never went away. Beth's heart went out to these people – a couple she didn't know and would probably never meet. They had all the sympathy and love that one small woman could send. She hoped they'd be able to feel it one day.

Beth's vision was blurred now, and she saw Katie's eyes had a tell-tale sheen, too. They were both thinking of their boys. Her friend offered her another napkin, but Beth just swallowed hard. 'There was one other thing that was odd. Do you have time? Can I just run it past you?'

'Absolutely,' said Katie. 'I'm in no rush. I've cancelled my morning class already.'

For a moment, Beth felt a pinch of worry on her friend's behalf. That wasn't the way to keep her yoga business ticking over. The ladies of Dulwich would no doubt be quite unhappy to have their regular stretching sessions whisked away at a moment's notice. And fitness was competitive round here. There were kettle bells, Pilates, Zumba and all manner of other options on offer.

But she ploughed on. 'I, well, I did pop upstairs after the, erm, discovery.'

'Beth! You didn't. Didn't you worry about what you might find up there?'

'Oh no, it was fine, it was once the SOCOs were in, so I knew there were no more nasties lurking.'

'But wouldn't you be contaminating the crime scene, poking about on your own?'

Beth felt a twinge of irritation at this. Like so many in Dulwich, Katie was hopelessly addicted to Scandi noir dramas, and so had a glancing knowledge of police procedure. Or at least, she thought she had. Beth waved away such concerns.

'It's not really like that, Katie. I wasn't "poking".'

'So, Harry knew you were looking?'

Beth continued seamlessly. 'Anyway. So, in one of the bedrooms, I found this odd little tangle of belongings. You know, a pile of hoodies. Some gadgets that teenage boys – or older ones – would use. A really nice laptop, stuff like that. It was almost as though someone had been living there.'

'That's weird. Not one of the owners, then?'

'I wouldn't say so. Wouldn't they keep their clothes in a wardrobe, like a normal person?'

'Well, maybe not teenagers or that sort of age group. I mean, look at our boys.'

Katie had a point. Jake wasn't a great one for tidying and sorting, and Beth was willing to bet Charlie wasn't either. Katie, of course, would fold her son's stuff away every night, if Beth knew her at all. That wasn't quite the service Jake was getting. But that was another story, thought Beth.

'I hear what you're saying. But there was something very temporary-looking about it. Like it was in a little pile so the person could take off at a moment's notice.'

'But no other signs of anyone else in the house?'

'Nope, the living room definitely had that unused air. And the kitchen, too, nothing personal in it. Apart from in that larder cupboard, of course,' said Beth with a shudder. 'Oh, well. We can't really do anything about it all while Harry's looking into it, I suppose. But I'll try and find out what's going on, and we can discuss developments, maybe?' She looked at her friend for confirmation.

'Sure, sure,' said Katie soothingly.

Beth wondered for a second if she was just being humoured. But never mind. Time to change the subject. 'So. Any looming homework horrors I should know about?'

Katie grasped the conversational baton and they both ran with it into the much safer byways of Latin tests and extra reading. Jake, of course, had not breathed a word to Beth about the fact his teacher had decreed that the whole class should expand their knowledge of the gladiators with a few books that weren't strictly on the curriculum. What was the opposite of 'going the extra mile'? she wondered. Some sort of tunnelling operation that took him away from the benefits of education? A very determined hiding of his lights under any available bushel? This was Jake's entire educational strategy. She sincerely hoped he was saving his energies for a last-minute sprint, just when it would count. Knowing him, that might well be moments before the A level invigilators said, 'You can now turn over your question booklet.' But would he still be able to hear the whistle blowing for the race, when he'd practised selective deafness for so long?

Beth told herself not to worry. Despite his extremely relaxed attitude to academic matters, Jake had still got into Wyatt's – a miracle in itself. She'd just have to keep reminding herself of that, proof positive that he could pull a win out of the bag when it was most needed, and try not to stress herself out. After all, she had a varied selection of other options if she wanted to get nail-bitingly anxious. But Katie was still talking.

'We could set up a sort of informal testing situation, say on a Friday night? Get the boys together and just go over all the new French and Latin vocab, and maybe the finer points of what they've covered that week in Maths too...'

Beth, who privately couldn't think of a worse way to spend

a Friday evening, found herself nodding along. Maybe she and Jake were peas in a pod. He was laid-back to the point of unconsciousness, and while Katie was a helicopter parent, Beth was a bit like one of those windmill contraptions they'd made out of paper and cocktail sticks in the playgroups she'd attended with Katie so long ago. Hers had never gone round when they'd been blown on, remaining stubbornly static instead and then falling apart. It said it all, really.

'Are you managing to keep the yoga going, as well as all your, um, Charlie's, homework?' Beth hoped she'd achieved a light tone, but she was genuinely curious.

Katie smiled. 'Oh yes, now that business with Billy is less, er, pressing, it's all getting into a rhythm again. You really must come along again,' she said. 'The classes are quite full, but I can always squeeze you in.' She looked sincere, but Beth thought she could detect a faint teasing note in her friend's voice.

'Oh, um, absolutely,' said Beth, knowing nothing would get her within twenty metres of a yoga mat at the moment. Then she met Katie's eye and yes, there was a distinctly satirical twinkle there. 'All right, no, there's not a hope in hell. What with all the house-hunting, and now this new thing... with the body and all...'

She knew, to a die-hard fitness fan, it would sound like a string of excuses as threadbare as the Village Primary's summer fayre bunting. But Beth really did have plenty on her plate, from steadfastly ignoring Jake's academic prowess – or lack of it – to avoiding finishing her outline for the definitive biography of appalling swashbuckler Sir Thomas Wyatt, the slave-owning founder of Jake and Charlie's school. And now the perfect displacement activity had plopped into her lap, in the shape of another mystery. Although, even as she framed the thought, the way the estate agent's hand had unclenched on the dingy tiled floor in what looked a lot like supplication made her brownie shift uneasily in her stomach.

'Are you really going to get involved in this business? I know I should tell you not to, but I might as well save my breath to cool my cappuccino.' Katie smiled. 'Just promise me one thing.'

'Of course,' said Beth, sitting up a little straighter.

'Please, please, try and keep yourself safe this time.'

There was no mistaking the pleading look in Katie's eyes. And Beth completely understood where her friend was coming from; really, she did. But if previous experience had taught her anything, it was that, if she were going to stop this killer from striking again, there might be one or two little glitches along the way. She crossed her fingers under the table and replied blithely, 'You know me, Katie. Promise.'

Katie groaned.

FOUR

Harry York sat at his desk at Camberwell Police Station, determinedly ignoring the pile of reports stacked about a metre deep on his desk. Petty crime rates, which had been tumbling satisfactorily for months, had shot up again. You didn't need to be a genius to work it out, he decided, glancing very quickly at a graph his subordinate, DC Narinda Khan, had carefully placed right on top of the tottering pile only a few minutes ago. Apple had just unleashed a new iPhone on the world, and every scrote in south-east London wanted to get their hands on one.

Much more serious – though he wasn't belittling the chagrin of the many posh schoolkids who'd had their shiny new mobiles swiped at bus stops and stations all over his patch – was the murder in Sydenham. If he had his way, every penny of his meagre budget would be poured into this investigation. As it was, his funds had to stretch, like cheap prosecco at a second wedding.

The murder. He was scratching his head about it. The post-mortem report wasn't in yet, but he'd seen enough of the corpse to have a few ideas. The most disturbing aspect so far was that it had been very freshly killed. When he'd got to the scene, not long after Beth's distress call, the man had been almost, but not quite, warm. That meant that Beth had been worryingly hard on the heels of the killer, if she hadn't actually coincided with his presence in the house. He didn't want to freak her out more than strictly necessary, but he was going to have to glean further information from her on any sounds she might have heard while she'd been, as she explained, examining the kitchen cupboards. He broke off here to hit his desk in frustration, the piles of reports all jumping a centimetre in a rather jolly fashion, which did nothing at all for his blood pressure.

Harry didn't usually waste a lot of time thinking about his circumstances, and certainly didn't bother bemoaning his fate. He was reasonably content with where he was professionally, although there was still plenty of the greasy pole to climb. Much of the time he was also quite content with where he was emotionally. There were days, however, when he wished Beth was safely trussed up in a 1950s-style pinafore, and preferably chained to any convenient kitchen appliance as well, although he knew by now it wasn't likely to improve her prowess in the culinary field.

Why, why did she have this propensity to get involved in murders? And why was she so accidentally successful at it? If only her incompetent blundering didn't keep on bearing fruit. Then he could persuade her to leave well alone, let the professionals – in this case, him – handle things while she waited nice and safely on the sidelines. But no. She was determined to get her hands dirty, put her neck on the line, risk all sorts of body parts that he'd much rather she kept well out of the way.

It was aggravating beyond words.

And then there was her recent behaviour. After initially agreeing to his logical proposition that they needed more space and therefore should move, together, to pastures new, a period of passive resistance had set in. During this time, he'd shown Beth umpteen properties on the moving websites and she'd pointed out infinitesimal flaws in all of them, which had made them utterly impossible in her eyes. He knew she loved her current home. He knew it would be hard for her to say goodbye to the village. But honestly! When she'd been reduced to complaining that one of the houses he'd shown her wasn't right because of the previous owners' taste in garden furniture, he wasn't ashamed to say he'd lost it a bit. Needless to say, most of these houses, any one of which would have done them proud, had since been snapped up by much less finickity buyers.

But now, after steadfastly stonewalling the whole project for many weeks, she was all of a sudden eagerly lining up more estate agent appointments, a mere matter of hours after finding a dead body in one of the few houses she'd got round to visiting. Did she seriously think he wouldn't notice what she was up to? 'Jesus Christ!'

'Sir?'

He looked up, and there was Narinda Khan, shaking in her boots as usual. If Beth had far too much spirit, Khan didn't have quite enough. So far, anyway. Despite his best efforts to train her up, she always looked one step away from the screaming abdabs. Harry sighed inwardly.

'Nothing,' he said heavily, trying to reassemble his features into a mask which wouldn't frighten her half to death. 'Except, have we heard back from forensics yet? On the Sydenham house?'

Instantly, Khan was combing through her laptop inbox for the report, and then she was straight on the phone to chivvy the department. She was keen, he'd say that for her. Though whether that was to make progress with him, or just so she could apply for a transfer elsewhere in double-quick time, he was never quite sure.

He breathed out with a gale force gust that sent the graph drifting to the floor. Khan held the phone away from her ear and looked over at him enquiringly. He shook his head, waved away her concern, and picked up the graphic crossly and slapped it back down on his desk.

It was his own fault. He should use his office – a little glass box just across the way. But he liked to sit out here with the others, absorbed in the camaraderie of office life. It helped him feel more attuned to his team. The downside was that the team got to scrutinise him in return. Normally this was fine, as he liked to lead from the front. While he didn't like to big himself up too much, he knew his dynamic approach got results. Yet, while he was this side of major exasperation with Beth, the odd expletive was going to escape – or there'd be plumes of steam pouring out of his ears instead.

All those lunches with Beth's yoga chum Katie and her hubby Mike hadn't been wasted; he'd picked up a few tips as well as noshing some seriously good food. He forced himself to take a few deep breaths and then turned back to his screen. Property websites. They were always quite calming. And at least this whole business meant he could browse through the available local housing stock without feeling he was slacking.

Charming features, in need of some updating, he read, scanning a description. He was becoming a bit more familiar with the jargon, and recognised that this meant a total car-crash before he even got to the photos of a dispiriting-looking house with lumpy, unmade beds and a huge stain on the living room carpet that would have had him calling in the SOCOs pronto. Once he got to the garden, he smiled broadly. This place made Beth's garden look like the Hampton Court flower show. No way he'd get her to look at it. And this wasn't even the murder scene. For God's sake, couldn't they even do the washing-up before the photographer came round? He was beginning to sound almost as house-proud as Beth, he realised.

That reminded him, he had a couple more boxes of books to bring over from Camberwell. He was gradually – some would say stealthily – emptying out his flat. Not much point keeping it on, wasting all that money in rent, when he could be paying off half of a massive mortgage somewhere else with Beth.

Part of him still found the very idea of a mortgage terrifying, and a joint one even more so. But it was a leap they had to take at some point. Surely. If they were really serious about each other and this relationship. In a way, he was testing the waters, bringing his stuff over bit by bit. For a neat-freak like Beth, the gradual incursion of a large number of cardboard cartons into her ordered space was stressful, he knew. But if she couldn't cope with his possessions, then how would she be able to cope with him, long term? And there wasn't much that was more long term than a joint mortgage.

Harry didn't mind downsizing a bit in the interests of the move, he really didn't. Though why it had to be him getting rid of his things, when he had so much less baggage than one tiny woman and child, he didn't know. Beth had a houseful of stuff, tidy though she undoubtedly was. And Jake had all the usual detritus of the growing boy – Lego and train sets he had outgrown but that he, or more likely Beth, couldn't quite bear to part with yet; pristine and unread classics on his shelves, undoubtedly presents from his granny, Beth's mum Wendy; and well-thumbed old copies of *Captain Underpants* and *Horrible Histories* scattered all round his small room.

Harry certainly didn't want to be the ogre responsible for whittling away Jake's childhood. And the truth was that Harry wasn't even terribly good at sorting out his own stuff. Every night that he actually spent in Camberwell – and there weren't all that many any more – he really meant to go through his bits and bobs, make piles to go to the charity shop, the bin, or the boxes. Trouble was, he was always too tired.

Beth wasn't going to be amused when she got the packing tape off those cartons and discovered that, as well as his comprehensive library of Golden Age crime fiction, he had also brought her heaps of stuff that he knew should have been on a one-way trip to the dump by now.

Well, they could go through things properly, together, once they'd finally found a place, Harry thought, rigorously closing his eyes to the many obvious pitfalls of this approach. He hoped this murder wasn't going to slow it all down too much. Although Beth had promptly upped her number of viewings, he on the other hand was unlikely to be able to get away to see anything for the foreseeable future. And they did need to make a joint decision. *God's strewth.* Much though he wanted to push such thoughts away, knowing how unhelpful they were, he was really feeling the pressure. He needed to get this case sorted out, and as soon as possible.

He forced himself to think about it slowly, clearly and dispassionately, as though he had all the time in the world. Although when was that ever the case with a murder in London? If it wasn't the mayor breathing down their necks, lambasting the Met in order to score cheap points, then it was a Westminster politician of one shade or another, doing much the same. Yet none of them, when they'd finally leveraged themselves into a position of sufficient power and influence, ever seemed to want to shower the force with the type of money that would make these problems easier to turn around. The public, time after time, had said what it wanted: the reassurance of the bobby on the beat. But that was nigh-on impossible to fund these days. And as for the other great pie-in-the-sky aim of modern policing – tackling terrible urban tragedies like knife crime, and getting anywhere near to sorting out the drugs problem that underpinned almost all the woes of the city – well, that required time, careful strategy, and money, money, money.

Was this Sydenham murder a one-off killing? Some sort of gang thing? The poor lad – an estate agent, as it turned out – was a bit too old, in his mid-twenties. He'd recently got himself on the first rung of what any parent might, with a bit of a sigh maybe, consider a respectable career path. It wasn't the pattern, the all-too-familiar scenario that played out in so much of Harry's patch – dysfunctional background, leading to low aspirations; truancy, leading to lack of qualifications; drugs, leading to very dodgy bedfellows; then all the jostling for territory which led to gang wars. He didn't fit that scenario at all, poor old Richard Pettit. Well, not even old, at twenty-five. And now the lad never would be.

Harry shook his head. Sometimes he just despaired at his job, and all the wrongs he couldn't right. But then, at least he was trying.

Had Richard Pettit just been in the wrong place at the wrong time? But why would an empty house that didn't belong to him be the wrong place? He was an estate agent; this was supposed to be his natural habitat. And what about the pile of clothes they'd found in one of the upstairs rooms? Were they Pettit's? Well, that was going to be easy enough to establish, once the DNA tests came back. Until then, it was all pretty murky, though one thing was for sure: Beth had arrived for her viewing at precisely the wrong time, as far as Harry was concerned.

It was so typical. All these weeks when he'd been pressing her to see much better places, then when she'd finally agreed to play ball, she immediately turned up a corpse and now had a perfect excuse to be too traumatised to do any more house-hunting. God, if he didn't know her better... But even in the quiet recesses of his own mind, Harry couldn't quite accuse his beloved of having offed an estate agent just so she could abandon the search for their dream house. And to be fair, so far she had done the opposite and stepped up her viewings instead – which was just as annoying in a different way.

Think. Think about the problem in hand, he told himself. Do not think about Beth, a problem that is usually very much out of hand. He concentrated. Sydenham, close enough to

Dulwich to be almost within touching distance, was too respectable to fit the drugs profile, wasn't it? Not that anywhere in London seemed to be immune from the spread of such troubles nowadays. But this hadn't been a shanking, as stabbings were called. Shankings were the hallmark of London drugs crimes.

He wondered, briefly, about a lowlife scumbag who had popped up in a previous investigation – a toerag by the name of Raf, who seemed to make a living preying on young, silly girls who were desperate for attention and could be manipulated easily. Moving into an empty house was the kind of trick this Raf would pull. And he'd been seen on Harry's manor not so long ago. But so far there wasn't a whisper about any girl being involved in this Sydenham business. And that was really Raf's MO.

All the clothes recovered from the house had been men's stuff – hoodies and the like. So Raf could be involved; though there was nothing tying him to the scene yet. Harry would keep an eye out.

But mostly, he feared, this was something entirely different. This was a Beth crime, if ever there was one. A white-on-white murder which looked as though it could be about something even sillier than who got the right to sell which drugs on which street, or which girl, for that matter. What had their last case been about? Not that he even wanted to call it *their* case, damn it, he corrected himself quickly. It had been a Met Police matter when all was said and done. But at the heart of the business, underneath the mysterious poisonings and about sixty ageing suspects, all with access to a wide range of legitimately prescribed lethal drugs, it had been about Bridge partners in the end. And who'd been mean to whom back in the 1980s.

'Jesus!' His hand came down with a crash on the desk, and an empty Costa cup skittered to the floor.

'Boss?' Khan yelped again like a whipped dog.

'Nothing, nothing,' Harry growled, getting up with resignation in every bit of his six-foot-four frame. He stretched lavishly, unknowingly drawing the eyes of all the women in the vicinity. 'Erm, just off to my office for a bit,' he said tersely, massaging the back of his neck and ruffling his rough blond hair. 'Give me a shout if anything comes up.'

* * *

Narinda Khan swallowed, watching him go with something curiously like regret in the quiet inky depths of her eyes.

His door shut with a decisive click and then, as he hadn't bothered to close the venetian blinds, she saw him lash out and appear to deliver a sharp kick to what could only be the rubbish bin in the corner. It had been full to overflowing earlier. He then mouthed what seemed to be a long, long string of colourful adjectives. Then he bent down, only to re-emerge with great handfuls of paper, presumably picked up from the spillage on the floor.

She wished she could lip-read. Maybe there was a course coming up? She quickly opened a new tab on her terminal and scrutinised the training opportunities on offer. She was always eager to acquire new skills. It was the only way she'd ever succeed in impressing DI York. And that was something she badly wanted to do. By the time she looked up again, all the blinds had been closed.

FIVE

Beth sat in the small, dark wine bar near Herne Hill Station and drummed her fingers lightly on the table. She'd been here ten minutes already. There was only so much idle scrolling through Instagram she could be bothered with.

Sometimes other people's beautifully curated lives were curiously soothing. At other moments, the total lack of shabby towers of crime paperbacks teetering in their picture-perfect sitting rooms could be quite distressing. In her mind's eye, she saw the scene she'd just fled. Colin and Magpie, both looking as though butter wouldn't melt, peacefully sitting foursquare in front of the sofa. She knew that wouldn't have lasted a second after she'd shut the door. They'd be lolling all over her best cushions, Colin drooling and Magpie shedding, both as though their lives depended upon it. And Jake would be wedged in the middle, getting as much forbidden weekday PlayStation as he could before even starting his homework, which was strictly against her latest diktat. At least they'd all be perfectly happy, though. What was it about flouting rules that was always so satisfying, she wondered, wriggling her feet out of her boots. There was a hole in one of the soles and her toes were distinctly soggy. Then she caught the eye of a scandalised-looking waiter and quickly shoved them back on again.

She looked around, leaving some time for her cheeks to stop flaming before she attempted to order anything. This bar was the trendiest place in the area, its plum velvet upholstery and brown walls offset by rose gold vases and pretty gilt candle-holders on the low tables. Not that there were a whole lot of wine bars to choose from in Herne Hill. Perhaps there was no need for them, as happily married couples outweighed singles by about a thousand to one in these parts, and Beth rather imagined it was the unattached who wanted to go out and sip expensive wine in dark places night after night.

But then, she acknowledged, she knew next to nothing about the dating scene. She'd tried to give it a go, a while back, but had only got as far as having a sedate cup of tea with a complete no-hoper in the village deli, Romeo Jones. It had hardly constituted a night out on the pull, and it had been stressful enough to cure her of any lingering curiosity. Besides, to everyone else's surprise as well as her own, she'd somehow ended up with an enormous policeman about the place, and that had come about without a single proper date or drink.

As usual, when she remembered that awful but exciting day at Wyatt's when she and Harry had first met, the images flitting across her memory were of clouds reflected in a lake the rich colour of Bordeaux, which had turned out to be a man's lifeblood, and a navy-blue peacoat that, even then, had looked like the most reassuring thing on earth.

Now, by contrast, she felt conspicuous and increasingly irritable. Where the hell was Nina? Her great friend, mother of Jake's little chum Wilf at the Village Primary, was a bit of a law unto herself. Beth knew Nina would have a tale to tell about why she was late this time, but she might well be too cross to listen to it by the time her friend finally rocked up. Even with Harry as more of a fixture in the house, it wasn't that easy for

Beth to get away. And she still had that feeling she'd had in the early days whenever she'd escaped the sleeping Jake for a night out. Every moment was precious, with a babysitter racking up fees and the inevitable tiredness bound to catch up with her the next day.

Nowadays, she was much more able to withstand the occasional late night, it was true, but the sense definitely persisted that any time away from the cares of parenthood should not be squandered. To her surprise, Harry had got home reasonably early for once. He was going to spend the evening looking through the case files, he'd said, but when she'd passed conveniently close to his hunched shoulders, she'd seen only property website tabs open on his laptop. When she'd asked him what the progress was on the whole murder business, he'd sent her off with a flea in her ear, some terse questions about noises in the Sydenham house that she'd answered in the negative, and a very vague mention of petty thefts being on the rise, which Beth was sure must be unrelated.

She felt he should be concentrating all the resources of the Met on the murder of the poor estate agent. Why wasn't he patrolling the streets, or briefing his team, or doing something typically decisive and action-packed? Why wasn't he doing anything, in short, but flicking through three-bedroomed houses with gardens on HomeSweetHome.com? It was very odd. A killing within a stone's throw of Dulwich was a crisis in her book. He should be cancelling all leave, like the TV cops did, and standing importantly in front of a whiteboard, having sudden maverick inspirations. But no, he was doubtless on the sofa, taking Jake's place, and by now being bookended by Colin and Magpie.

On the other hand, she definitely wasn't going to turn down a bit of free childminding when it offered itself. As soon she'd realised that Harry was home for the whole evening, she'd been on the phone to Nina, and then out of the door before he really knew what had hit him. Nina had promised to join her as quickly as she could.

So, where on earth *was* Nina? The minutes were ticking by, and there was still no sight of her familiar white puffball of a coat. Now that Beth thought about it, perhaps being annoyed with her friend wasn't the right reaction. Perhaps she should actually be worried. After all, Nina had recently changed jobs, leaving her cushy number in the admin office at Wyatt's for what Beth privately thought was a step down – a post in the new Herne Hill branch of Fester and Hock, the estate agents. And suddenly her new career didn't seem the safest of choices. With any luck, though, it was going to help Beth in her search for whoever had committed the ghastly deed she'd uncovered last night.

One of the questions Beth was planning to get to the bottom of was why Nina had swapped a sinecure of a job for the hurly-burly of estate agency, just when the UK housing market looked like it might just possibly tumble off the white cliffs of Dover into the crash pundits had been warning about for years.

Beth knew that she definitely had a bias against anything that wasn't Wyatt's. For her, the school had always represented the acme of her aspirations. And the fact that Jake had squeaked in – despite all her doubts and fears – was still a source of tremendous satisfaction, though she did her best not to glow too smugly. Nina, on the other hand, had a much more robust – even, Beth acknowledged, a more balanced – view of Dulwich, being a relatively recent incomer. And she also seemed to like switching it up a lot, job-wise. So far, she had worked at a solici-tor's, the school, and now the estate agent's, and Beth had only known her a year or so.

She looked around aimlessly, unfortunately catching the eye of the waiter behind the bar. She'd been nursing a tap water all this time, and it looked as though it was time to either ante-

up and get a real drink, or abandon ship and trail home to
Harry.

Just as she was deciding a glass of wine on her own might be
preferable to an evening with her lover and his hoard of
whodunits, the door opened and a familiar round figure burst
in. It was Nina, flinging off her white coat, ordering a large
mojito, kissing and hugging Beth, and throwing herself into the
seat next to her, all in one go.

'Fought I'd never get away. Blimmin' office. They're all
going crickets over this Sydenham business.'

Crickets? Beth took a moment to try and decode. One of the
many reasons Beth loved Nina was that she spoke a language of
her own, full of merry malapropisms and circumlocutions. Beth
enjoyed it, but sometimes she did feel she needed subtitles.
Crickets/crackers, she decided.

'I'm not surprised. What are people saying about it?' Beth
was on the edge of her seat now, after having been slumped in
the corner for so long.

'Just, you know, all the worries. Was it a punter gone nuts,
after getting to the house and discovering it didn't have a new
broiler, for instance? They can get a bit narked, the viewers, if
the place isn't quite what it says on the perpendiculars,' Nina
confided. 'Or was it a random crazy who just got lucky and
bopped the guy on the head? I dunno, but it's not great, is it? Bit
like the time that girl went missing, you know, back in the day.'

For a moment, Beth thought Nina must mean the teenager
who'd briefly disappeared in Dulwich. She'd been at the acade-
mically super-shiny but socially pressured girls' secondary, the
College School. But that had only been a few months ago, and it
was before Nina had even moved here. No, she couldn't mean
that.

Beth racked her brain a bit more and then caught hold of a
memory that had been hovering on the edge of her consciousness ever since the horrible moment in the Sydenham kitchen.

It was a ghastly episode that had happened years and years ago, when she'd been tiny, but it had seemed to cast a shadow over her childhood. An estate agent had vanished after a bogus appointment, and had never been seen since.

Even Beth's mother, Wendy, fairly lackadaisical about her daughter at the best of times, had suddenly become almost clingy in the aftermath, and had done her best to monitor Beth's free time with a bit more interest. But as Beth had been a loner, happiest with her nose in a book, there was little scope for Wendy to work up much of a drama, and she had soon relapsed into her customary apathetic parenting, channelling her energies as before into her own preoccupations. A name suddenly came to Beth.

'Wait a minute. Do you mean Suzy Lamplugh?'

'That's her. Poor love.'

They were both silent for a moment, contemplating the awful unsolved case. Suzy Lamplugh had faded now from a flesh-and-blood twenty-five-year-old with the world at her feet to a blurred photo. That fuzzy image, showing a carefree, pretty blonde with a pageboy cut and jaunty smile, had looked out from a thousand front-page news stories – and had become a haunting mockery of itself. Never found, gone forever.

Both women grabbed their drinks and took a hefty swig. Beth put hers down, but Nina raised her mojito to her lips for a second time.

'Absent friends,' she saluted. Beth sipped along.

There was a pause. Beth tried to shake off the sadness of that case. It was surely the most horrible thing that could befall those who were left, those who'd loved that promising young woman. But this case in Sydenham was very different. The man had already been found and there was nothing to suggest that he'd been lured, as Suzy had been, to a bogus appointment. *Mr Kipper*, Beth remembered with a shudder. That was the alias Suzy's nemesis had apparently used. But the killing of a man seemed to betoken a different sort of crime, less eerie and, she fervently hoped, a lot more solvable.

The disturbing sexual element, the cautionary tale of an innocent lured to her doom, the wickedness of the predator – surely those would be missing in this case? It was probably an open-and-shut thing, a grudge, a manly dispute... though even as she framed the thought, Beth realised that there had been plenty of creepy elements to the Sydenham slaying. The silent, empty house, that had seemed to be waiting. The body stuffed in a cupboard. Even the scattering of possessions upstairs. None of that suggested a fight that had got out of hand, or a simple argument ramped up into an accidental fatality.

No, there were elements of premeditation here, suggestions that the killer had had the time and opportunity to get his victim into the house, and then known precisely where to stow him. And, if Beth hadn't been so nosy, would the body have been there still? It wasn't the equivalent of Suzy's disappearance from the face of the earth, but there was stealth there. All the more reason for Harry to be out and about searching for the perpetrator, not comparing architraves and bathroom fittings at home.

She shook herself away from the memory of the Sydenham house and looked at her friend anxiously. Now she wondered whether to confide in her. Nina was a massive gossip, who made most sieves look waterproof. Her store of outrageous tales was one of the many things Beth loved about her, but it did make her circumspect about trusting Nina with information. This time, though, she might have to make an exception if she wanted to make any progress. She made up her mind.

'You know I was there when he was found, don't you?'

Nina almost choked on a sprig of mint, and Beth had to thump her on the back. 'You're kidding! No one said,' Nina said, eyes streaming, as soon as she was able.

'I'm hoping no one knows. Don't say a thing,' Beth said

quickly, wondering if she'd been mad to even mention it to Nina. 'I mean, I didn't *actually* find him,' she added, wanting to distance herself as much as she could from the business, in much the same way as she'd taken that involuntary leap back into the sink. Just thinking about it gave her a twinge. Her back was quite badly bruised from the point of impact, but that was butlers' sinks for you. The details had made much of the fact that it was a lovely ceramic double-drainer but, from where Beth was sitting, quite uncomfortably, it was just horribly hard. 'The estate agent found him.'

'Wait a minute, I thought he *was* the estate agent?'

'No. I'd made an appointment with him, but when I got there, it looked like no one had shown up. Well, now I know why. But I rang the office, made a bit of a fuss... so a girl came out and showed me round instead. Well, started to... and she was the one who opened the cupboard.' Beth glossed over the fact that the girl had only done it at her own request. Or, in fact, helped Beth out when her little wrists proved unequal to the task. 'But you won't tell, will you? I know I've already got a bit of a reputation...'

'Yeah, I'm surprised Chapels don't follow you around with a hearse. Would save them a lot of time and trouble on pick-ups,' Nina said. Chapels was the closest firm of undertakers. It was based in South Norwood; Dulwich didn't really like to acknowledge an inconvenience like death. 'But don't you worry, I won't say a thing. Mum's the bird,' she said, performing an elaborate mime of the zipping of her lips and the throwing away of a key that would have shamed her son Wilf, if he were ever to get promoted from background ruminant to a proper acting part in the school nativity play.

Beth rolled her eyes but was mollified. There was no going back now, anyway.

'What do you think it'll do to the housing market round here?' Beth asked, unable to repress an ignoble surge of hope

that there might be a sudden price drop which would enable
her to upgrade without leaving the sacred confines of SE21. She
knew it put her on a par with the monied types who spent every
dinner party discussing the ups and downs of property as
though their livelihoods depended on it – which they probably
did.

'I wondered that myself, for about five seconds, then the
calls started to come in,' said Nina. 'It went blimmin' nuts.
Everyone and his mog has booked a viewing. We think they're
all hoping there'll be a huge price drop, but I'll tell you something for nutmeg, that's not going to happen.'

Beth tried not to look too disappointed. 'Are you sure?'

'The Sydenham market might take a hit, yes. But that's not
going to dent the stock in Dulwich itself. Come on, you know
what prices are like, even here in Herne Hill. They're more
buoyant than, well, that posh fatty Doris Johnson and his
flaming ego.'

Only Nina could get *his* name wrong. Beth shut her eyes
briefly at the image of the irrepressible blond politician
squeezed into a frock. Then she shook her head a tiny bit,
clearing her vision. 'You don't think it's going to have any effect
round here, then?'

'If anyfing, it'll be the reverse, honey. Hate to say it, and I
bet that's not what you want to hear. Did you think Dulwich
Village was suddenly going to be cheap as quips? Fought you
wouldn't have to move out after all? Nah. Not going to happen.
Abso-bloomin-*lutely* not. It's going to make Sydenham cheaper,
yes. No one wants to get bumped off in their own home, after
all. But Dulwich is going to soar. Because it's safe, see? It's just
made the contrast with those other areas outside even more
obvious. It's almost like that was the idea all along.'

Beth looked at Nina, arrested. Her friend was quite right.
She just hadn't thought of it like that. She'd hoped this crime
might somehow benefit her, which she now felt rather ashamed

about. But she knew what she should actually be asking Nina about, and it wasn't cross-dressing Tories or the tatters of her own home-ownership dreams. 'Did you know the estate agent who died, then?'

'Richard Pettit?' said Nina, swigging again from her tall glass. Beth wasn't surprised that Nina already knew his name. She herself had gleaned it by sneaky – ahem, *careful* – eaves-dropping, but Nina was plugged into information systems that she could only dream of. And, if Nina knew it, then undoubt-edly it was now common currency all around the parish.

'I didn't know him personally, poor guy. Didn't work at our firm, did he? But yeah, I knew *of* him. He worked for Worthing-tons – you know, they have the branch in the village. Quite new at the job. Well, he was young, wasn't he?'

Beth thought back. She'd averted her eyes from him as quickly as she could. But there had certainly been something boyish about him, even in violent death. The floppiness of his hand had given him a sort of youthful, uncontrolled air, like a colt taking its first steps. She realised now that was probably due to the lack of rigor mortis in the body. But he'd also seemed gangly, skinny even, which she normally associated with youth. All the boys in the upper levels of Wyatt's School had that same disjointed quality of being slightly too big for their bodies, less than totally in control of limbs which had grown sometimes by a foot in a matter of months. Those who were keen on rugby tended to bulk up quickly and were soon pretty indistinguishable from grown men. But others left the school in a stringy sort of state, and the estate agent, slight though her acquaintance with him had been, seemed to have been in this camp.

Did she know Worthingtons itself? There were a few estate agents in the village, nestling amongst the scented candle shops. There seemed to be some sort of understanding among the retailers that if you could afford to spend forty-five pounds on a lump of neroli and frankincense-flavoured wax, then you could also stump up three million for a house that needed updating.

Up until recently, Beth had walked swiftly past the estate agents, oblivious... although she'd often been tempted by the candle emporia. But with Harry's sudden enthusiasm for the move, she'd taken to slowing down and sticking her nose up against the shiny property shop windows, like everyone else in Dulwich, even though the detached redbrick mansions on Calton Avenue and the Georgian gems in the village itself were as far out of her price range as a two-bed on Mars.

Yes, now that she thought about it, she realised she definitely did know Worthingtons, though she'd never been inside. She'd made her appointments via the website, and never particularly bothered which firm she was dealing with. There was always a number at the bottom of the listings and that put you through, using, Beth suspected, some sort of premium-priced line which was probably the way HomeSweetHome and the others made their trillions.

'What was he like, this poor Richard guy?'

'Hmm. Hard to tell, really. As I say, never met him meself. And now it's a speak-ill thing, innit? No one will, not for a while anyway. So, I haven't heard anything bad, but that's not to say there isn't anything,' Nina said darkly.

'Do you think there *was* something?' Beth was a little surprised.

'Nah, but he was an estate agent, after all,' Nina said airily. 'Bound to be somefing.'

'But, Nina, so are you?' Beth's eyebrows said it all.

'Nah, bless you. I'm just a filer, that's me. Admin, pure and simple. Sending out the snappers to take the pics, getting the perpendiculars sorted to give out to the punters. And the meeting and greeting, I like that, when people come into the office. Much busier than that last but one job at the solicitors—' She broke off and both women remembered the inoffensive beige office that had held so many awful secrets. 'Yeah, this job is way better than that. I love this set-up, I do. But I wouldn't do what the actual estate agents do, lie their heads off all blimmin' day long, not for anyone's money.'

'I'm confused. I'm not sure why you took the job if you don't actually like estate agents?' *And I really don't know why you gave up a post in the best school in the world in the first place,* Beth added silently.

'Simples. Money, innit? This job pays me more. I know you love that whole Wyatt's schtick, but they're a mean bunch, when all's said and done. That's how the rich get rich, and stay that way, hon. Haven't you noticed that yet? Plenty of gold on them gates, none in my pay packet. Maybe you've got things different, but I need to pay the bills,' said Nina.

Beth couldn't help nodding. Much though she loved Wyatt's, she had to admit she wasn't exactly being showered with ingots herself. Having a regular income was a blessing, as she had existed for so long on a precarious footing with a port-folio career of tiny editing jobs that added up to about ten pence more than starvation most months. And true, her job descrip-tion at Wyatt's had a useful ability to fit the very few hours she found she could spend on it. But it was also true that Wyatt's was holding firm to many of the precepts of its founder, who'd been an unabashed enthusiast for exploitation and plunder.

That suddenly reminded her. Jake's *termly account* was going to be due soon! This was the prim little phrase Wyatt's used to describe the thumping great sum they'd demand in exchange for educating her lad, and she still had very little idea how she was going to pay it. The thought usually rushed in on her in the dead of night, causing her to wake up in a cold sweat. The fact that it was now infiltrating her waking hours meant it was all getting a bit too pressing.

She had a few savings. She'd throw them at the problem first. And maybe she could offer them a job lot of second-hand crime fiction, still boxed up, in lieu of payment? It was the only thing in the house that there was definitely a surfeit of at the moment. But worrying about the school fees was only going to send her into a tailspin. She consciously turned her mind away from all that, and back to Nina and the murder.

It was hard to believe that Richard Pettit had been hiding a horrible character. Beth had only had the slightest acquaintance with him... if you could call jumping away from his dead body an introduction at all. But, although the sight had been grisly, it had partly been because he'd lain there so helplessly and uselessly, like roadkill. You averted your gaze as fast as you possibly could, but you didn't blame the poor creature for having ended up like that.

Richard Pettit just didn't seem old enough to have done anything truly awful, or even to have worked up a properly lethal secret. Yet there he'd been, as lifeless as any squirrel that had run out of luck on the South Circular. There must be a reason why he'd ended up dead.

Beth thought hard. 'Have you had any suspicious calls recently? It's just that, with Suzy Lamplugh, someone rang her office and made an appointment, didn't they?'

Nina looked blank, but Beth filled her in. 'Don't you remember, a Mr Kipper? Does that ring any bells? You know, I bet they even laughed about it in the office before she went off to meet him. And then she never came back. Can you imagine? Have you had anything like that? Someone ringing up using a funny name, or anything?'

'Yeah, no. That's the first thing they say to the newbies these days, especially the girls, soon as they get taken on,' said Nina. 'There's the jokers, the ones who try and get us to arrange a viewing for Mr C Lion or Mr I P Freely. Then there's the plain dodgy creepers. It's different for me as I'm chained to the desk, but for them that does the showing, there's a whole special prototype now. They're way more careful about that stuff than they used to be. They get people to register, get all the details, address, phone, then check them out, ring them back, do the background as far as they can. No one would just rock up to do a viewing alone with a complete stranger off the street. Not any more.'

Beth slumped a bit in her seat. In one way, it was a huge relief to know there was increased vigilance nowadays. At least no one would walk into whatever hell had awaited Suzy Lamplugh that day. But on the other hand, it did mean they were no further on. Richard Pettit had been going to meet her, so she would be the name in the diary that had been thoroughly checked. Did that mean she was the chief suspect? Not again. She'd had that once before, and clearing her name had been the impetus behind starting her first investigation. With Harry on the case, she couldn't really be in the frame, could she? It was all such a puzzle.

'Well, nevertheless, it looks as though someone wasn't quite careful enough, doesn't it? Richard ended up dead, no matter how hard anyone checked,' Beth said slowly.

'We don't know that it was a punter gone rogue, though,' Nina pointed out, sucking the last drop from her drink with a ferocious rattling from her straw. 'Maybe this Richard guy actually arranged to meet a friend at the house before your appointment, and maybe they had a row and things went wrong? Or it could have been a burglar...'

'If it was a burglar, they must have been really disappointed. There was nothing to steal in that place, unless you like dusty pink cushions, or pizza leaflets,' said Beth. At the time, the house had seemed quite benign and she'd happily imagined them living there – at least until she'd got to the kitchen and its horrors. But now, in her imagination, it was beginning to loom as large and as sinister as the Addams Family mansion. 'Whoever owned it had moved out, quite a while ago by the looks of things. It was empty, except for a few bits of furniture that no one in their right mind would want to keep.'

'Yeah, but you get my point? Just because he was an estate agent killed in an empty house doesn't mean that the murder had anything to do with his job.'

'Well, true,' said Beth reflectively. 'But it's the only thing we've got to go on at the moment.' 'We? Not sure about that, hon,' said Nina, shifting away from Beth slightly.

Beth was a little hurt. First Katie had declined to join in with her latest quest. Now Nina seemed to be washing her hands of the matter, too. And while Katie had brought enthusiasm (and some strange outfit choices) to their one shared adventure, Nina was sitting on something much better. A mountain of potential leads.

'All right, don't panic, I'm not roping you into anything,' Beth said quickly, trying to allay Nina's obvious fears without entirely shutting the door on her participation. 'But I admit I did just think, well, I sort of hoped... you are quite well placed to ask a few questions. I mean, you do know a lot of estate agents,' Beth wheedled.

'So do you! You're the one looking at houses,' Nina protested, her cherubic face outraged.

Beth gave up the subterfuge. She'd never been proficient at charming people into doing things, and apparently age had not added to her skills. 'Oh, come on, Nina. I'm not asking for much. Just the odd little query. And then you can just fill me in. It's not like everyone won't be discussing the whole business, anyway.'

Nina thought for a moment. 'Well, that's true. It's the big news, that's for sure. And it makes a nice change from all that Fartygate malarkey.'

Beth suppressed a snort, then smiled at Nina. It was partly out of relief, knowing that her friend would now make some enquiries for her even if she didn't really want to, and partly out of sheer affection. Nina never failed to cheer her up.

'Now, drink that dry, babes, and let's have a couple more before we both have to call it a night,' Nina said firmly.

Beth obediently necked her white wine, wondered for at least half a moment whether she ought to have another, then gave in to Nina's cheery urgings. She didn't want to look as though she was no fun. She hardly ever had a night on the tiles – or the comfy cushions of SE24 – like this. And she certainly had a lot of things on her mind that she could really do with blotting out.

SIX

Beth lifted her head from the pillow very slightly, just enough to squint at the time on her phone. Things took a while to come into focus, and then she rather wished she hadn't made all that effort.

It would be wrong to say she had a killer hangover. She just had a feeling that someone had borrowed her skull in the night and had been using it to play football with in the scrubby back garden. She thanked her stars that Harry wasn't here to say, 'I told you so.' He'd given her a lecture last night about taking paracetamol and drinking lots of water before bed and, of course, she'd then refused to do either on principle. She could see the tablets lying there on her bedside table, on top of the alarm clock so she couldn't miss them, as well as a large and untouched glass of London's finest tap. Huh.

As she moved slowly down the stairs, clutching the banister on one side and the wall on the other, Colin appeared out of the sitting room to greet her with his waggiest tail and his worst breath.

'God, Colin, have you been eating dead badgers all night? I wish you'd brush your teeth,' she said, pointing her face away but giving the lovely old creature a gentle pat all the same. It was impossible not to respond to his simple joy in the new day and, more particularly, his enthusiasm at the sight of his mistress – even if she was looking more than usually rough. Beth felt her doldrums lift a tiny bit as she stroked his warm chocolate fur with unusual care, trying not to make any sudden movements that would jar the extremely painful contents of her head.

And then her spirits came crashing down again, as Harry emerged from the kitchen, tall, commanding, bristling with energy, and with an I-told-you-so look all over his face. 'Good morning,' he said, using, in Beth's view, an unnecessarily loud tone of voice.

'Is it?' she said quietly, trying to sidle past him. That was never an easy operation, given his size, but was even more difficult these days with the volume of boxes stacked in the narrow hall. She'd been so sure he'd already left for work. Now there were going to be all kinds of recriminations. She'd really been counting on having a bit of time to herself, just a short but necessary interlude, during which she could pull all the corners of her cranium back together again with a very strong coffee, or three, before getting to grips with the day. But it seemed that chance was very much gone. She sat down carefully, shutting her eyes against the shafts of watery autumn sunshine which seemed to be hitting the backs of her eyes like laser beams.

Sure enough, Harry tailed her into the kitchen, but just when she was expecting the tirade to begin, he seemed to unbend from his great height and said, in quite a kindly way, 'This is for you.' A brimming mug of tea was set before her on the freshly cleared table. 'I was just bringing it up to the bedroom, but you beat me to it.'

She looked into the tan-coloured depths and sniffed. It was builder's, of course. He'd never got the hang of making a proper cup of Earl Grey. But beggars couldn't be choosers, and it would save her the horrible business of tangling with the kettle all by herself this early in the morning, which seemed like an insurmountable palaver in her weakened state.

'You're quite late. Jake's already been and gone,' said Harry.

It might have been her imagination, or even her guilty conscience, but the momentary kindliness now definitely seemed to have been replaced with a censoriousness tone. It was as clear as if he'd written it out in capitals on a Post-it and left it on the table in front of her: *BAD MOTHER.*

She wondered, yet again, why she'd stayed on and had that last drink – well, the last few – with Nina. They'd both ended up having to trickle home alone as they lived in opposite directions, which was not the best idea with a killer on the loose. Last night, though, they'd both laughed uproariously at the hilarious idea that they might get murdered. In fact, they'd got to the stage where absolutely everything was funny, from the school fees to the boxes of books to Nina's not-so-nice new boss, and most of all the bartender who'd firmly shooed them out onto the streets of Herne Hill at closing time and locked the door behind them.

Beth winced again as she thought of the state she must have been in when she'd finally reached Pickwick Road. She vaguely remembered steadying herself on the letterbox in the main street, outside the defunct post office, and then tottering from lamppost to lamppost, like Colin on a mission to leave his calling card the entire length of Dulwich Village. Well, never mind. She'd made it back in one piece, eventually. And had a few hours of sleep.

I'll soon be fine, she thought, wincing slightly. It wasn't as though she got tiddly that often. And she hadn't said or done anything really silly, had she? That would have been the worst thing.

'And as for what you said to me last night...' Harry raised his voice as he strode down the hall and stood by the front door.

Her head whipped up. Ouch. *Oh God, no!* 'What?' she asked feebly.

'Don't worry, I won't tell a soul,' he said with a wink, and then he was gone.

Beth sighed in frustration. Drat the man. She couldn't tell whether he was joking or not, though for the sake of her mental equilibrium she decided it was much better to be sure he was. Or else she'd spend the rest of the day trying to reconstruct a conversation they may or may not have had.

She wasn't going to let herself feel too guilty about Jake, either. As Harry kept telling her – when he wasn't deliberately trying to make a point, that was – her son was a big boy now. To say he wasn't keen on walking to school with her was a massive understatement. He'd try every trick in the book to make sure that he either outstripped her, or he fell back and trailed behind. Anything to ensure that no one would ever think the two tiny, dark-haired, grey-eyed people walking in the same direction to an identical destination were, in fact, closely related.

Oh, never mind, thought Beth, and shook her head to clear it. That was a terrible mistake, but it did get her fumbling to her feet and moving slowly over to the high cupboard where she stored the medicines – out of Jake's reach, but out of hers as well. She'd picked the cupboard for safety's sake when he'd been an inquisitive toddler. Now the precaution was irrelevant, but she'd never quite got round to changing things. It meant she either had to jump to snag the paracetamol packet, or drag a chair across the kitchen. The second idea seemed like an impossible hurdle, so she tried the first. The operation jarred her skull and its already scrambled contents horribly, and made the tablets doubly necessary once she'd finally reached the little carton and plucked it out of the cupboard. Why couldn't she just have taken the ones that Harry had so kindly left out for her? But she harrumphed at the idea, and swallowed back the paracetamol with her last swig of tea, sliding the rest of the packet into her handbag just in case, and crossed her fingers that the day could only get better.

Just then, she heard the mail. Their postman was quite erratic and could appear any time from 8 a.m. onwards, depending on how many Boden, Brora, White Company and Lululemon parcels he had to deliver that day. This was quite early for him, which was surely a good sign. You never knew, it might even be a cheque from one of her freelance gigs. Several must be just about due.

She got up slowly and carefully, dodged Magpie and Colin, who were milling around looking expectantly at their bowls, and made her way over to the mat. She bent gingerly and picked up the little pile of envelopes, flicking through them as she carried them back over to the table. Catalogues from companies who still thought Jake was five; catalogues from companies who thought she could afford cashmere; even a catalogue for Harry from a company that thought he could do with more books – she chucked *that* in the bin straight away – then bills, bills, bills. And, lurking at the bottom, a letter with that distinctive Wyatt's crest. It couldn't be, could it? Not already.

But it was. Jake's first whacking great invoice from the school. She unfolded the crisp white pages, dismayed at the sheer number of them, and squinted at the total. No, that couldn't be right. She rubbed her eyes. Maybe all the alcohol had given her some sort of visual impairment? She blinked a few times, and even tried to take a hearty swig of her tea, before realising there was none left. But nothing helped. The figures at the bottom still danced up and down, shouting a total that was making her headache feel worse by the second. What on earth was she going to do now? Perhaps Wyatt's took body parts in lieu of payment, though she doubted they would give much for her liver, the state it was in today. Maybe a nice kidney, though? Would that do the trick?

She sighed gustily and whacked the pages down on the table, shocking Magpie who ran straight for her cat flap and was out before you could say bankruptcy. Beth knew she'd been slacking lately on her freelance jobs. That had obviously been a massive mistake. She needed to ratchet up the work, big time. And make sure she didn't lose the Wyatt's job either.

She looked at her watch. *Lord.* It was about time she got in there and did something to make herself look indispensable.

SEVEN

By lunchtime, Beth was beginning to feel normal again, thanks to two more paracetamol, a drenching on the way to school which had acted as a refreshing cold shower, several strong coffees from the staff canteen, and a lot of deep breathing while she tackled her inbox.

Things weren't quite as dire as she'd first thought. She'd remembered that Wyatt's had promised to pay her extra for her biography of Sir Thomas, the ghastly rake who'd founded the school, and assuming she could just cobble that whole story together as quickly as possible, and then make it a massive best-seller, that should almost cover the first term's fees. What she was going to do after that was a little more opaque, she had to admit.

Was there anything else she could do to make some money? Write a book about how to catch murderers, for instance? Beth rapidly dismissed the idea. She had no gift at all for fiction. Even telling a lie was beyond her, though she had a black belt in prevarication – or would have done if she'd just got round to taking the exam – and what she really knew about crime scenes and police procedures could be written in huge letters on the back of one of Magpie's cat treats. Despite her hopes earlier that morning, she was pretty sure no one would be interested in buying a used body part from her. Or even renting one, which meant prostitution was probably out, too. There wasn't much of a market in Dulwich, as far as she was aware, and she refused to travel far for work. She was also willing to bet that it required shaving her legs a lot more often than she was prepared to contemplate. This was leaving aside the glaring fact that she was quite unlikely to get much custom, unless she signed up with a madam who had an equine theme amongst her stable of girls. The certainty that Harry wouldn't be impressed was a consideration too.

Much though it pained her to admit it, moving from her lovely house in Pickwick Road to something a little – or, actually, a lot – less pricey in an outlying area was the best prospect. The only realistic one, in fact. Releasing equity, they called it, didn't they? It would give her a chunk of money that she could then throw at the fees. People around here often moved, and some were quite open about why they'd taken the plunge. She wouldn't be the only person making the ultimate sacrifice by a long chalk. But she'd find it very hard. And, of course, once it was done, that was her main asset disposed of. Unless she kept shifting to areas that, from a Dulwich snob's point of view, were less and less desirable. She'd probably have to end up in the Outer Hebrides by the time Jake finished at Wyatt's. And there was still university to pay for after that.

Hard though it was to imagine young Jake ever getting any sort of job, except as a test pilot for new PlayStation games, he would one day have to make his own way in the world. And by the time he'd finished school, that would probably involve multiple degrees. Nowadays, she was willing to bet even the awful waiters in Aurora, the worst café in Dulwich, had qualifications in hospitality or event planning or numerology or astrophysics or *something*, though there was precious little sign of intelligent thought in the way the place was run.

Ugh. She felt like a hamster on a wheel, getting nowhere fast but fated to spin around forever trying to support her boy. But she mustn't get too far ahead of herself. He was happy, he was doing fine, and Wyatt's would mean he had the chance to go on to great things, which was surely what it was all about. She mustn't pitchfork herself into despair – especially not when she had a headache this bad. 'Sufficient unto the day is the evil thereof,' somebody somewhere had once said. Beth was now willing to bet they'd been looking at a school fees bill when they'd opened their mouths.

For a long time, she had just been keeping going, a little bit at a time, not gazing too far ahead, keeping their heads above water as best she could. And hoping it would just work. But she now recognised that a move really was the only solution.

From the outside, it was going to be business as usual. She'd been looking at houses for a while. But she'd only been doing that to keep Harry quiet, she now admitted to herself. There was always going to be something wrong with a house that wasn't in Pickwick Road. She'd imagined herself regretfully saying no to every property she saw, for the foreseeable future, until Harry was finally forced to admit that there was nothing out there which was a patch on Beth's lovely little house.

Yes, Harry was trying to make things difficult by bringing over all his awful books, she knew that. He was making the point that they jointly needed more space. But she'd thought that eventually even he would get fed up with tripping over boxes, and would weed out his collection of his own volition.

Now, though, Beth saw that she'd actually boxed herself into a corner. She'd always known she couldn't really afford Wyatt's for Jake. Resolutely not thinking about the fees had been a way of avoiding the problem, not of sorting it out, she now had to concede. The long-looming crunch had come. And the house, her beloved house, had to go.

Just as Beth felt her headache creeping back – this time through sadness rather than alcohol abuse – she realised that this decision, though tough, did not have to be a disaster. Leaving Dulwich was not the end of the world. Or rather, it didn't have to be.

People did it all the time. Moving vans were no novelty where she lived. She'd waved off friends and neighbours loads of times. People like her who'd decided to set off on new adventures. Human life was sustainable outside SE21. Even her old friend, Jen, had done it, Beth realised, and had set up home in Camberwell. Although look how that turned out, she thought glumly.

Best to concentrate on the fact that leaving Dulwich was a well-worn path. Even Nina lived in Herne Hill, not Dulwich proper. Beth always erred on the side of inclusivity, using the catch-all description of 'Dulwich' for areas stretching all the way up to Sydenham Hill on one side and Dog Kennel Hill on the other. But she knew others – Belinda McKenzie, for example – preferred to chop the place into tiny demarcations, the better to emphasise the exclusivity of the slices they lived in themselves. East Dulwich, West Dulwich, Honor Oak, Dulwich borders; she'd heard them all in her time. She, of course, lived firmly in Dulwich Village. The best address. The one that carried the highest price tag. And this was her part in the bargain she'd unwittingly struck with Wyatt's, when Jake had got in. Her son's education would come at the cost of her house.

Yes, she would always have some regrets – but she'd never begrudge Jake the finest schooling she could get for him. She owed him a great start in life. His father wasn't around to do all that he would have so loved to have done for Jake. Although that wasn't Beth's fault – James had been just as guilty as she had of downplaying his symptoms and failing to get treatment – she was the one carrying the can. So, this can was just going to have to be kicked up the hill, literally, all the way to Sydenham, and that was that. And they would be fine. Absolutely fine.

Plus – and it felt really quite odd to be adding this as a bonus, but nevertheless Beth realised she did think of it as one – house-hunting would give her a good excuse to find the estate agent's killer.

She sat back in her swivel chair and looked around her. Even though her future might not always involve her living in the heart of Dulwich, she'd still be working in this lovely place. She'd therefore still be a part of life here, and would labour, as she had been doing so tirelessly, to keep it and the rest of south London safe.

And that was her second decision of the day. For once, Beth realised she wasn't going to second-guess her interest in the crime she'd been dragged into. She wouldn't wish it away or try and find a thousand reasons why she shouldn't get involved. She wouldn't even allow Harry's inevitable disapproval to put her off. She'd been a witness to the discovery of poor, pale Richard Pettit, and that meant she owed him something. She could busy herself finding her little family a new home, and at the same time have a proper dig around in this mystery.

As she fired up her laptop and started scrolling through properties in Peckham, Sydenham, South Norwood and beyond, for the first time she was almost looking forward to getting a move on.

EIGHT

Beth edged forward in the darkened hall, her index finger to her own quivering lip, on tippy toes as she bounced lightly from one side to the other. Whose idea had it been to replace the tiles with rubber and put the whole lot on a ship pitching in stormy seas, she wondered, trying to avoid crashing into Colin. He padded over to her, unperturbed by her weaving gait, tail wagging with the sheer joy of seeing her back in her rightful place at long last.

'Hi, Colin, shhhh,' she said, giggling as he slobbered on her hand and made a rare attempt to goose her. Usually, he knew not to try this old trick with his mistress, though all other women were fair game. But something told him she wasn't quite as vigilant as usual this evening. Beth shrieked as his cold wet nose tried to probe and batted him away frantically. 'Don't do that, Colin, you'll wake up Harry,' she told him in a stage whisper.

'Too late. Harry isn't asleep,' said a deep voice from the sitting room. Instantly, Beth's cheerfully sozzled mood evaporated. Oh no. She was in trouble again. She knew her behaviour, heading out for drinks on successive nights and getting unmistakably squiffy each time, was out of character.

But somehow the judgemental air Harry had had this morning, added to the strains and stresses of facing her financial situation head-on for once, had meant that when Janice and Sam from work had suggested a drink in the evening, Beth hadn't slipped into her normal default mode of deferring. After all, if Janice, with her tiny baby, could manage to get a precious evening out, then wasn't it time that Beth did the same? Her boy at home was much too strapping to be used as a reason to rush home, and she had an even more strapping built-in babysitter these days. No excuses, the girls had said, and she'd allowed her arm to be gently twisted.

They'd had a great evening, snorting with laughter about subjects that were normally off-limits. Beth had done her damnedest to get Janice to spill the beans about what Belinda McKenzie had said to Dr Grover in their recent meeting. She reckoned even the fly on the wall would need a hefty number of counselling sessions after witnessing that little fracas. But, despite umpteen white wine spritzers, Janice remained the soul of discretion on that intriguing topic. Or maybe she was too scarred by it to wish to relive the debacle.

She redeemed herself, though, by dropping the bombshell that Tom Seasons, the former bursar who'd been Beth's bête noire, was now suing the school for constructive dismissal. He'd finally flounced out of his job after the dramatic conclusion of Beth's last case – not a moment too soon, in Beth's opinion. He'd had various swings at her over the past couple of years. Now, in what seemed like a similar spirit, he was trying his luck against the mighty Wyatt's itself. Beth's blood boiled at the thought that he was now attacking Dr Grover and the school in this way, when he'd pretended for so long to be a faithful servant. Honestly, that man...

She'd nearly fallen off her bar stool in her indignation, and only the loud cackles of her companions had brought her back to the present and the great joy of being able to laugh about a bully instead of having to face him day in, day out. And at least he'd stopped hiding his true nature from the world. Everyone now knew he was toxic; it wasn't just Beth dealing with him alone, while he bamboozled others under the heavy-handed cloak of 'banter'.

They'd spent the next few hours putting the world to rights, escaping and ignoring domestic cares, and laughing again and again at the injustices and absurdities of their lives. Sam was single and childless, so she wasn't bowed down yet by the chores that both Beth and Janice faced. But she did have plenty of tales to tell from her adventures on Tinder. These made Beth feel that much more than her fair share of cooking and cleaning might not always be such a terrible exchange for having a man about the place, after all. When Sam wasn't being ghosted by swains who'd previously professed hopeless adoration, she was having her arm twisted to get up to shenanigans that Beth had never even heard of and didn't wish to try, but was very happy to shriek with laughter about. She honestly felt ten foot taller and a stone lighter by the time they'd finished and were decanted back onto the streets of Dulwich.

Unfortunately, though, it was her second drunken foray in a row, and it looked like Harry, for one, was not enjoying her spreading her wings. She looked up a little nervously now and felt herself shrink, Alice in Wonderland-style, as he appeared in the sitting room doorway, hands braced far up on the door jamb. Even in the darkness of the hall, she could see his blue eyes were as full of harsh questions as they must be when he contemplated some appalling suspect in the police interview rooms.

She took a deep breath and drew herself up to her full, not very majestic, height, then wobbled slightly on legs braced against a gentle swell. She wasn't wearing heels – when did she ever? She'd never got the hang of them and would need a

Zimmer frame, or stabilisers, to negotiate the streets of Dulwich in anything more vertiginous than a one-inch wedge. But right now, she felt as though she was wearing stilettos on a ski slope. It was just about possible that she'd drunk a whole lot more than she'd realised.

She put one hand on Colin's collar for support, while the other braced itself on a tower of boxes. And then she glared up at Harry. It was actually his fault that she wanted to go out – the place was filling up relentlessly with his rubbish. It wasn't the cosy home she'd known for so many years any more. Could he blame her if she didn't want to spend the evening trying to squint at the telly through a thicket of cartons?

Apparently, he could. He coughed drily. 'Fancy a herbal tea? Or perhaps a very, very strong coffee?' He didn't even wait for her answer but strode off to the kitchen and snapped on the overhead light. Beth shut her eyes briefly. In some ways, it was a relief. She'd been expecting something a lot more blistering than the offer of a hot beverage. But she was left feeling a bit tottery.

'Come on, boy,' she said to Colin, and they trudged into the sitting room.

Harry was using one of the taller cardboard boxes as a makeshift occasional table, and it still bore signs of his lonely supper. She supposed she was meant to feel guilty about that too. Well, she wasn't going to, she thought, collapsing onto the sofa as far away as possible from the dirty plate. And she was definitely going to resist the temptation to pick it up and wash it immediately.

The telly was flanked on both sides by low walls of boxes, and there were more stacked – quite tidily, she had to admit – in the corner by the window which overlooked the neglected back garden. But although they'd been arranged neatly, they did completely destroy the spacious feel of the room. Every time she glanced over at them, she felt herself becoming crosser.

Had James had this much crap? Did all men drag such great

volumes of baggage around with them? She felt as though she was the innocent victim of a hostile takeover, with her own possessions slowly becoming edged out by his. She'd been looking through her own bookshelves recently, deciding what she could bear to get rid of to make room for his collection. But she didn't really want to lose anything. She'd had to sort through the lot following a recent burglary and her shelves were not only squeaky clean but very well-ordered too. Why should she have to chuck out her stuff to make room for his? He wasn't making any effort at all to downsize.

And what about Jake? What would he be making of this incursion into their home? True, he'd shown not one single sign, so far, of caring about the volume of Harry's things in the house. As long as the PlayStation controllers were within easy reach, the boxes could tower right up to the ceiling and he'd still be happy. But was there a deeper level, at which he was secretly uneasy at his father being replaced, at a new man moving in? Beth's head hurt just thinking about it.

Maybe now, after her night on what passed in Dulwich for the tiles – naturally, they'd be Fired Earth's finest handmade artisan variety – was not the time for soul-searching. She reached for the remote and flicked on the TV. It was the local news. Immediately the screen was filled with a huge image of a house – the very one she'd been looking at when the estate agent had flopped out of the cupboard, limp and lifeless as a pennant on a still day. Yellow crime scene tape now closed off the gate, and a bored-looking policeman was scrupulously avoiding the camera lens.

Beth's eyes wandered over the exterior of the house. It had been evening when she'd been house-hunting, but this footage had been shot in daylight. The house really was handsome. She admired the detailing of the red brick, something she hadn't been able to appreciate on her visit, partly because of the darkness, partly because of the horror within. Those windows were a good size, and you could see that the tiny front garden, although not as well-maintained as that of its neighbours, could be sorted out very easily. The place definitely had kerb appeal. Not bad, she found herself thinking, then stopped in horror. What kind of a ghoul was she?

Harry appeared in the doorway in the nick of time, allowing her to leave the question dangling unanswered. 'Did you hear me?' he said, stepping over a box of books and presenting her with a piping hot mint tea.

The mug burnt her hands; she set it down as quickly as she could on a box and some of the steaming liquid slopped over the rim. She tried to suppress the ignoble hope that it was seeping inside and wrecking lots and lots of books. He eyed her with beady disapproval.

'Sorry, what did you say? The telly was too loud.'

He turned on his heel and said over his shoulder, 'Oh, nothing really. Just reminding you that there'll be more boxes coming tomorrow.'

Suddenly, Beth's temper went from nought to sixty, and her pleasant feeling of wavy drunkenness evaporated like morning mist.

'What! You're kidding, right? That's a joke, isn't it?' she barked at his departing back, and then rather wished she hadn't as her skull ached.

He turned round, arching an eyebrow in mild surprise. 'Just a few more things. But we're at the halfway stage, or nearly.'

'Halfway? *No!* You can't bring anything else here. There's no room,' said Beth, leaping to her feet, and throwing scalding tea over herself in the process. The toothpaste smell of mint rose up from her wet jeans. 'Damn.'

'Well, where are you expecting me to put my boxes?' Harry asked, all sweet reasonableness, head on one side.

'I don't care! Just not *here*. You can see the place is full to the brim already with your stupid paperbacks.' She gestured

wildly at all the boxes lining the room and caught her hand on
one. 'Ouch!' Her cheeks flushed with heat, though whether it
was the after-effects of the alcohol, the pain, or her sudden rage,
she didn't know.

'Oh, I see. My books are stupid, are they?' Harry asked, his
voice raised, too. He took a step towards her.

Beth knew she had gone too far. Harry adored his crime
fiction library, and she'd always found his enthusiasm rather
endearing. A detective, who didn't mind reading an entire genre
which was predicated on the idea that an amateur with no rele-
vant or useful experience could always beat the police? It spoke
of an inner confidence and a willingness to be generous-spirited
which, in the past, she'd found very attractive. But that was
before the whole of his library had come home to roost. Now
she found herself standing up and charging towards him, as best
she could through the steeplechase course of boxes.

'Yes, they are stupid when there's no room to move in here,
when we're tripping over 1930s poisonings every time we turn
around. You must be able to see there's no space for any more.
It's getting ridiculous.'

Harry now had his hands on his hips, and an expression of
righteous indignation spread across his handsome face. 'Oh,
right! So, you don't want my stuff here? How am I supposed to
take that? We're supposed to be moving in together, aren't we?'

He'd lit the blue touch paper now. Beth let fly with another
tirade. Before she knew it, she had roved far from the books and
boxes. In fact, she found herself dragging into the arena every
single niggle about Harry that she'd been incubating since the
day they met. The way he dumped his coat on the banisters; the
fact his plates never wandered back into the kitchen unless she
escorted them herself; his determination to exclude her from all
investigations; his habit of leaving the loo seat up; even the way
he left her texts wafting unanswered forever in the ether. She
was puce and out of breath by the time she'd finished, and the

silence seemed to ring with everything she'd said. She looked down for a second, trying either to take a breath for a second wind, or to compose herself to apologise. Even she wasn't quite sure which.

When she lifted her gaze to Harry's again, she immediately became aware of another set of eyes on her – this one peering down on the scene from near the top of the stairs. *Oh no!* Colin and Magpie had made themselves scarce long since, but it seemed Harry and Beth's raised voices had been loud enough to wake Jake.

'Darling! Oh, I'm so sorry. We were just discussing...' Beth stumbled, moving forward past Harry, who was as still as a stone policeman now. And about as useful.

'Discussing! Right,' said Jake. His voice was sleepy, but his words were unmistakably sarcastic.

Beth hurried up the stairs towards him, tripping slightly and clasping the banister, wishing fervently now that she hadn't drunk so much, hadn't reacted to Harry's news, hadn't kicked off...

She couldn't remember the last time Jake had woken up in the middle of the night, but it had been a while. And he'd never, ever in his life been woken up by a blazing row. That was partly because he'd been so young when James had died. Both she and James had been exhausted by parenthood, much too tired to rise above gentle bickering about whose turn it was to put the bins out and other small niggles. In any case, they hadn't had the kind of relationship that was ever punctuated by seismic rows. Their aims and backgrounds had been broadly similar, their views on childcare meshed well. There really hadn't been that much to get heated about.

She recognised that might have led to its own troubles, eventually. They had been morphing into a brother/sister rela-tionship, Beth could see it now. But at the time she'd relished the peaceful support James had always given her so unstintingly. And now, she missed it all the more.

She was crucified by the fact that they had not only woken poor Jake up in the middle of the night, which was bound to make him exhausted, cranky and less able to cope at school tomorrow, but that he had witnessed such a horrible drunken rant. Beth couldn't remember the last time she'd let her temper rule her like that. In the moment, it had felt quite liberating and she'd certainly got a multitude of things off her chest. But now she was filled with regret. Honestly, she wasn't fit to be in charge of a child.

By the time she reached the top of the stairs, Jake was back in his own room with the door firmly shut. She knocked on it gently, only to hear him say in a muffled voice, 'Go away, I'm asleep.' She hung her head in shame, and trailed slowly down the stairs. Harry was waiting at the bottom.

NINE

Beth braced herself for round two, but Harry, who seemed equally exhausted, just looked down at her pinched and miserable face and took her in his arms instead. Immediately she felt safe again. It didn't stop her bitterly regretting what had just happened. But it was enough to help her drag herself upstairs with him, crawl into bed and fall into a dreamless sleep.

The next morning, as well as the now-familiar crushing headache, Beth had a very bad case of remorse. If this was a life of heavy drinking, then you could keep it, she thought to herself as she tried to brush her teeth without moving anything from the neck up. She rushed downstairs – as fast as she could – so that she didn't miss seeing Jake, as she had done the day before. But he might as well already have been absent, for all the interaction he was interested in offering. He confined himself to giving his mother and Harry watchful glances.

To Beth's jaundiced eyes, it felt as though he was bracing himself every time Beth opened her mouth to ask Harry to pass the cereal or the milk, in case open warfare broke out again. After an awkward silent period of munching, during which

Beth failed to come up with any anodyne topics of conversation and Harry busied himself only with scarfing down enough calories to sustain his daily battle against south London's criminal elements, Jake pushed up from the table, dumped his bowl in the sink and looked as though he was about to make a run for it.

'Jake. I just wanted to say... anything you heard last night – I mean, it doesn't mean anything... I hope you weren't upset, that's all I'm trying to say,' said Beth, her face aflame. She was used to blushing, but she couldn't remember a time when she'd ever felt so ashamed in front of her own child.

Jake took a long hard look at her, then squinted under his brows at Harry. She must make him a hair appointment, Beth thought. 'Whatever,' he said with a shrug, then shouldered his backpack and slammed the door behind him.

Colin, hearing footsteps, came out of the sitting room a little bit too late and sat on the mat, staring at the door, wagging his tail in a slightly hopeless fashion. Beth knew exactly how he felt.

She pinched the bridge of her nose with her finger and thumb, trying to cut off her headache, and was lost in her own little world until she felt Harry's warm hand come down on her arm.

She looked up, dreading another awkward conversation or, even worse, a telling-off, but he looked as unsure as she did. Then they spoke at once.

'Look, if this is too soon...'

'Look, if you've changed your mind—'

They laughed at each other, the tension suddenly dissolving. Beth got up awkwardly and they embraced amid the breakfast debris. When she was in his arms, her doubts had a habit of evaporating, like night frights vanquished by morning sun. She just hoped that this time her present feelings of rightness, of love and certainty, would persist. This was a big step. There was so much riding on it, not least the happiness of one small boy. Beth simply couldn't afford to get this wrong. Home was where the heart was, didn't they say? And, like it or not, she seemed to have thrown her lot in with Harry.

Walking along to school later, and realising yet again that she was going to be late, Beth decided not to reproach herself too much. The inevitable detour upstairs for an energetic rekindling of their relationship had not only been necessary but actually mandatory. She now felt a lot more clear-headed about the road ahead.

Passing the grand doorway to reception, she caught sight of Janice's blonde hair. Her friend was tweaking the handsome display of school prospectuses into ever more perfect alignment on the coffee table. Parents would flick through these later, taking in nothing of the impressive statistics and fabulous photographs, while waiting anxiously for their offspring to come out of their all-important interviews.

Beth quickened her pace a little, not wishing to get into a post-mortem on what had, at the time, been a fabulous evening, but was something she now looked back on with regret.

It was going to be her last outing for a while, that was for sure. Even if she could have faced more hangovers, she certainly didn't want to be looking at Harry's stern face and Jake's distress any time in the near future. Although she wasn't keen for her brace of censorious men to put the kybosh on her fun, there were plenty of serious issues that needed her attention, apart from her lovely gossipy friends.

She wasn't footloose and fancy-free, like Sam, or half of a Dulwich power couple, like Janice. She was someone who had always needed to work to keep her head above water. She supposed her finances might ease somewhat when Harry was a permanent fixture, but they hadn't really talked about how this house business was going to work. Would they have a joint account? Who would pay what towards the mortgage? Her main aim in moving was to sort out the school fees, but could she expect Harry to help her with those? And how much did a policeman actually earn, anyway? There were always so many questions. And the morning after their first truly blistering row didn't seem the moment to broach any of them.

No, it was definitely a day when she needed to get her head down, do some atoning, and get on with serious hard work for a change. And luckily, she had something she could really get her teeth into. She marched across the tarmacked acres of playground, unlocked the door to her little archives office, and sat down decisively at her desk. On the right-hand side was her groaning in-box. For an instant, she even contemplated pulling it towards her. But then she got out a pad of paper instead.

There was something serious afoot in the area, and she of all people needed to focus on what really mattered. Her previous successes in discovering murderers weren't an accident, however slipshod her methods of deduction had sometimes appeared and however much her success had seemed to astonish everyone around her, including Harry. The truth was that she was actually quite good at working this stuff out. And there was the side issue that investigations had always proved to be wonderful distractions from the other, more intractable problems in her life. Yes, she lived in a house infested with crime novels. Yes, paying the school fees was going to clean her out more efficiently than her most intense bout of OCD ever could. And yes, she did have a mountain of actual work piling up. But none of that seemed nearly as important, at this moment, as the unexplained murder on her books.

All right, there was no particular reason why one little archivist should feel it was up to her to make a difference in the case, particularly when, as she knew full well, the mighty Metropolitan Police Force would happily declare the whole thing unsolved at the drop of a hat. But she'd seen that pale hand unfurl; and, more chillingly still, she'd been the reason the man had been at that house in the first place. She had a stake in the game.

Not, she reminded herself, that you should ever really call a murder that.

The second thing Beth did, after getting up from her desk and cracking a window to let out a bit of the Colin smell, was to flip open her laptop and go to the Rightmove tab. She jotted down a couple of quick notes and tried not to feel the obligatory stab of guilt as the rich aroma of old Labrador dissipated. She hardly noticed it when Colin himself was there. And his presence was so reassuring; all she had to do was look at him and he thumped the ground enthusiastically with his tail. It was like having her own cheerleader sitting in the corner, though admittedly, his cocoa-brown coat wasn't quite as glamorous as the traditional little red skirt and pair of pompoms.

She shook her head to get rid of the image of Colin in full costume and on top of a pyramid consisting of a furious Magpie and the other neighbourhood moggies, and tried to concentrate on her screen. Doing this sort of research was no hardship. She didn't mind admitting she actually loved delving into the property websites. She was keen to see whether any new properties had been added since she'd last had a look yesterday; and also wanted to see if, by poring over the details of *that* house in Sydenham, she could tease out anything at all that might constitute the first glimmering of a clue.

Rightmove was addictive stuff. Even if you weren't entirely sure whether you wanted to up sticks at all, there was something about the glossy parades of photos that could make you feel that it was the best idea in the world. Of course, that was at the top end of the price range. Lower down, and things sometimes took a comical turn. Unmade beds, half-finished plates of food left just in shot, and gardens infested with the sort of plastic chairs that were destined, along with cockroaches, to inherit the world after any nuclear winter.

Unfortunately, with the sort of joint budget that Beth and Harry were looking at, they were more at the moulded plastic end of the market. But that didn't prevent her starting her search today by having a quick scan over the upper echelons of the Dulwich market, even though these were precisely the properties she couldn't afford and was having to move away from.

Luckily, there wasn't anything new. Indeed, some of the houses had been there forever. And although their website pictures were as fresh as the day they had first been posted, to Beth they were now looking distinctly unimpressive, no matter how ginormous the price tags. There must be a reason why these places weren't selling, and it wasn't just the unrealistic number of noughts tacked onto their asking prices. Sometimes you could work out the problem by looking at the floor plans – inconveniently located loos; a dearth of bathrooms; third or fourth 'bedrooms' that were really cupboards. That reminded Beth of the Sydenham house; hadn't the girl from the agents said the very same thing?

Beth changed the postcode parameters at the top of her search and a new set of results popped up. The top listings here were much more affordable, but somehow that meant the whole process was less fun. She just couldn't get as excited about projecting herself into any of these perfectly decent houses, with their nice-enough kitchens and reasonable number of reception rooms. What she truly wanted, what she'd always had her heart set on, was the sort of Georgian pile smack bang in the centre of Dulwich Village, with six bedrooms and a secret garden door opening into Dulwich Park. Or, failing that, one of the swanky 1960s townhouses, like the one owned by the late graffiti artist Slope, which weren't that easy on the eye of the beholder but did afford their owners peerless views over the village, beautiful Belair Park and the lovely grounds of Wyatt's Museum of Art.

But she wasn't doing this to have lots of fun playing ideal homes, Beth reminded herself sternly, as she tried to zero in on *that* Sydenham house. This was serious research she was doing, for the very important purpose of getting a proper grip on her investigation. Ooh, but that was a rather nice house there, with the magical words 'New Instruction' pasted over the photographs. She'd just have a quick look...

Twenty minutes later, Beth had finally clicked on the tall, handsome, but curiously forbidding façade of the Sydenham house. Looking at it now, she was quite surprised that she'd ever agreed to go and give it a once-over. It wasn't the kind of thing that usually appealed to her. Not that there was anything wrong with it, as such. But still. Was she reading too much into the photos, particularly now that she knew what had happened in the place? She looked through them, trying to imagine she was seeing it all for the first time, and definitely trying to push away the memories...

There was the dusty pink sitting room again. And the kitchen. She nipped past that frame as quickly as she could. The upstairs was interesting. Four bedrooms, all fine but shabby; the smallest was, just as the estate agent girl had said, tiny. Which one had that pile of clothes been in? Ah, the second-largest bedroom, next to the bathroom. And, more importantly, who on earth had they belonged to? They hadn't looked like the kind of clothes a young estate agent would be wearing. Richard Pettit, from her very brief acquaintance with him, had been in the shiny suit brigade, as far as she could recall from her epic long-jump away from his body. He hadn't looked like the hoody type. But maybe when he was off duty? And if the clothes weren't his, then who did they belong to?

Beth shook her head. She mustn't get ahead of herself. For now, she just needed to cast a dispassionate eye over the place. Could she see the house as an outsider would? Or was she now so jaundiced by the events of that night that it would forever be, as the local media had christened it, a 'house of death'?

It was so hard to say. In many ways, it just looked like the kind of bog-standard place that someone would want to get shot of. Beth was confident that when they finally took the plunge and bought somewhere (she wasn't going to say *if* they did), she could make it look nice – well, as nice as her current house, at any rate. Whoever had owned this place, their days of taking pride in their home seemed to be long gone. It hadn't had a lick of paint, let alone a good vacuuming, for yonks.

Maybe they'd been elderly, with children who'd flown the nest? Had they rattled around, waiting only for those Sunday lunches that had left their distinctive aroma behind in the kitchen?

Beth sighed. Would that be her, one day? At the rate she was going, she wouldn't be surprised if Jake never came home once he'd finally got out. And she couldn't even tempt him back with her roast potatoes, unless she somehow learnt the knack of making them golden and crispy instead of flabby, wan and stuck so hard to the pan that they left half of themselves behind when scraped onto a plate. But Jake wasn't shallow enough to think only of his stomach. He'd come back to see her, to spend time with his beloved mum, to chat. Yeah, right, she thought to herself. They'd had some in-depth talks recently, hadn't they? She remembered his last withering 'Whatever' with a pang.

She turned quickly back to the website. Did this house maybe have a sadder aura than others on the website? Was it something about the place itself, rather than the estate agent, that had provided the conditions for murder? She knew she'd felt somehow resistant to seeing it, and the estate agent, poor Richard Pettit, had been quite persuasive. What was it exactly he'd said? It was so hard to remember. Over the last couple of weeks, she'd listened to any number of spiels from these people about the charms of the places they were selling, most of which had just gone in one ear and out the other. She thought he'd mentioned the tired décor, but of course he'd done a switcheroo on that and presented it as a massive positive, 'offering tremendous scope to put your own stamp on things'.

This did suggest he hadn't been a great judge of character. She was pretty sure she didn't come across as the type who'd find inner fulfilment in sanding down doors and stripping floors for six solid months to make the place presentable. But then, as she was from Dulwich, maybe Pettit had taken a bet she'd be in the Belinda McKenzie mould. Belinda was a relentless improver who constantly had a full team of workmen tweaking something somewhere in her house, if only the tiebacks on her curtains. Even Katie, the sanest of the sane around here, had still gone full-on Kelly Hoppen in her bijou holiday cottage, becoming frantic when the right shade of priceless taupe seagrass matting that she'd sourced for Charlie's room had been discontinued.

What else had Pettit mentioned? She was pretty sure he'd said the place was chain-free, but that was an inducement that was frequently bandied about, and more often than not turned out to be a total lie. Could she remember anything at all he'd said to shed a glimmer of light on this whole business?

Think, Beth, think. But try as she might, the only thing that came to mind was the cast-iron fact that it was a long time since breakfast, and she was starving already. She looked at her watch. God, five minutes past nine. It was almost literally a thousand years – as Jake would have put it in the days when he was still talking to her – till she could respectably take a break, let alone down tools for lunch.

It was perhaps just as well that there was a soft tap on her door at this point, as her thoughts were becoming distinctly gloomy. She wondered who could have wandered off the beaten path and found their way to her little archives institute, then realised by far the quickest way to find out was to open up. This was a far less scary prospect than it had once been, when her bête noire, Tom Seasons, had prowled the grounds of Wyatt's, and always seemed to be looking for an excuse to come and have a go at her. Now that he was long gone, she just felt pleasant anticipation, right up until the moment when she shot to her feet to open the door and her hangover reared its ugly head again. She tried not to wince, but then gave up the ghost as she saw Sam's head peeking round the corner.

Sam, now in her early thirties and determined to wrestle as much fun as possible from life before she was forced to settle down and get serious, gave Beth a wink. 'Headache? Tense, nervous headache?' It was the tagline from an old painkiller advertisement, and it pretty accurately summed up Beth's current status. She nodded carefully, and Sam produced a packet of ibuprofen and a bottle of sparkling water.

Beth looked up at her in gratitude. 'You're a saint. Thanks so much. I'm such a lightweight at this. I seriously shouldn't be allowed out.'

'Ah, don't worry, you'll get into practice,' said Sam airily.

Beth shut her eyes briefly. Perhaps this wasn't the moment to announce she was never going to drink again.

'I just came by to see if you'd heard the news,' Sam continued, throwing herself into the seat in front of Beth's desk, and crossing her legs nonchalantly.

Beth couldn't help envying her yards of thigh in opaque tights, below a neat little Jigsaw frock. It was the Wyatt's School staff's unofficial uniform, which Beth had never been able to adopt. She couldn't have begun to afford it – and would have looked terrible in it anyway. She tucked her own be-jeaned stumps further beneath her chair and wished she was wearing a less scrubby jumper. Not that Sam gave two hoots about her appearance, but Beth was sometimes very conscious of the fact that she was the least stylish person at Wyatt's, probably for several centuries.

'What's that?' asked Beth, distracted as she unscrewed the mineral water and took a grateful gulp to wash down the pills. The bubbles prickled her nose and made her eyes water. 'News, did you say?'

'Don't tell me you haven't heard? They're only saying they've already got that estate agent's killer.'

TEN

Later on, Beth couldn't help but be ashamed at the feeling of disappointment which engulfed her. The murderer had already been caught! And without any help at all from her. At the time, she was just astonished.

'I haven't heard a thing! Who was it? And why?'

But Sam, having got her effect, wasn't enormously bothered about the details. She'd heard the report on the radio as she'd driven in from her flat in Bromley – a suburb that was far enough out of central London to be a little cheaper than Dulwich, but which was still very well-heeled. As was Sam, Beth thought, admiring her gorgeous suede shoes.

'Something about gangs, as usual. You know, they can't go a day without stabbing each other,' Sam said idly.

Beth thought this a little strange. She didn't want to judge the other woman too harshly, but she hoped she herself would never be quite so dismissive of a blight which took so many young lives in London. For her, the rumbling drugs war served only as a reminder of how lucky some kids were not to feel the hopelessness which led others to get involved.

More to the point, she didn't think the killing had the look of a drug murder at all. Usually, those were done in plain sight, out on the street or, at a pinch, in the communal areas of blocks of flats. The bodies weren't hidden away; they were left where they fell, and they usually fell somewhere quite obvious. They certainly weren't stuffed away in a cupboard. What would be the point? These killings were used to mark territory or to settle scores – they were warnings to rival factions. Concealing them would have been counterproductive. Beth frowned heavily.

'Are you all right?' Sam asked. 'You've got a strange look on your face.'

'I'm fine,' said Beth, readjusting her features a little. 'But I'm not convinced this is a gang thing. Apart from anything else, the man who died... well, he didn't look like any sort of gang member I've ever seen.' Her thoughts switched inevitably back to that horrible slide out of the cupboard, the long pale arm, the dark clothes. She'd been too horrified to remember at first, but was now pretty sure the corpse *had* been wearing a suit. Hardly the usual gangbanger's outfit showing at least two inches of logo-covered neon underpants elastic, and finished off with glaring white trainers.

Admittedly, Beth was taking this information from *The Wire*, which was about the only cop drama that Harry would consent to watch. So, it was a distinct possibility that what worked as a casual dealer look in Baltimore would not really pass muster on the streets of south-east London. But dark suits? Beth was willing to bet they hadn't been in vogue for criminals since the 1960s, when the Kray twins had stalked the capital in outfits that made them look as though they were off to a really stiff job interview.

'And you've seen a lot of gang stuff, have you?' smiled Sam, unknowingly underlining the point.

Even outside of the necessary wardrobe, Beth's knowledge of organised crime was minimal. For all she knew, estate agents could suddenly have become a vital part of the drug world's communications network. And suits might be the new hoodies.

'You've got something there,' she admitted. 'It's just, well, if I'd had to guess, I would have said this was more... more personal.'

'Well, I'm just glad they've caught them, aren't you? No more worries about making it home safely after a night out. I must admit, I looked over my shoulder a couple of times walking back yesterday, did you?' Sam performed a theatrical shudder, causing her pretty dress to shimmy fetchingly.

Beth nodded, but she was deep in thought. If, as she suspected, this death had nothing whatever to do with the drug crime riddling London, then this comfortable confidence that the whole thing had been neatly wrapped up could be fatal. Literally. Another estate agent, or some other innocent victim, could well be struck down because everyone assumed the streets were safe again.

'Beth? You're miles away. Didn't realise your hangover was that bad.'

'Sorry, Sam. It isn't. Well, it's awful, but it's not that. I was just wondering...' Beth wasn't sure if Sam was really the person to share her morbid concerns with, but luckily Janice chose that moment to knock on the door.

'Early lunch, anyone? Well, very early... maybe we should call it brunch? I don't know about you two, but I can't concentrate at all this morning. No idea why.' She smiled. Despite the new era of 2 a.m. feeds, and now a stonking hangover on top, Janice was still managing to look fresh from the Brora catalogue in a lilac cashmere jersey. Beth didn't even want to imagine what she'd looked like when Jake had been as tiny as Janice's baby, Elizabeth. Probably the Creature from the Black Lagoon.

'I'm thinking some stodge and a nice full-fat Coke might replenish the odd brain cell. That's if I've got any left.' Janice's smile was droll.

'Brilliant idea, just give me a second to shut down... I'll see you in the restaurant,' said Beth.

Sam and Janice swished off gorgeously together. The pause, when her little domain was silent again, gave Beth a chance to reorder her thoughts. No, she was certain that someone had got this wrong. The murder was not a drug crime. She wondered briefly if Harry was responsible for tying this up so quickly and neatly, and trying to shove it into his out-tray. She'd have a go at discussing her own theory with him tonight; if he wasn't doing his usual oyster impression, that was.

She flipped down her laptop, collected her bag, and locked up carefully. A jolly brunch would be just the thing to get her back on track again, though she'd have to dodge any suggestion of a repeat of last night's outing. She didn't want to admit that she'd more or less decided never to leave Pickwick Road in the hours of darkness again – well, certainly not if it involved trips to wine bars. She hadn't been banned from going out; Harry hadn't set down any prohibition – she hoped he'd know better than that by now. But he'd be relying on her own reluctance to cause Jake any more disquiet. And if she was entirely honest with herself, she doubted she was really cut out for regular roistering. The hangovers – and the fallout – were just too terrible.

ELEVEN

The next Monday, Beth was almost shining with virtue as she sat in her swivel chair at work and contemplated a tiny in-tray and a flourishing out-tray. The brunch on Friday had, as she'd hoped, really put her back on the straight and narrow. Once they'd all got over their fragility by ordering the greasiest stuff on the menu and chewing away in silence for a while, they'd made a collective recovery, and the gales of laughter coming from their table had proved to Beth that she didn't always need to drink her weight in cocktails to have fun.

That night, and throughout most of a peaceful weekend, she had blamelessly read her book on the sofa. Unfortunately, Harry had not been around to witness this sedate display. Presumably he was at the station, making his team work overtime, brushing the estate agent case under a very large carpet. This was doubly galling, as the novel she was gripped by was one of Harry's whodunits.

On Sunday night, she had even been contemplating complimenting him on his collection. But then immediately suggesting that once they'd both read a book, maybe there was a faint possibility that it could be released back into the wider book-reading community, via a second-hand bookshop like the Oxfam one down in Herne Hill. She didn't really rate her chances, though. On the other hand, now she had dipped a toe into his literary obsession, she found she was actually loving it. There was something curiously soothing about a mystery that wasn't going to remain so for long. She could finally see why they appealed to Harry so much, contending as he did with life in all its southeast London messiness.

Jake had been on the PlayStation right next to her, but had studiously ignored her as he killed various ant-like soldiers. For a while, she was aware of the strength of his determination to blank her from his consciousness. It was in the defensive rounding of his shoulders, the way he gazed straight ahead and didn't turn once in her direction, even when she gasped at a particularly spectacular leap of intuition from the amateur sleuth she was reading about.

But as she got drawn deeper and deeper into the pages of her book, she forgot to feel the force of his disapproval. If she had looked up, she would have noticed that he kept shooting her little glances as the evening wore on and his screen time grew close to running over. When she'd eventually solved the case and thrown the novel aside, Jake was no longer on the sofa beside her. He'd stomped off to bed all by himself in disgust. Result, thought Beth, though not without the usual flicker of guilt that accompanied any milestone in parenting. Would she have done things differently if James had still been with her? Well, undoubtedly. For a start, the house wouldn't have been overrun with another man's library, and she wouldn't have been so knackered having had to do everything alone for so long. But even James would probably have conceded that a boy of twelve could clean his own teeth without chivvying. And sending his mother to Coventry, whether she noticed or not, was just plain rude.

By the morning, normal relations had pretty much been

restored. Jake had even smiled briefly at her over his Weetabix, and she was relieved and thrilled that they'd then gone on to have quite a merry discussion. It was enough to warm an anxious mother's heart. There wasn't really time for an in-depth chat, but just having a bit of a joke was enough to be very cheering. As usual, the pets were a useful topic when the rest of life was a bit fraught. Today's debate was whether Colin could actually understand every word they said or not. Both agreed he had a very good grasp of any vocabulary that touched on food – a point proved when Jake unwisely mentioned dog biscuits and Colin presented himself, panting, at the boy's feet a second later, with a face as hopeful as only a greedy Labrador's can be. Beth and Jake both laughed themselves silly, and she felt that Colin had once again earned his weight in Pedigree Chum.

Harry was still nowhere to be seen. Beth dimly recalled him returning in the small hours of the night, but he was gone again by the morning. It was aggravating, as she wanted to cross-question him over the arrest that had been made, and whether it was true that he'd wrapped up the case already. Sometimes the press exaggerated. And sometimes the police spread disinformation to the media, for its own reasons. But as usual when Beth had a million questions for him, Harry was conspicuous by his absence.

A few blameless, fairly early nights, away from anything containing even a unit of alcohol, and it was amazing how much you could achieve, thought Beth rather smugly as she sat in her swivel chair. Outside, there was the reassuring sound of kids in the playground. Once she had found the random whoops and yells disconcerting, but now it was just white noise. Especially as one of the yellers was her own son.

On her computer screen was a version of her book outline – now pretty polished, if she did say so herself – and on the pad in front of her was a to-do list that was only sixteen items long. This, in itself, was a major victory. Was it possible that she was finally, after years of delaying tactics and avoidance, getting on top of her prevarication habit? Or was that something she was still going to have to get round to? Beth smiled to herself and picked up her mobile. For once, it was right there in front of her, not hidden in the depths of her reverse-Tardis handbag or buried under a pile of filing on her desk.

'Nina? Could I pop in and see you at some stage? I've got some ideas I wanted to run past you.'

She listened and nodded as Nina checked the office appointments diary, dropped it on her foot, searched for and found a pen, and eventually suggested a time. 'Two thirty is perfect. See you then.'

Sighing a little with the satisfaction of being organised – so much more organised than Nina! – and having a very shiny halo, Beth jotted the time down on her desk calendar and felt she deserved a treat. She clicked on her current guilty pleasure, the Rightmove tab. These days, it was always open on her laptop.

She was browsing through a nice collection of photographs on a property which had just been listed, when there was a knock at the door.

She was halfway through making sure she looked busy by clicking back onto her book outline, and simultaneously saying a breezy 'Come in', when Janice rushed into the room, hair flying everywhere and, most unusually of all, a large wet stain on the front of her cashmere cardi. Without asking, her friend hurled herself into the seat opposite Beth and then, most extraordinarily of all, burst into noisy sobs.

Beth sat for a moment, utterly poleaxed by this turn of events. After a beat, she realised a response was most definitely required, and she got to her feet and awkwardly put an arm round Janice, whose shoulders were still heaving with emotion.

'Can I get you anything, Janice? Tissue? Glass of water? Maybe I should fetch Dr Grover?'

At this, the frenzied crying redoubled. 'No, no, not him. Don't say a word to Tommy!' came a muffled voice. Janice had buried her head in Beth's stomach, but was now, at least, trying to bring her sobs to an end. After a few wrenching hiccups, which Beth did her best to soothe with some ineffectual pats, Janice reached out, took a handful of tissues from the box on Beth's desk and blew her nose loudly. Beth stepped back, relieved to be out of the fray but completely unsure what to do next.

Finally, she stepped briskly to her little conference table and grabbed one of the dusty bottles of mineral water which were waiting very patiently for the day Beth convened an archives meeting. She unscrewed the top and passed it to Janice, who took a hefty swig, then wiped her eyes on her cashmere sleeve. This alone seemed such a breach of normal etiquette that Beth was all jitters again, but at least the storm of tears was over.

Rather gingerly, Beth sat back down behind her desk and eyed Janice as though she were a suspect package instead of the calm friend she'd come to rely on so much. Finally, Janice had recovered enough to speak.

'I'm sorry, Beth. I know you hate this sort of thing. But it's all been getting to me.'

'I can see that, and don't apologise for one moment... but what on earth is the matter? And what can I do to help?'

'Thanks, Beth, that's so sweet of you,' said Janice, her voice full of enormous relief.

Immediately, Beth realised she'd inadvertently signed herself up to something. What could it be? God, she hoped it wasn't going to be too time-consuming. What with the estate agent business, which she still couldn't believe was quite over yet, Jake, the boxes and the rest, she wasn't sure she had much mental capacity left for anything else. That wasn't to say she didn't want to do her bit for Janice; of course she did. But she was already stretched thinner than a piece of greying chewing gum. She wasn't left wondering for long.

'It's Tommy, you see.' As usual, Beth had trouble squaring the breezy nickname with the oh-so-daunting figure of Dr Grover, the amazing head who'd done so much to burnish the reputation of Wyatt's. There had never been a time in the past three hundred years when the school had exactly been under-performing, but thanks to Dr G it had reached giddy new heights of late. Wyatt's was the top of every exam tree, the star on the wish list of all the Dulwich mummies, the one coveted school that everyone, all over London, wanted to cram their kids into – as Beth knew only too well. Even the little matter of their original founder's disgusting dabbling in the slave trade had somehow been spun, by Dr Grover, in such a way that admissions requests had gone up instead of down.

'Is he stressed or something? He always seems fine,' asked Beth, struggling to understand.

'Oh, there's nothing wrong with *him*. Quite the contrary.' Janice didn't quite sniff her disapproval, but there was something in her tone that had never been there before when she'd mentioned her husband. Instantly, Beth was on red alert.

'What's up, Janice?' she asked gently.

Janice's beautiful eyes went glassy with tears again, and Beth was stricken. *Oh no, not another waterfall!* But this time, Janice straightened her spine, took a breath, and spoke instead of crying. Her voice wavered a little, but what she said was clear enough. 'I think he's having an affair.'

Now it was Beth's turn to sit up straight, but she couldn't manage speech, not with her jaw on the desk. Dr Grover! No, it couldn't be true.

'You look surprised, and yes, I agree it's shocking. But I really think something's going on.'

Beth, her mind windmilling wildly, asked carefully, 'What makes you think this? Is there any... evidence?' Somehow, she recoiled even as she put the question. She really didn't want to think of Dr Grover cheating on lovely Janice. If that was what had happened to their relationship, so soon after the hearts and flowers phase which had been evident to all, what hope was there for anyone? And what hope, in particular, for Beth herself?

Her romance had never reached anything like the lovey-dovey heights that Janice had enjoyed, as far as Beth knew, and it was now full of grumpiness. If Janice, having found unalloyed true love and bliss, was now having her eyes opened to something awful, how long could it be until Beth herself had to confront something like this? Or maybe something even worse?

Beth caught herself before she got too carried away with her train of thought. Poor Dr Grover shouldn't be tried and found guilty before a shred of proof had been produced, even if Janice was her friend.

'Look, tell me what's worrying you. Ten to one, it isn't what you think. Dr Grover adores you; everyone knows that. He's the last person I can imagine cheating.'

'But isn't it always the last person you'd think of that turns out to be the first person after all? I mean, come on Beth, you should know that with all your investigations.' Janice shrugged. 'Believe me, I hope it's not true, I really do. But don't forget, he's cheated before. I should know. I didn't behave well, I know... I knew he was married. But he told me, swore blind, that it was all over between them. And he said they never really got on anyway...'

Beth remembered when she'd first arrived at the school. There had been mysterious liaisons between the head and the school secretary which had actually meant that at one point she'd wondered if they were mixed up in a murder themselves. Finding out it was a secret affair had actually been rather a relief, though she doubted that Dr Grover's previous wife had felt the same way.

But as far as everyone in Dulwich knew, his eventual divorce had been an amicable business. The first Mrs G was an actress who'd forged a steady career in TV soaps, turning up in *EastEnders* to start with, before graduating to *Casualty* and then *Holby City*, clawing her way up the fictional medical profession at the same time. Her first role had been as a hard-pressed health visitor to the residents of Albert Square, but she was now playing a lofty consultant gynaecologist having a smouldering affair with a male nurse.

But maybe things hadn't been as smooth between the Dulwich head and his first wife as they'd seemed? Certainly, as an actress, his ex probably wouldn't want to draw attention to the fact she'd been supplanted by someone younger; that wouldn't enhance her reputation. Scorn, thinly disguised as pity, would no doubt have been heaped on her by the gloating tabloids, who loved to dish it out to anyone in the public eye who didn't keep hold of their man.

'And you know what they say,' Janice continued ominously.

'Once a cheater...' Beth started obligingly, then realised she was hardly helping. Better to get down to the nitty-gritty. 'So, what's made you suspect that something's, erm, going on?'

Janice let out such a hefty sigh that the handful of papers left in Beth's in-tray were ruffled in the breeze. 'Oh, you know, at first it was just really tiny things. He'd say he'd be coming home early, then he'd be an hour later than he said. Then he'd swear blind he'd be back in time for Elizabeth's bath, and he'd be nowhere to be seen. And then, he's always on his phone.'

'To be fair, everyone's always on their phone,' said Beth, trying to be the voice of reason. 'And a lot of men try and avoid bath time and stuff like that. You know how exhausting it can be, and that's without being at work all day running this place.' She got a sour look from Janice for her pains.

'Yes, well, I know he's a busy man, I know he's over-stretched, and I know he has to be available. If it's not the school governors bending his ear, it's some parent who's got hold of his number. Honestly, some of them just won't leave him alone. Don't they realise he's entitled to a private life? So, I'm used to that. But it's the way he is with his phone, all of a sudden. Once, he would have just left it lying around anywhere; now he's always got it on him. And he's got a password, out of the blue, when he never had one before. When I asked what it was, he just laughed and changed the subject.' Janice's bottom lip wobbled again.

Beth pursed her lips together and thought. This didn't really sound good. A new password was highly suggestive. 'I hate to ask this, but have you, erm, tried to break into it?'

Janice tried to feign shock for a moment, then gave up. 'Yes, all right, I admit I've had a couple of goes. But it's nothing obvious. It's not my birthday, or Elizabeth's.'

Beth suppressed a smile at Janice's egocentricity, but at the same time she acknowledged that Dr Grover's world did revolve entirely around the two girls in his life. Or, at least, it had.

'Do you have any idea of, erm, who...?' Beth left the sentence delicately unfinished, but it was enough to get Janice sniffing again.

'No, no I don't. But it could be anybody...'

'Well, not really, Janice. I mean, who is he likely to come across, to have made any sort of connection with? Not that I'm saying that's what's really happened,' she added quickly as Janice looked increasingly tremulous. 'We just need to consider all the possibilities.'

'So, you think it might be someone else... at the school?' Janice held the tissue up to her mouth and looked around her, as though a floozy might burst out from behind one of Beth's shelves of school programmes.

'Look, I really don't think it's someone else at all, full stop,' said Beth, trying to sound as convincing as possible.

True, the phone stuff sounded odd, but it was hardly proof

positive. And even if something really were going on, there was
no point in pushing Janice over the edge until it was established
beyond all reasonable doubt. The poor thing had a tiny baby to
look after, and really didn't need this extra stress. Beth thought
hard, but then decided to take the plunge. What the hell. She
had at least two moments spare a day. And she did love solving
a mystery. 'But I will have a root around if it will put your mind
at rest. I'm not sure how to go about it, though.'

Janice gave a smile of relief, her equilibrium seeming almost
restored by the thought that someone was going to catch her
husband out. Be careful what you wish for, Beth thought to
herself, as Janice got to her feet, throwing her sodden tissues
into the bin with an almost jaunty flick of her wrist.

She whisked out into the corridor, leaving Beth wondering
if the first Mrs Grover was the only actress in the family. Then
she paused at the door.

'Oh, you'll know what to do. You're like the Mounties these
days, you always get your man,' Janice said, in quite a breezy
tone of voice.

But I don't know if I want to get *your* man, Beth thought,
once Janice was safely on her way to collect Elizabeth from the
admin offices, where she was being cooed over by half the staff.
From her window, she watched Janice push her state-of-the-art
buggy across the playground, ostentatiously giving the square of
brilliant green in front of the head's office a wide berth. That
pram was so space-age Beth could almost imagine it taking off
into the stratosphere and flying the little duo home. Janice's
figure was more rounded after giving birth, but it suited her,
adding a new lushness that hadn't been there before.

Was it really possible that Dr Grover had lost interest in
her? It was hard to credit. Such a short time seemed to have
elapsed since they had first got together. But it was true that Dr
Grover had seemed securely married before, and that had all
unravelled in double-quick time.

It had been largely before Beth had arrived at Wyatt's, but the head was a well-known face around Dulwich (especially for someone as obsessed with Wyatt's as Beth had always been), and his ex-wife had that TV glamour that gave the couple even more cachet. She was sure she'd seen them both at a couple of Belinda McKenzie's dreaded Christmas drinks parties – while Beth had still been on the guest list. From the outside, the replacement of one wife with another seemed to have been managed with the bare minimum of pain and suffering, but that was, Beth acknowledged, only on the surface. Just because neither party had taken to *Hello!* magazine to scream about their agony didn't mean that there weren't bitter regrets.

Would Dr Grover seriously risk getting embroiled in another divorce only a couple of years after his first? Even if he were looking for more excitement than a recent mother could provide, surely the prospect of being hauled through the courts for a second time would be a brake on even the most ardent lust.

Yet, as Beth knew, there was nothing like the arrival of a baby to put a bit of a damper on things between its parents. People often thought having children would glue together the cracks of their relationship – but it was much more likely to force fault lines apart. Her own marriage had weathered parenthood but then come to an abrupt end thanks to the grim reaper. She sometimes wondered if she would have taken poor James's complaints about headaches and sniffles more seriously if she hadn't been so busy with Jake. But then, he hadn't taken it all very seriously himself. Until he was in the hospice.

Maybe Dr Grover was feeling pushed out, neglected. Maybe he was looking for a bit of fun on the side. Beth sincerely hoped he wasn't. She admired him as much as everyone else in Dulwich. She really didn't want him to turn out like Sir Thomas Wyatt – on the face of it, a force for good. Underneath, frankly, a cad.

There was also the worry that this new quest would derail

her vow to find whoever had done for the estate agent. Harry, according to Sam's sketchy report, must be confident he'd got the perpetrator banged up, but Beth had a nagging feeling that this was wishful thinking. Now that she considered it, wasn't there a possibility that she could combine the two investigations? She'd have to be zooming about south London quite a lot, on viewings, in order to find their dream house – and keep the area's estate agents under surveillance. What better cover for a bit of snooping on the movements of Dr Grover?

Beth decided not to hesitate any longer, but to get straight on to the one person who could sort out both of her investigations. She dialled.

'Nina? It's Beth. I've got a favour to ask. I know we had an appointment at two thirty – but could I just come round now?'

TWELVE

Beth sat in a big spongy orange chair opposite Nina and hoped the décor wasn't going to give her a migraine. The estate agent's office down in Herne Hill had recently been given a makeover and was now desperately trying to be 'funky', but in a way that suggested the designer was as posh as they came, and had never encountered anything truly edgy in their life. The place bristled with incredibly uncomfortable designer chairs like Beth's orange number, which was currently contriving to jab her in the bottom and be so high off the floor that her feet didn't touch the ground.

There was a massive fridge full of bottles of mineral water which seemed distinctly unfriendly, environmentally speaking, and pointless in the autumnal chill. And not even a very interesting drink to offer customers. There were large signs on the wall saying *Buy Buy Buy* and *Sell Sell Sell* in shrieking neon, and the desks were a vicious lime green. Beth was glad to see a huge blow-up map of the area behind Nina's desk that was at least quite useful.

'Interesting redesign,' said Beth, looking around and raising her eyebrows.

'Tell me about it,' said Nina. 'Had to wear sunglasses the first few days, but we've got used to it now. So, listen, what can you do for me?'

'Um, it's the other way round, Nina. I want to ask your advice. Two things, really. First, have you found out anything about our, er, friend?'

'Which one?' Nina leant forward, her cherubic features marred by a frown. 'Ah, the dead geezer? Why dincha say so?'

Beth bit back a retort. It was no good stressing discretion to Nina. If she hadn't currently worked in the estate agents, her dream job would have been town crier, complete with a medieval-style tabard and hand bell as she went around announcing items of juicy gossip to all and sundry. 'Yes, er, that... and something else now, too.'

Suddenly Beth wondered what on earth she was doing. If she told Nina anything at all about Janice's fears, they'd be the lead item on the evening news. No, she'd have to keep this aspect of her investigation quiet. Trudging around south London looking at possible homes was going to be the ideal cover for a bit of surveillance. She'd just have to make sure that Nina didn't always tag along.

But then, the long-dormant sensible bit of Beth's brain reactivated. Wouldn't this mean putting herself in danger? In her mind's eye, she saw the estate agent's pale arm flopping forward again from that extremely useful larder cupboard. It didn't take a huge stretch to imagine one of her own limbs crashing out of it, although she doubted that even in death she'd manage to emulate that languid bloodless grace that had simultaneously fascinated and repelled her. It almost decided her on the spot – she definitely didn't want to be a stumpy corpse. But was it a good enough reason to abandon ship?

She sat there, hesitating, while Nina eyed her across the bright green plastic expanse of the desk.

'Somefink you're not telling me, I reckon, babe,' she said levelly.

But luckily for Beth, Nina didn't do resentment. She'd unerringly sensed Beth's reticence, but she also knew when to leave well alone. Probably just too sensible to want to get involved, said the rational bit of Beth's brain, overjoyed to get so much airtime all of a sudden. But she shut it down relentlessly. She'd do what was necessary for the sake of her investigation. Well, investigations, plural, this time.

'So, have you heard anything? I bet all you estate agents chat the whole time,' said Beth brightly. Nina narrowed her eyes briefly.

'Well, I'm not an estate agent, per sage,' she sniffed. 'But yeah, I'd say there's some chat. Nothing that's going to help you, though.'

'You don't know that. I'd love to hear what people are saying.' Beth leant forward, and the uber-stylish chair tipped dangerously. She craned back again.

'Yeah, no sudden moves, babe. The person who chose those chairs wasn't a total idiot. People have to sit still and listen to all the agents' chitty-chatty, otherwise they're on the floor.' Nina chuckled.

Beth waited patiently and, as she'd expected, Nina began to spill the beans. After Beth's request, Nina had tapped into the unofficial estate agents' network which ran round London like the South Circular. It was a bit like the Twilight Barking in one of Beth's favourite films of all time, *101 Dalmatians*. This involved people, not dogs; but they actually were a bit barking. This wasn't just her opinion, Beth told herself. Nina had often hinted that some of her colleagues were a couple of snaps short of the full brochure.

Perhaps it wasn't surprising. There had been a time when the market had been so buoyant that any house in the area could more or less sell itself. Then had come a period of crushing stasis during which estate agents had got jumpy, rushing at potential buyers like passengers on the *Titanic* spying under-occupied lifeboats. Now the Dulwich market at least seemed back to buoyancy again, though war and the cost-of-living crisis were waiting in the wings with the potential to derail it all over again. It must be stressful, see-sawing constantly like this. No way to make a living, Beth thought.

This fancy refit of Nina's office seemed very much like an act of bravado. Beth was willing to bet there wouldn't be enough commission coming in soon to pay for one of the ridiculous orange chairs, let alone a carefully mismatched set of six. Probably financing all the mineral water bottles would be a stretch. It was sad. But from Beth's point of view, it was actually excellent. If there was someone out there preying on estate agents, she wanted the community nervous enough to sing like the Dulwich Amateur Operatic Society getting ready for its Christmas rendition of Handel's *Messiah*. She looked hopefully at her friend.

'Yeah well, a couple of the girls from the offices roundabout have quit. Not surprising, really. And everyone that's left has decided they should text when they arrive at a place, and when they leave as well. As if that's going to stop anyone whacking them on the head, but I s'pose if they feel safe...' Nina's eyebrows said it all about this idea.

Beth was puzzled. 'But the official story is that they've caught the murderer, Nina. Why is everyone so worried?'

'Why are you still on the case? Do *you* think they've caught him?' Nina shrugged. 'Looks like your boyfriend isn't fooling anyone, this time.'

For a moment, Beth felt stung. Poor Harry. All the work he'd no doubt done, the arrest he'd made, all the evidence-gathering and presentation of facts to the Crown Prosecution Service... and people still thought there was a killer on the loose. Then she realised it was pointless feeling for him. She'd been entirely unconvinced when she'd heard the whole thing had been put down as a drug-related matter. So, there was no reason why anyone else in Dulwich would buy that story either. It might be partly because no one in Dulwich wanted to think that drug crime was now on their doorstep. But it might also be because the whole business really seemed to have absolutely nothing to do with traditional drug turf wars at all.

'Listen, the buzz is all about the bloke what got it – Richard Pettit – having done a few well dodgy deals,' said Nina. 'And the person who offed him, they're saying it's someone who wasn't that pleased with paying an enormous commission for nuffink, put it that way.' She folded her arms and smirked in self-satisfaction, as though she'd cracked the case single-handedly.

Beth stared at her. 'But, Nina, that could be anyone who's ever bought a house, surely? No one likes paying the commission. And most people come away from a deal feeling they've been hard done by, whether they're the buyer or the seller. One has to pay a huge whack to the estate agent, and the other buys a house riddled with dry rot or whatever and is furious at being diddled. That's just business as usual in the property market.'

'Yeah, I did tell you it wasn't going to help,' said Nina, unrepentant.

Beth sighed. She couldn't pretend she hadn't been warned, but she'd definitely expected a bit more from her friend. 'Can you keep your ear to the ground, though? Just in case you get wind of anything that's a bit more... definite?'

'Course, babe. Consider it done and busted.'

Beth blinked but said nothing. The phone suddenly shrilled, reminding Beth that it had been silent during the entire time they'd been chatting.

Nina lifted the handset and chirruped, 'Fester and Hock, how can I help you? Oh, it's you, Mum.' She looked over at Beth and raised her eyebrows, as though for permission to chat. Beth smiled her thanks at her friend and left her to it.

As she walked away down Half Moon Lane, she reflected that the phone ringing only once in all that time was really not a good sign. And the fact that it had been Nina's mother and not a potential client was even worse. People were always predicting that the London housing market was going to collapse. When and if it did, that was thousands, millions, *squillions*, being wiped out.

For Beth, moving from an expensive area to a cheaper one – or at least braced to do so – it was potentially good. But for all the solid Dulwich residents who'd sat in their expensive houses for decades, watching a theoretical fortune tot up in bricks and mortar, it was very bad news indeed. Beth had seen the mess of flats that had been flung up in places like Lewisham – she had to drive through it on the way to visit friends in Blackheath – and had heard that they mostly stood empty, either bought by overseas investors who'd soon consider dumping them if things didn't improve, or left unsold. At least the *Daily Mail* would be pleased. The paper had been confidently predicting a crash for decades. It was a bit like being a stopped clock, Beth supposed. You had to be right eventually.

One thing was sure. The housing market really did seem to be dead – in Nina's office, at any rate. Every bit as dead as that poor estate agent.

THIRTEEN

The case was dead, thought Harry, as he sat at his overburdened desk in Camberwell Police Station. Through a thicket of files, he could just about see his sidekick, Narinda, who was listening patiently to a caller and making notes. If he knew her, these would be neat, legible, to the point – but would probably contain little they didn't already know or couldn't have guessed. Although it was great that the public called in and tried to help out on murders like this, that didn't make their having seen a suspicious character several months ago in an entirely different location any more helpful.

Harry sighed and ran a hand through his rough dark blond hair. It felt a bit long to him. Maybe he should get it cut at the weekend? Assuming the case didn't break and put paid to any free time. Maybe he should take Jake with him. The poor boy's hair was getting so shaggy now that he could hardly see out from under his fringe.

Thinking about fringes meant that a certain luxuriant curtain of hair swung inexorably into his mind's eye. Beth. What on earth was he going to do about her? She seemed so pissed off these days. Was it the boxes? Was that why she'd been out so much with her friends?

He supposed he couldn't blame her for wanting to let off a bit of steam. She'd been through enough in the past months to have a lesser person lying on a therapist's couch for months on end, for sure. A few late nights and chats would probably do her loads of good. But all the drinking worried him. It wasn't good for her, for their relationship – and the shouting the other night had definitely not been good for Jake, either.

It *was* the boxes, he knew it. He'd always suspected that his belongings would be a sore trial to someone as tidy as Beth. She liked things neat and orderly – apart from her own appearance, of course. But everything in the house had its place, and there seemed to be not an inch free for anything of his. He'd been testing her resolve, bringing so much stuff over. How willing was she really to accommodate him in her life?

It had been a bit unfair. She'd tried, she really had. But she now seemed to be feeling the strain. Interesting, that she could put up with the two tins of paint that had been languishing in her hall for as long as he could remember, but his boxes were beyond the pale. But wasn't that always the way? People could tolerate their own mess but were much less apt to put up with other people's. Well, the truth was that a good sort-out of his books was long overdue. Maybe he'd get going on that this weekend – again, if he wasn't otherwise engaged with this murderer. He didn't want to get too much ahead of himself, or promise to do something that he'd then have to let her down on. But he could at least stack them up so they were a bit more out of the way. Arranging them around the telly had been a bit of a tease. It had definitely fallen flat.

By the time Harry had got home that evening, three more potential leads had gone by the wayside, including Raf, the good-looking ne-er-do-well, whom he'd been half-hoping he could pin this whole business on and had very much enjoyed banging up for a while.

Though Raf had been spotted lurking on the Penge and Sydenham borders only a few days ago, Harry had taken a call from a colleague in West Hampstead that afternoon to ask about his form. Bloody Raf had been caught on CCTV in the NW3 area just when the estate agent was getting offed. The north London nick hadn't realised Harry had got Raf in custody, and when he told them as much and revealed they'd just given him an alibi, they had all shared a brief moment of depression at the news that he wasn't guilty.

The NW3 squad was pretty sure Raf was grooming girls at a Hampstead private school in the hopes they'd become his latest stable of unpaid handmaids – and worse. His usual practice, it seemed, was to feed such girls compliments, then drugs, then suddenly withdraw affection and stimulants unless they agreed to turn tricks for him. It was simple, and the tragedy was that even teenagers from privileged backgrounds had such low self-esteem that he had a surprisingly good hit rate.

In many ways, it was excellent news that Raf was taking his bad-boy good looks and viciously effective business plan north of the river. But Harry would have loved to have had the chance to hang the estate agent murder on him.

Raf was safe, though, and it just reinforced Harry's growing conviction that the murderer was long gone. There was a golden twenty-four-hour window with these things that was now very much closed. After that time had elapsed, people's memories grew hazy, CCTV images got taped over, and even the impetus to report an oddity faded away.

Telling the press that they were on to someone, had made an arrest and had tied the case up to a drug bust in a different part of the capital had been a big gamble. And one which, he was now forced to admit, had not paid off. They'd thrown everything they had at Raf – not literally, of course – but it turned out the arrest was based on a tip-off from someone he'd got on the wrong side of once too often. Raf could charm the pants off teenage girls, but went down extremely badly with his own sex. This time it was a pusher who'd suggested that he'd seen Raf hanging about right outside the Sydenham house.

As there had been no teenage girls in the picture, Harry had been sceptical, but it had most definitely been worth a try. So, he'd rounded Raf up and dumped him in custody, and they'd scurried around trying to find anything they could that might connect his lazy sexual charm to the hapless dead estate agent. But it had been no dice.

It should have made him angry, being used by some stupid gang to clear Raf off the streets. No doubt the scumbag had failed to cough up the money for a drug deal, something he'd almost certainly blame on whatever girl he had working for him at the moment. But at least it meant these petty drug pedlars were talking to the police, if only to waste his time by dobbing each other in. Harry didn't feel cross; he just felt tired. And a bit dispirited.

Tomorrow, he'd have to go out there and admit that they were releasing Raf. Their suspect had been buying cigarettes near a posh girls' school just at the moment when Richard Pettit must have been stuffed into that cupboard. With London Transport the way it was, there wasn't a hope in hell that he could have got from one side of the city to the other in time to have done the deed.

CCTV, God. It was a blessing, and a curse. When you needed it most, it was always broken or the perpetrator found a blind spot. When it worked, it only ever seemed to prove that someone couldn't have done what he was accusing them of. He sighed and gave up. Time to go home. He'd leave the perp who wasn't the right perp in the cell for the night, concentrate his mind a bit, then let him go in the morning. At least Raf wouldn't be able to commit any new crimes for the moment.

He looked up and realised everyone except Narinda had already left. 'Off you go now, Khan. See you in the morning,' he said.

He'd forgotten that if he didn't actively tell her to leave, she'd stay by his side. He couldn't help making the comparison with Colin's dogged loyalty, though of course that was doing the poor girl a terrible disservice. Her breath never smelt like the old Labrador's. Thank heavens.

The streets were quiet as he swished back through the fine drizzle. Each street lamp had its own little Van Gogh nimbus of light. Apart from these tiny golden globes hanging in the air, Dulwich Village appeared almost like a black and white photograph, beautiful and stark and still. He could imagine the way it had looked a century ago. Pretty much exactly the same, minus the stupid cushion shops. He smiled wryly as he signalled to turn right into Pickwick Road. What would they have had instead? A place that sold covers for your piano's legs? An aspidistra emporium?

He could see why Beth loved the place. But it definitely lacked oomph. He spent his days on streets that teemed with life and energy, so it felt odd coming back to a place this staid and respectable. For a cop, it was... well, a bit of a cop-out. Still, he knew better to present this argument. Saying they needed to live somewhere rougher was never going to appeal to a woman with a child to bring up. And there was a lot to be said for calm and stability. Though he definitely wasn't going to miss the parking, he thought, as he tried to nuzzle his car in between two SUVs, hoping neither had an alarm fitted as he strayed perilously close to their bumpers.

'I'm home,' he shouted five minutes later, opening the front door. But the place was quiet, apart from the click of Colin's paws on the hall tiles as he came out of the sitting room to do his bit as official greeter, drooling on Harry's shoes and wagging his tail as the big policeman unbent to pet his velvety head.

'Where's your ma, then, boy?' said Harry.

No reply was forthcoming, but plenty more drool unspooled while Colin did his best impression of a dog that hadn't been walked for a hundred years, or fed for about two hundred. Harry dodged round him and went into the sitting room. He had to admit the place did look like a branch of one of those storage firms, or possibly even the very last few frames of that old classic, *Raiders of the Lost Ark*. He sighed. Was it worth him sorting through the boxes now before piling them up in a more unobtrusive arrangement? Or should he stack them and then have a rummage later...

As he debated the matter, the sofa started looking more and more inviting, despite Magpie's fierce green glare. She was sprawled right across the cushions and there was a hollow next to her which, he was willing to bet, was a forensic match with Colin's bottom. Honestly, Beth needed to be a bit stricter with her pets, he thought, as he wedged himself in with some difficulty next to the cat, careful not to dislodge her and attract that razor-tipped paw. He turned a determined eye away from the towering cartons and switched on the telly.

Beth, getting home an hour later with Jake after an impromptu fish supper at the sit-down part of Olley's in Herne Hill, was not amused to be greeted by the sound of loud snores. Jake peered round the sitting room door and then sprinted upstairs without passing comment. Once upon a time, he would have woken Harry up and insisted he play some game or other with him, but these days he seemed to be enjoying his own company more than any interaction, even via a console. Beth hoped that wasn't due to the row he'd overheard the other day and that it was just a manifestation of pre-teen disdain for other life forms.

She paused in the doorway. It was quite a scene. Magpie and Harry were sprawled across the sofa, the cat taking up a furry three-quarters of it. Harry's head was back, his mouth was open, and the timbre of the snorts he was producing was rivalled only by Colin's. The old boy had been relegated to the floor, and was lying sprawled across Harry's feet. Despite his place in the pecking order, the dog still looked like a very happy chap. At that moment, he snorted so loudly he woke himself up with a little shake and then gazed at Beth out of one brown eye, his mouth curving into what could only be a wide smile of welcome, before gravity got the better of his eyelid and he drifted back off to sleep again.

Beth knew she should be dragooning him out for a turn around the block to get his night-time ablutions out of the way. But she'd let Harry deal with that when he finally woke up. She wondered for a second whether she should spread a blanket over the sleeping giant, but decided all Magpie's fluff must be keeping him warm enough.

She picked up the remote from the armrest and clicked off the telly. Ironically, it had been showing *Grand Designs* – the aspirational makeover show – while all around the room was the cardboard evidence that the only thing Harry seemed to have designs on at the moment was every inch of space Beth possessed. She tutted silently and padded off to the kitchen.

A few minutes later, she was tucked up on her side of the bed with a camomile tea. It was still quite early, but she had a great book to read. She opened up another of Harry's whodunits with a smile of anticipation. Jake seemed happy enough in his room. She'd listened at his door for a bit and could hear the canned laughter of something or other on Netflix. Once upon a time, she would have breezed in, sure of her welcome, and snuggled up and watched with him.

For a moment, she wondered if the programme – whatever it was – was suitable, then she shook her head. She couldn't wrap him in cotton wool forever. It was doubtless the must-watch series of the moment that all the boys would be talking about in the playground. She didn't want to make Jake too different or stop him from following the crowd if that's what he wanted to do. Anyway, anything with a laughter track would at least be upbeat.

She sighed and started to let the crime story absorb her thoughts. She knew she ought to be even crosser than she was about the way she was having to take refuge up here because her sitting room had been turned into some sort of depot. But with a killer on the loose, she knew Harry would have precious little time for sorting out his stuff over the next days or weeks.

It made it all the more important that she should help him out with the murder – whether he wanted her to or not. If it was anything like the book she was reading, it shouldn't be too hard. She could pretty much guess whodunit already.

FOURTEEN

It was a bright autumn morning and Beth sniffed the crisp air. She loved days like these. The year might be sliding downwards into the endless British winter, but in Dulwich at least it was doing it in style, with the red of the acer trees in Court Lane blazing for all they were worth against the clear blue sky.

Unfortunately, she was no longer in Dulwich, but driving out to Norwood.

Her property net was being cast wider and wider, and it wasn't all due to her interest in the murders. There simply wasn't anything in their price bracket nearer home. All her hopes about an imminent freefall seemed to be coming to nothing. The figures in Dulwich were actually edging up, as Nina had warned, in a response to the killing in Sydenham. Was it just her, or did Dulwich seem a lot less scary than outlying areas? Yet she was willing to bet the zeros would slide off SE21 the moment she signed to move out of the postcode forever. It was just sod's law.

Anyway, this place she was on her way to was actually gorgeous – or it had certainly looked it on the website. A Georgian terrace, 'in need of refurbishment', or in other words, a bombsite, its potential shone through, or so Beth had convinced herself. She'd spoken to the agent just a few minutes ago to confirm they'd be there to meet her. One thing this experience had taught her was that she was definitely never going to risk going into a house all alone. Even with the woman from the agency there the other night, it had been unimaginably horrible when that cupboard door had swung open and... No, don't go there, she told herself, as she pulled up outside the property.

The front garden was like a small explosion in a weed factory, but that could easily be dealt with. The façade of the house was pleasant and, aside from cracked paint, the structure looked solid enough.

Ah, and there was the estate agent. On the phone, she'd been well-spoken and extremely enthusiastic. In the flesh, she was a bouncy and very attractive twenty-something, and immediately Beth felt a little older and a little shabbier by comparison. She girded her loins, though, opened the rusting garden gate, and stepped forward. Now what was the girl's name again? Pippa, was it?

'Hi, I'm Beth,' she said, holding out her hand.

'Poppy,' the girl replied and shook it, her dangly earrings quivering slightly. She was so pretty, and so well-turned-out, that Beth wondered what on earth she was doing becoming an estate agent. Surely she should be getting started in publishing, or PR? Particularly in these murderous times. If she'd been Poppy's mother, she'd have warned the girl off. Before Beth could stop herself, she'd plunged into speech.

'I hope you don't mind me asking, but aren't you a bit, well, worried, turning up for viewings in light of, ahem, recent events?'

For a second, Poppy looked as though she was going to pretend she didn't know what Beth was talking about. Then she caved in. 'Why do you think I'm waiting outside?' she said simply.

Beth was a little startled by the girl's frankness. It didn't entirely inspire confidence. Although she approved of the way Poppy was exercising caution, she had hoped they'd be looking at a guaranteed murderer-free house. Apparently, that was too much to ask these days.

But there couldn't really be a killer lurking within the tall, cream-painted building. Could there? If there were, Beth wasn't sure that she really brought a lot to the party, defence-wise. Poppy, who was only three inches taller than her and looked as though she would snap in a breeze, would stand almost as much of a chance alone as with her in tow. Technically, people always said there was strength in numbers. But they were probably thinking about battalions. Not women and, in her case, someone who didn't exactly have a track record of physical fitness.

Lately she'd even given up trying to open difficult pickle jars, but simply passed them to Harry, Jake or even Colin rather than attempting to prise the lid off herself. She wasn't up to fighting a killer with her bare hands, and nor was this Poppy. Still, the idea of calling for a man to shepherd them round the house, on grounds of safety, was just too ignominious to contemplate. She'd much rather risk her life than admit there was anything a woman couldn't do.

She squared her shoulders. 'Well, shall we?' she asked as boldly as she could.

They walked up the steep stone steps. These would have been a nightmare in Jake's buggy days, Beth acknowledged, but were fine now. Though, if they bought this house, they'd want to stay... and she hoped Jake would do the decent thing and provide her with grandchildren at some point. In which case, it would be hell dragging the babies' pushchairs up here. But she was getting ahead of herself. Just a smidge, she thought with a smile.

Poppy, seeing it, grinned back. 'Magnificent period entryway and original part-tiled vestibule, isn't it?'

'Or front door and hall, as I sometimes call them,' Beth countered, hoping she was going to nip in the bud any hyperbole that Poppy planned to throw at her.

But it rapidly became clear that Poppy was the type of estate agent who'd recently swallowed a thesaurus whole, and wasn't the slightest bit afraid, scared or worried who knew it.

'Are you loving the encaustic ceramic work as much as I am?' the girl trilled.

'I doubt it,' said Beth, hoping she didn't sound quite as sour as she suddenly felt.

There was nothing like a bushy-tailed young thing to make you feel the weight of your years, she decided. Poppy floated around the sitting room like Tinker Bell on helium, ooh-ing and ah-ing about quite normal bits and bobs like a cracked marble mantelpiece and the coving, which was marred by a mysterious brown stain that didn't augur well for the efficiency of whatever bathroom or shower was oozing away in the room above.

As long as Beth zoned Poppy out, she found she could actually quite appreciate the house. All right, it wasn't where she wanted it to be, but it did seem to have all the stuff they needed. In a nutshell, this was the one thing you'd never actually find in a nutshell – more space. The layout again lacked Pickwick Road's unusual geometry. Beth wasn't surprised; she'd never seen a road like hers anywhere else in the UK. It was named (probably) after Samuel Pickwick, the character from Dickens' first novel. Dulwich residents still loved to remind each other that the famous writer had been a regular in the Crown and Greyhound pub over the road.

For some reason, Pickwick houses had as many acute angles as any tangram. Perhaps the original architect had hoped to fit a few more inches in by sticking a window out here and a wall out there. Maybe they'd just been a massive triangle fan. There were disadvantages to the result – it was hard to work out where to put beds and sofas in rooms where nothing was square or straightforward. And long before fitted kitchens were the norm, Pickwick Road residents had been forced to go bespoke in order to use their space effectively. Even now, the size and shape of Jake's room, with its odd pointy shape, made it impossible for him to put anything away tidily. Or so he said.

But Beth still loved it.

This Norwood place, though, was actually fine, she thought, as she stood in the centre of the sitting room and turned round slowly, admiring the fancy ceiling rose. The current owners were a little more house-proud than the ones at that ill-starred Sydenham semi. The sofa here was newish and quite posh; the framed prints on the walls were Tate Britain rather than Ikea.

There was so much snobbery in buying houses, Beth realised. Having grown up in Dulwich, she had both an instinctive nose for it and a sneaking suspicion that she was not nearly as immune as she'd like to think. There was definitely a process of like calling to like. If you appreciated an owner's taste in art, you were more likely to be able to imagine yourself taking over their home.

She knew it should be all about projecting yourself into the space, no matter what was going on there at the time when you saw it. But it was just a lot easier if it wasn't a huge leap of the imagination. Maybe this was why she had gravitated towards empty houses, Beth thought. Although, after her recent experience, she certainly wasn't feeling that pull any longer.

Poppy, pirouetting around in the hall, called out excitedly to her, breaking into her thoughts. 'Shall we have a look at the lovely west-facing eat-in kitchen?'

Eat-in, muttered Beth to herself. Honestly. Where on earth were you supposed to eat, if not in a kitchen? But that wasn't right, she acknowledged quickly. Once upon a time it had all been about separate breakfast rooms, kitchens and dining rooms. Now the amorphous open space was the dream – a free-for-all footprint that you could zone the way you liked.

Although maybe not at her budget, thought Beth, trotting obediently to the end of the corridor. Then, like a showjumper refusing a fence, she came to an abrupt halt.

Although she realised the chances of lightning, or murderers, striking twice in the same place were very slim, she still felt quite reluctant to go further. She waited until Poppy caught up with her and then ushered her onwards. Let her find the body, she thought. No, that was silly, there definitely wouldn't be another. Would there?

She followed at a snail's pace, to find Poppy standing in the middle of the kitchen, looking at her quizzically.

Of course, it was broad daylight, which made things much better. No mean, stinging neon light, no dark garden looming beyond. And, she hoped, no large larder cupboard. That had gone from a must-have to a no-no in her book.

Then she realised there actually *was* a cupboard, over there by the fridge. She hadn't seen it at first, because its door was so similar to the run of kitchen units that it was almost camouflaged. Even though it was on the other side of the kitchen and looked half the size, it was suddenly all much too reminiscent of that house in Sydenham.

'Er, what's in there?' she asked Poppy, pointing.

Poppy gave her a swift glance, turning from bright young thing to a much less frivolous creature in under a second. It was all the proof Beth needed to be sure that Poppy, and probably every other estate agent in south-east London, knew exactly where the body was buried. As it were.

They both walked slowly towards the door. It looked innocent enough on the outside, but Beth knew full well that appearances could be deceptive. They exchanged a glance as Poppy reached out and put a hand tentatively on the small brass knob. Then she drew a breath, grasped it more firmly and turned decisively. The door swung outwards, and there was a nasty rustling sound. For a moment, Beth thought she was going to be sick on the spot. But it was only a monumental stash of bags for life tumbling out – a fortune in plastic, as each was worth a princely ten pence these days. She took a deep breath and tried to control her nausea.

They both laughed nervously. 'Someone's not thinking about the planet,' Beth quipped.

Poppy tittered obligingly in return then fiddled in the cupboard, snapped on a light, and they both saw that, apart from the bags, there was nothing more sinister stored there than a collection of spiders' webs that would have done Miss Havisham proud.

That didn't mean the whole house was clear yet. There was still upstairs. Would there be another weird little collection of belongings hiding somewhere, showing someone had been camping out? Beth breathed in. Was it going to be like this every time she viewed a house from now on? Because this was seriously preying on her nerves. She was going to be white-haired and shaking by the time she'd found their dream home. Assuming she ever did.

But twenty minutes later, she and Poppy had encountered nothing more threatening upstairs than seriously bad taste in wallpaper, and they were back outside again.

'So, what did you think?' asked Poppy brightly.

Beth tried to give an honest answer, but it was very hard to disentangle terror and relief from the more normal boredom of seeing and judging other people's taste in soft furnishings. 'Well, I suppose it's got the sort of space we need...' she said, wrinkling her nose. Even this equivocation was enough to get Poppy so excited that Beth worried the girl would do herself a mischief.

'So, shall I get you in for a second look?' she asked, almost jumping up and down on the spot.

'Hang on a second, I've only just had the first one. Give me time to, erm, let my impressions settle,' she said mildly.

'But if you're buying with a partner, wouldn't they like a chance to see, too?' Poppy had her head on one side now, like an inquisitive bird. She wasn't going to let this glimmer of a potential commission disappear off, like a juicy worm wriggling into reverse and burying itself back under a suburban lawn.

'I'm sure my partner would love to, if we get that far. But it's important that *I* like the look of it first,' said Beth firmly. She was secretly rather annoyed at the idea that the views of a theoretical partner might trump her own and seal the deal.

'Oh, absolutely, yes, yes,' said Poppy, but it sounded automatic.

Beth wondered what ploy she'd come up with next, and started edging away. She'd quite like to get back home now.

'We have had a *lot* of interest in this property, though. I'd hate someone to snatch it from underneath your nose,' Poppy said, with a small and patently synthetic smile of sympathy.

'I suppose I'll just have to take that chance,' Beth said, starting to walk quite briskly down the path towards her little Fiat.

Poppy bounced ahead and was in front of Beth again before she knew it. 'Just let me know, and I'll do my best to try and secure another viewing,' she said, as though it was going to be a Herculean task.

'Yep, definitely,' said Beth, sliding behind the wheel of the car.

For a moment, she'd thought Poppy was going to get in with her, but the girl just leant down and did lots of thumbs-up signs through the window as Beth tried to ignore her and turn the ignition. Even when Beth had slammed the car into gear, Poppy couldn't stop herself giving the roof of the car a quick pat – very quick – as Beth finally zoomed off.

As she met the snarl of traffic snaking back to Dulwich Village, Beth found she did have plenty of time to think about the house, and the one in Sydenham. Things were always

knotted up at this time of day, which was one disadvantage of
living smack in the middle of Dulwich. Everyone else always
seemed to want to drive around the few streets she used,
whether they had a right to or not. And, of course, the bigger the
car they were driving, the more they acted as though they
owned the whole place – roads, shops, houses and people
included. That would be one thing she wouldn't miss if – *when*
– they finally moved out.

Beth flicked on the radio and turned to the local news.
She might as well see what, if anything, had happened to
what she already thought of as 'her' case, in the last twenty-
four hours. Harry, as usual, was being miserably tight-lipped
about the whole thing. Honestly, what was the point of
having a police inspector as a boyfriend if he didn't give you
any information? Though, remembering their rapprochement
the other night, she acknowledged that there were certain
advantages that really didn't have anything to do with
murder.

The reminiscent smile was wiped off her face as she
suddenly tuned back into what the radio announcer was saying:
'...*the body of a second estate agent, the police have confirmed.*'

Immediately, she signalled to turn off and edged out of the
traffic into a handy parking spot. She was very lucky to find one,
and the car behind her tooted angrily at having been pipped to
it. Normally, Beth would have been crowing. A space within
spitting distance of the St Barnabas parish hall? At this time in
the afternoon? It was unheard of. But Beth hardly bothered to
register either her great good fortune or the sound of the hooting
driver behind. She was concentrating feverishly on the radio. Of
course, no sooner had she cut the ignition than the bulletin was
over, and the announcer switched to a plug for a show the
next day.

Beth changed channels, wondering if another station would
cover the story. 'The leader of the opposition, who has been

engaging in talks with other parties on the effects of the cost-of-living crisis...'

She snapped off the radio in frustration. All right, it was a very serious matter. But there was a murderer still on the loose here. And would they cover it properly? No, all their reporters were outside Westminster as usual, giving minute-by-minute coverage to a mess which seemed as insoluble as the tangles in Magpie's coat.

She started up the car again and was about to attempt to edge back out into the stream of traffic, when there was an imperious tap on her window. She looked out, only to do a double-take. It was Belinda McKenzie.

Once upon a time, Belinda had been a frenemy – one of those women who pretends to like you but actually chips away at you unobtrusively like a stealthy sculptor, leaving you feeling just a little less complete after each encounter. For almost a year now, Belinda had switched off the pretence of friendliness and been a lot more upfront about her feelings for Beth. She loathed her.

Belinda had deliberately excluded Beth from all the 'Welcome to Wyatt's' coffee mornings she'd taken it upon herself to host last half-term in a transparent bid to draw all the newbie mums into her cult. And poor old Jake had been the only child in the whole of Year 7 (one hundred and fifty kids!) not invited to Belinda's son Billy's lavish twelfth birthday party, even though he actually got on quite well with the boy.

Although Jake had failed to snag one of the gilt-edged – yes, *gilt-edged* – invites, he certainly hadn't been the only boy to be a no-show on the day. After much soul-searching, Beth's great friend Katie had decided to whizz off for a tactical weekend away in Cornwall at the very moment when Belinda had thrown her home open to the world. And Katie hadn't been the only one. Numbers, according to Beth's sources in the school, had been well down on previous years. It wasn't very edifying or at all grown-up, but Beth had smirked quite a bit at hearing that news.

Seeing Belinda's curiously unlined face at such close quarters now was very disconcerting. The woman had been avoiding her for so long, only coming anywhere near when Beth was with Katie. As Katie was almost Belinda's next-door neighbour in Court Lane, it wouldn't have been tactical for Belinda to freeze Katie out as well. There was also the fact that Katie was probably one of the nicest people in the world, and you'd have to be even more nuts than Belinda to want to deprive yourself of her friendship.

Belinda tapped on the window again, harder, and though her features didn't move, her eyes glittered dangerously, which Beth diagnosed as extreme irritation. Unwillingly, she pushed the button to wind down her window a little. But only a little, mind. What on earth did the woman have to say to her?

'*There* you are, Beth,' Belinda started, as though Beth had been deliberately hiding from her for months instead of going about her business very visibly. Belinda could have caught up with her any morning if she'd really wanted to. Or sent her son a party invitation.

Very reluctantly, Beth pinned on a social smile. 'Yes, here I am. In my car. Can I help you with something, Belinda?' she said, trying to sound as business-like as possible.

'Just wanted a quick word,' Belinda went on.

Lord. Did she have to? Beth suddenly felt a pressing need to get away, to be anywhere else. But really, where could she go? And this parking spot, though it wasn't ideal, was probably as close as she'd get to her own home at this time of day, with all the mummies of Dulwich on the streets picking up their kids from essential extracurricular activities like toddlers' tae kwon do and mother-and-baby Mandarin classes. Also, if she stayed in the car, then Belinda would tower over her throughout their conversation as though she were knee-high to a grasshopper.

Reluctantly, she snapped off her seatbelt and stepped out onto the pavement.

Unfortunately, Belinda was still towering over her. On an ordinary school day when she had, surely, nowhere much to go and no one to impress, the woman was wearing stacked heels, which made her about four foot taller than Beth, at a conservative estimate. Beth sighed and leant her back against her Fiat instead. She might as well be comfortable, even if she could never be tall. The car was still warm from her excursion and she took comfort from it.

She slung her bag casually over her shoulder and heard the tell-tale scrunching of old Haribo packets. Her eyes flew automatically to Belinda's bag, which as usual was the biggest, juiciest, newest fruit to have fallen from the Mulberry tree. Although it was huge, it probably only contained a space-age phone and the keys to the most expensive home in Dulwich, Belinda's life was so streamlined. And, thought Beth suddenly, so pointless, actually.

Now both women were on the pavement, standing awkwardly, and blocking the way for a procession of women with buggies. Belinda tutted as though it was all Beth's fault, and took her by the arm. Beth fought her instinct to shake the woman off, and found herself being led over to the recessed entrance to what had, until recently, been one of the only useful shops in Dulwich. It was the much-lamented post office, which had closed down and then started up again as a cushion shop. Then it had shut again, and was now a pop-up greetings card concession, as likely to totter and fold at any moment as its own wares.

Beth and Belinda stood awkwardly together, Belinda's enormous bag between them. Beth eyed it again and thought irresistibly of the buffer states created to keep the European powers from war at the Treaty of Versailles. It was almost the size of Poland.

The silence stretched, and Beth looked mulishly up from the bag to its owner. Belinda was gazing into the far distance, apparently waiting for Beth to make the first move. Well, she was damned if she'd speak first. This had all been Belinda's idea. From this angle, the woman's face looked as taut and shiny as one of the balloons that had no doubt been tied onto the gatepost of her multi-million-pound home on the occasion of young Billy's birthday jamboree.

'So... how are you?' Belinda said abruptly, switching her gaze to Beth for a second. She raked over her outfit like an expert on *The Antiques Roadshow* asked to assess a pile of third-hand *Peppa Pig* DVDs. She didn't wait for a response but steamrollered on. 'Just wanted to hear what's going on with the estate agents. I mean, you're the one with your ear to the ground... in all ways,' she finished off with a titter, which did very little to endear her to Beth.

'Oh, you know, this and that.' Beth was at her most non-committal. She was reluctant to admit how scanty her knowledge really was, despite her best efforts to pump Harry and Nina for information. And she had no intention of parting with even an iota of the little she'd gathered. 'Why are you interested?' she countered.

She wouldn't normally have asked such an abrupt question, but she felt beating about the bush was redundant with Belinda. The woman was always rude to her. Beth herself would never stoop – quite – to outright impoliteness, but why couldn't she be direct back? And she really didn't want to keep gazing up at Belinda like this. It was giving her a crick in the neck.

Belinda looked at her for a silent moment or two. Despite herself, Beth quailed. She knew how Belinda's au pair, gardener, dog-walker, cleaner and even her husband felt when they'd displeased their mistress. But she stood her ground.

'Property's always been an interest. One knows so many people in the business, too. Like Barty's friend, Piers Frampton.'

There was a definite pause here, presumably for Beth to murmur in awed recognition. Belinda had mentioned Piers Frampton like someone dropping quite a brick of a name, but it meant nothing at all to her tiny and unappreciative audience. After a beat, Belinda carried on. 'When you're in one of the most beautiful houses in Dulwich' – here she left another little gap, presumably to allow Beth to murmur sycophantically, but Beth merely continued to stare crossly at her and it went unfilled – 'then you have a responsibility to keep up with these things. But maybe you wouldn't appreciate that,' she said condescendingly.

Beth, who despite herself felt a tide of red sweeping up from her collar to her ears, still said nothing. She knew that Belinda's house was, indeed, second to none in terms of square footage, but even though she'd stolen lots of Katie's decorating ideas over the years, it had a chilly lack of charm that said much more about its owner than she'd ever realise. Beth could have added that many considered Pickwick Road to be a very fine address indeed, as far as Dulwich properties went. But she took a deep breath instead.

'OK then, Belinda,' she contented herself with saying as neutrally as possible, and hoisted her bag further up on her shoulder, about to walk the short distance home.

But Belinda put out a hand again and stopped her. 'So, what do you know? You haven't actually said.'

'Haven't I?' said Beth, trying for mysterious and realising she was probably just achieving smug. She was not parting with any of her precious few facts, however avid Belinda was to know them. The woman wasn't entitled to every single thing she wanted. Whatever her expectations.

'So, you don't actually know anything. That's, well, a bit sad,' said Belinda, turning down her mouth a minuscule amount in mock-sympathy.

Despite herself, Beth did suddenly feel a powerful urge to

prove Belinda wrong and pretend she knew tons. But she knew she had to resist it, and try not to fall into Belinda's trap. She flicked a little on-off social smile back and prepared to walk off again... only to find that hand had shot out again, and was now lightly circling her wrist, the razor-sharp red acrylic nails pressing into her skin. It was the sort of warning shot of severe pain to come that Magpie tended to give Beth when she was a bit slow filling her bowl with nuggets. It was *not* what Beth expected from a fellow school mum. This was too much. Beth shook off Belinda's grasp and looked up angrily.

Belinda's expression was entirely unruffled. 'Well, we must get the boys together soon, anyway,' she purred. 'Billy's just got the latest PlayStation console. And Barty picked up the new games when he was in Hong Kong for work last week – *all* of them. Jake loves his gaming, doesn't he?'

Beth knew this was the most lethal weapon in Belinda's armoury. Access to her children's playdate schedule was only permitted to the chosen few. If Jake was suddenly invited to Court Lane, then he would be made for life – in Belinda's eyes, at any rate. But Beth wasn't going to be bought.

'I'm so sorry, Belinda, but Jake's really busy at the moment,' Beth said over her shoulder, and she walked off briskly before the woman could see her nose growing faster than Pinocchio's. Jake? Busy? That would be the day. Despite the homework burden at Wyatt's, which seemed to keep both Charlie and Katie working for hours every night, Jake seemed to be sticking to his beloved primary school position that almost everything was optional.

Every afternoon, he raced through any compulsory tasks with slapdash abandon, while doing his best to evade any discussion with his mother, and if there was anything left, he would rush through it at school before the register was called. Beth didn't love his system, but she had to admit it was working so far. And it did mean that she didn't have to spend her afternoons googling quadratic equations, as Katie did.

She wondered how Jake would feel about the way she'd just turned down something Belinda definitely considered to be a golden ticket. Would he be cross? Or would he consider that his mother had dodged a bullet on his behalf? He got on fine with Billy, but did he want to spend more time with him? Beth hoped the answer to that was no, as it was definitely off the cards now. Belinda had been vacant-faced with shock. Mind you, she looked like that the whole time these days.

Beth could feel the woman's eyes still burning into her back, and she did her utmost to resist the urge to run. She was extremely relieved to turn down Pickwick Road at last, and she did trot the last few yards, knowing she was safely out of sight. Her breathless arrival at the front door startled Magpie, who'd been basking in the last rays of autumnal sunshine in the window box, which Beth had lovingly planted with pansies only a week ago. She shot to her paws, gave her owner a look of outraged disgust, and sauntered off, leaving squashed and trampled stems in her wake.

'Magpie!' Beth said in exasperation. She so rarely had the impulse to cultivate anything, as her front and back gardens attested. But she'd seen the pansies in the supermarket and, inspired by her last case, had thought she'd get a few and try out this whole outdoorsy lark. Look where that had got her. A lovely al fresco mattress for a very naughty cat. She opened the front door disconsolately. First Belinda, now Magpie. How much worse could the afternoon get?

Immediately, she stepped on something horrible just as she was shutting the door. Oh God. Wet. Squishy. She didn't even want to look down, but realised she had to.

Thank the Lord, it was just Jake's sopping swimming things. She'd forgotten he'd even had swimming today, and was amazed he'd looked out the kit himself this morning. Had it been washed after the last trip to the school pool? She couldn't remember, but it was irrelevant now. Well, if Jake could now apparently find his swimming things on his own, he could have taken them the extra few steps to the washing machine, couldn't he?

'Jake!' she yelled up the stairs. No answer, but she heard the sound of his door shutting. Great. That wasn't supposed to be the way it went. He was supposed to troop down obediently and stand, preferably with his head bowed, while she told him off. Well, it looked like those days were over.

She picked up the swimming things between thumb and index finger and took them, dripping, into the kitchen, flipping open the drum of the washing machine and tossing them in. There. One thing dealt with. Turning to the table, she saw that someone had left the remnants of a snack – a hearty one – lying all over the surface. There were breadcrumbs, a rank-looking bit of ham and an empty crisp packet standing like silent witnesses to a feast.

'Jake!' she shouted again. And again, there was a deafening nothing in response. *Boys.* Then she thought of Belinda. *Women.* And Magpie. *Cats.* The whole blinking lot of them, in fact. She made a cup of tea and took it into the sitting room, immediately coming up against what seemed to be a solid phalanx of boxes. Had they moved in the night? Or had Harry been shifting them around again? *Men,* she added to her hitlist.

She flopped down on the sofa, attempting to block out everything, and searched for a local news bulletin. She now considered it her bounden duty to get herself as well informed as possible on the whole estate agent thing, to get one up on Belinda if nothing else.

But ten minutes later, she was forced to admit defeat. There seemed to be nothing since she'd heard those words on the radio. A second estate agent had been killed, though, she was absolutely sure she'd heard that. Even the rolling news channels were devoting themselves solely to the latest Westminster kerfuffles instead of goings-on in south-east London. She sighed and wandered back to the kitchen where Jake's swimming trunks were now being whirled round and round in a soapy world of their own. She felt a pang. She should have put some other stuff in there, too, and made a dent in the washing mountain.

She opened the fridge and tried to find inspiration in contents that were either too dried-up or not dried-up enough. It would have to be pasta. Again. Oh well, at least she didn't have any culinary heights to live up to. Belinda was probably having to whip up some amazing three-course extravaganza at the moment – or was shouting at someone else to do it for her. Even Katie would be hand-carving a delicious range of organic vegetables for Charlie to turn up his nose at. There was a lot to be said for a simple sauce out of a jar.

Tonight, she'd stay up until Harry got home, and she'd interrogate him properly on what on earth was going on with the estate agents. First they'd had someone in custody, but there had been no charges. Now, there had been another death – if she hadn't been hallucinating before Belinda had come along and distracted her at exactly the wrong moment. If the suspect had still been banged-up when the second murder had been committed, then Harry had an obvious problem on his hands. Surely he'd want to expound his theories to a very willing listener? It always worked so well in the books he loved.

She and Jake had supper tête à tête and, thank goodness, everything seemed to be fine again. Maybe her boy was just too much like his dad to hold a grudge for long. James had had an equable, not to say sunny, temperament – just one of the things she'd loved about him. Jake was looking more and more like him, she realised, as he forked in his pasta while telling her the latest playground jokes.

'What do you call a Russian with Covid?'

'No idea, love. Eat up before it goes cold,' she answered.

'Ivor Chestikov,' he said triumphantly.

She was still smiling as she cleared up a little later, leaving Harry's helping under a plate for when he got in. Though she and Jake had spent a lovely evening together, and she'd been reassured at the fact that his jokes were still those of a young boy, not a teenager at all, she hadn't quite dared broach her conversation with Belinda. Once, she would have been certain she'd done the right thing in turning down the woman's offer flat. Charlie was the Batman to his Robin, or the Tonto to his Lone Ranger. Spending tranches of time at Billy's would have been a mere sideshow, distracting him from the main event. But maybe all that was changing?

She found herself nostalgic for the days when Jake had never stopped talking from the moment he'd woken up every day. Many was the time she'd sat at this same table while a stream of chatter had swirled over her head, and she'd just thought about other things. Tonight had seemed a little more grown-up; until the jokes, at least. But it had seemed fragile, after the past days of discord. She hadn't wanted to risk their newfound peace.

Beth wondered whether Billy would allude to his mother's plan in the playground tomorrow, and would reveal that Jake's own mother had blighted it. She thought it was quite unlikely. Billy had always been a nice enough child. But he was much larger and heftier than Jake, taking his physique directly from his meaty dad, Barty, who must surely have played very expensive games of rugby at his own school in past years, while Belinda was as tall as a poplar tree. Billy must, consequently, be even further on in the dreaded game of puberty which often seemed to rob boys of the manners their parents spent so long instilling.

While Beth busied herself with the dishes, Jake disappeared upstairs. It seemed their quality time was over. He was spending more and more hours shut in his room. She wondered idly whether she ought to get him some vitamin D supplements. But presumably he still saw a bit of sky at breaktimes at school.

She settled herself down in the sitting room, for once brave enough to shove Magpie off the sofa. Colin immediately took up his usual station at her feet, occasionally peering at her with a hopeful eye to make sure he hadn't missed an offer of a snack or walk.

With the BBC rolling news on low, just in case the second murder made a showing, she plucked another of Harry's novels off the pile beside the sofa and started thumbing through it. Maybe it would give her some tips she could use in her investigation. Unfortunately, this particular sleuth's secret weapon was a butler who, when not cross-questioning suspects, ran a stately home with one hand, chauffeured with another, and could still rustle up a mean three-course meal, maybe with his feet. It was all good fun, but Beth wasn't sure the skills were really transferable.

One lesson she was learning, though, she thought as she raced through the pages, was that it was a lot easier to solve a mystery if you had the police tugging their forelocks at you before spoon-feeding you all the information you could possibly require. And it was handy having a nice big room to hold the final confrontation in. Her phone beeped with an incoming text message, but she was too tired to look at it. I wonder if any of those houses on HomeSweetHome have proper libraries, was her last waking thought, before sleep claimed her.

FIFTEEN

Today can only be better than yesterday, right, Beth thought, opening one eye and squinting into a new day. She'd finally staggered up the stairs in the early hours of the morning, but Harry had either already gone or hadn't come back. His half – well, three-quarters – of the bed had been cold when she slipped beneath the sheets. She told herself it was a good thing, as she could skimp on her beauty routine. But as that usually just consisted of brushing her teeth, she realised she was only fooling herself. She'd probably need fillings now.

As she reluctantly lowered the duvet, she realised the house felt suspiciously cold. Once out of bed, she clutched a radiator and got the confirmation she'd dreaded. The heating wasn't on.

Half an hour later, and having poked and prodded in the forbidding boiler cupboard, there was still no sign of the comforting dancing blue flame that meant piping hot water and warmth. After a chilly shower, she got out her phone to call the boiler engineer. There was the text she dimly remembered arriving last night. She opened it up. The number was with-held. *If you know what's good for you, you'll keep away from*

Sydenham. She'd been cold enough already. Now it was as though ice cubes had been poured down her back.

She racked her brains. Who could this be? Who wanted to stop her investigations? So far, only Harry, and this wouldn't be from him. Would it? She shook her head, baffled. Anyway, she couldn't stand here in a howling draught worrying. She got straight on to the engineer, thanking her lucky stars that she still had his number and that he wasn't off in one of his amazingly swanky holiday homes, bought with the sacks of money that a grateful Dulwich clientele had had no option but to part with over the years.

'How old is the boiler? Well, it's virtually new. Erm, that is to say, about twelve years old?' she said, as the chap sucked his teeth and made doubtful noises, rather like a surgeon on being told the patient was an obese smoker who tucked into vodka for breakfast and had eaten burgers thrice daily since birth. Eventually, she cajoled him into agreeing to a house call, which was going to cost her as much as Jake's blazer which was lying crumpled on the stairs. Her newly rebellious son hadn't even bothered wearing it into school today. Well, that had been worth the money. *Not.*

She remembered now that he'd been a baby when they'd got the new boiler. Of course, that had been an awful time to be stuck without heating. A squalling infant, a million Babygros to wash, bottles to sterilise... Looking back on all that, perhaps she had it easy now. But the boiler breaking down did make her think that, maybe, it was time they moved on from this house. If the infrastructure was going to pot, it might be a good moment to cut their losses and let someone else deal with the joys of a Victorian property beginning to feel its age.

Mind you, anywhere they moved to would probably have its fair share of issues. None of the houses she'd seen so far had had state-of-the-art wiring or electrics, she was willing to bet. She hadn't peered into the fuse boxes, particularly not at the

Sydenham house. It was hard to think of sensible questions about circuitry when you were screaming and running for your life. But at least if they got a new house, the problems would all be different ones.

This thought, and the fact she now had to stay in to wait for the engineer, meant she'd had to let Janice know she wouldn't be sauntering through the Wyatt's gates today. Janice was lovely about it, of course.

'Don't worry, Beth, I know you'll be super-productive when you *do* come in. Will that be tomorrow?'

'Um, yes. Yes of course,' said Beth, her fingers only lightly crossed. She hoped she wasn't being paranoid, thinking there might be a slight edge to the way Janice had lingered with that almost imperceptible extra emphasis on the 'when you *do* come in'. It was almost as though she was implying Beth didn't actually visit her desk that often... But the shocking truth was that she didn't. She must put that right. It was her own guilty conscience nudging her, she was sure. Not Janice nagging, in the politest and most Dulwich way possible. Or at least she sincerely hoped not.

The horrible thought gave her the impetus, of course, to do something entirely different. She got straight on the phone to Nina.

'Nina, I urgently need to see some new properties – some good ones this time, hopefully! Plus, I need any info you've got on the murders. Is there anything fresh on the grapevine since we last spoke? I can't find any more details on this second murder; do you know anything about it? There was an announcement on the radio yesterday that I heard two seconds of, then nothing on any of the news later... I've had a quick look online this morning and in the paper too, but it's not covered.'

'Yeah, you won't find nuffink. They're trying to shut it all down, innit?' Nina's response was both succinct and indistinct. If Beth had to guess, she'd say her friend was stuffing herself with some sort of cake at her desk while her colleagues were out. She could just imagine the crumbs. Beth closed her eyes briefly.

'Who is shutting it down? And how can they do that, anyway?'

'You know, the estate agents, the top brass. They don't want the viewers to get the wellies, do they?'

Beth could sympathise. The idea of a corpse on the premises while you were trying to look at a house was enough to give anyone an exceptionally bad case of the *willies*, as she could herself attest. And as for an actual, real live one... Well, she wasn't sure what could be worse than either wellies or willies – wallies or wobblies? – but that was definitely it.

'Can they do that, though? Suppress the news?'

'I fink the police is helping. They don't want to reveal details, say there might be copycat killings. Yeah, right.'

As so often was the case, Beth found herself sympathising with Nina's terse and cynical summing up of the situation. *Yeah, right* definitely seemed to cover it. Copycat murders? Of estate agents? They weren't the most popular people – estate agents regularly came lower even than journalists and bankers in surveys of distrusted professionals – but that was no reason to go round randomly bumping them off, surely? There had to be something else connecting these killings.

'Is there anything that ties the two victims to each other? Apart from being estate agents, I mean?'

There was a pause, and Beth could clearly hear Nina chomping away. If that was a muffin or a bun that her friend was devouring, it was really stale.

'Both houses were in Sydenham. And, don't say I told you, but there's a story going round that both geezers actually worked for the same firm.'

'Really?' Beth sat bolt upright. Now they were finally getting somewhere. A connection like this could point to a problem at the company, a relationship between the victims, a real reason for the deaths. Apart from the fact that some people would die – or kill – to buy a house in Sydenham.

'For Worthingtons?'

'You aren't going to do anything silly are you, hon?' asked Nina, her voice clearer now as she swallowed down the remnants of her recalcitrant breakfast.

'Not at all. You know me,' said Beth, crossing her fingers. Well, she couldn't do anything silly for ages, that much was true – she was stuck at home for the moment. The boiler engineer had given her the usual window of 'between ten and two, love', which more accurately meant any time from now till eternity. 'But you could give me a hand tomorrow,' she added. 'Not for anything dangerous. Just to drive past the second property involved.' The mysterious text message telling her to avoid Sydenham must mean she was on the right track. 'Your bosses wouldn't mind, would they? If you said I was a potential client... Was it definitely that firm, by the way? Worthingtons, like I said? They both worked there?'

'Hmm. I'll ask and I'll let you know. They might be OK about it. And as for the company, babes. People are *saying* they were both with Framptons. But they're wrong. Richard Pettit was actually with Worthingtons, I fink you told me that already. People must have their driers crossed because the house you saw was with multiple agents, and so was the one where this other guy bought it. So, people are making assignations.'

Beth took a moment to be impressed at Nina's new mastery of the jargon. Multiple agents, indeed. It looked like selling houses was really starting to suit her. Though that might be a shame, as it seemed to be rapidly turning into a very dangerous job.

'Aha, I can see why people are getting confused. So, it's not the same agents; it's two different ones. It's so hard to know these days. I made the appointment via the website, so I was never sure which firm I was dealing with. That doesn't seem such a great idea now, in the circumstances. Don't worry, I'll be more careful in future. Do you know much about Framptons?'

'Nah. Just that they love a bit of that Sydenham action. The Thorpes, that's that great area with all the nice stained glass and stuff, is really highly sought-after. And all the roads have names with Thorpe in them.'

'You'd better watch it, Nina, you're really starting to talk like one of them,' Beth said.

They finished the call on giggles, but Beth was thoughtful as she put down her phone and fired up her laptop. Framptons. Now, where had she heard that name recently?

SIXTEEN

Beth bundled her still-damp hair more securely into its scrunchy and tapped her fingers restlessly against the steering wheel. All the relaxing benefits of a long, and gorgeously hot, shower were evaporating as she waited for Nina outside the Herne Hill estate agents. She blessed yesterday's boiler wizard. Not only had he shown up within the allotted timeslot – just – which already marked him out as something special as far as south-east London tradesmen were concerned, but then he had successfully repaired her boiler. True, he'd spent the obligatory amount of time shaking his head at it, asking her winsomely whether her last repairers had been wearing big hats when they tied up their horses outside (it took her some time to realise he meant they'd been cowboys), and muttering about putting her poor old Potterton out of its misery. But Beth had persuaded him that it was much too young to die. While she'd been off making his umpteenth cup of strong-Typhoo-with-two-sugars, she was pretty sure she'd heard him whacking it with a spanner. But when she'd come back with the tea, it was purring away as happily as a snuggly little kitten. Despite his eye-watering call-out fee, she decided he was worth every penny, as the cost of a new boiler would have had them all out on the street in one of Harry's many cardboard boxes.

She did have a nagging feeling that it was a terrible shame Harry was so busy. Surely he, as a man, should have been able to fix the boiler for her? She realised this was appallingly sexist, and she would have been furious if he'd assumed she was better at making cakes than him (although she was) or was the only person in the house qualified to wash up (although apparently this was also true; both he and Jake were strategically incompetent at it). But it would have been great if he could have done something with the boiler. Especially if it had really only required a good sharp blow with a blunt instrument. That would have saved them an epic line of pound signs. Oh well, maybe he'd be more hands-on in their new home. If they ever found one.

Beth's smug feeling that a crisis had been averted began to dissipate when she drew up at the estate agents. Nina was taking an inordinate amount of time to extract herself from her desk. Beth could see her through the big picture windows, passing Post-it notes to colleagues, rummaging through her enormous collection of plastic bags, almost making it to the door and then trailing back for her phone. It wouldn't have mattered a jot, but there had been nowhere to park, so Beth had simply stuck on her hazard lights right outside on Half Moon Lane and was now obstructing traffic. As well as a bus filled with bored commuters, there was now a caravan of much more antsy mothers behind her, all getting to the tooting stage in their very big cars. Exhaust fumes were pouring over Herne Hill like a miasma of disapproval.

'Come on, Nina, come on,' Beth said through gritted teeth, pretty sure she was going to be thumped by someone soon. She could almost hear the whirr of windows being wound down.

Just in the nick of time, Nina popped out of the office like a cork from a bottle, hands full of carriers as usual, and a cherubic smile on her little face. One of the mothers unwisely chose this moment to let fly with a beep on her horn, and Beth watched Nina veer in her direction. The mother thought better of it and burnt rubber instead, skirting round the Fiat like a Formula One driver taking a crucial corner.

'Ah, that's better,' said Nina, flopping into the seat. 'Fought I'd never get away from that lot. 'Smuch better there in the afternoons when they're all off on viewings. I can really get a lot done then.'

Beth gave her friend a sideways glance, but decided not to comment, and they moved off – to the relief of most of Herne Hill. Soon they were bowling up Village Way and joining the stop-start traffic chugging past the Village Primary. Nina craned out of the window to see if she could spot Wilf in the playground, though he was probably inside by now.

'He's learning the Black Deaf in History,' Nina confided to Beth.

Beth thought for quite a long moment. She was still only half awake, but this really sounded massively politically incorrect, even for a place as privileged as Dulwich. Then she decoded the Nina-ese. She remembered Jake tackling the plague – the enormous global catastrophe which had wiped out a quarter of the UK population in the fourteenth century. She'd thought at the time it was enough to give anyone nightmares, but Jake had got quite into rats and fleas and sores. She wasn't quite sure why the government considered grotesque mass extinction such a suitable topic for primary-age children. Unless it was to prepare them for the advent of another global pandemic, and the fact that public health preparations hadn't moved on enormously from the 'nail a bunch of herbs to your door' school of preventative medicine, followed swiftly by a 'bring out your dead' attitude to its failures.

Beth felt very nostalgic about Jake's years at the little Primary, and she, too, craned out to look at the playground with its snakes and ladders and hopscotch grids marked out in yellow, green and red paint on the tarmac. It all looked so much smaller to her than it had last year. And as for Jake, he'd soon see it as positively Lilliputian. Now that he was being bombarded with Latin vocabulary and nasty bits of physics, she looked back on those checklists of symptoms of the bubonic plague with misty eyes. Though, come to think of it, that had probably been one of the first signs.

They swished on past and up towards the South Circular where the traffic predictably ground to a halt. There was no point getting cross about this; it was a fact of life. Beth simply pulled on the handbrake and turned to chat to Nina, as people in all the cars in front or behind were doing. At least Beth had adult company, while many of the mothers, so high up in the seats of their Land Rovers, had to crane over their shoulders to make baby-talk with offspring who were in lonely splendour in the back. They all inched along like a caterpillar hoping to make it, one fine day, to a tasty leaf.

Eventually, they reached the junction with Lordship Lane, and Beth turned right. She never really liked passing the distinctively rounded clock tower of the Horniman Museum. It had been a favourite spot to take Jake when he'd been little, and the petting zoo and grounds were gorgeous, but now it just reminded her of a dear friend who'd got married there and had had high hopes for happiness – on that day at least. It was easier when there was someone else in the car.

'You haven't brunged Colin along for the ride,' Nina observed.

'He looked so happy on the sofa this morning, I thought I'd leave him to it. Mind you, Magpie's probably given him hell since then. I'll make sure he has an airing when I'm back home. Have you ever thought about getting a dog? I know you love old Col.'

It was Nina's turn to give Beth a glance. Both of them knew

Colin's habit of goosing every woman in the vicinity went down very badly with Nina. Being short and round, she was at precisely the right, or wrong height, depending on whether you were looking at it from the point of view of a pervy Labrador or not.

'Nah, got me hands full with the cat, innit? Plus, Wilf doesn't seem bothered.' Nina's enormous ginger tom was one of the few cats around who might have given Magpie a run for her money, Beth reflected. Just as well one lived in Herne Hill and the other in Dulwich Village. She hoped they would stay a postcode apart, for everyone's sake. Otherwise, it would be a confrontation like the Jets versus the Sharks, only with less swishing of skirts and probably a lot more blood. A West Norwood-side story. Beth smiled to herself.

They were chugging up Sydenham Hill now, with Beth's Fiat not enjoying the stop-start progress. That was one advantage a massive SUV had, she realised. None of the gear-crashing and brake-stomping she was having to do so much of. Oh well, maybe it would tone up her thigh muscles. It was the closest she was going to get to an exercise routine, anyway.

Once they'd finally hit the mini-roundabout at the top, things moved a bit more freely, and soon they were coasting along, passing the bridal shop on the corner and turning left into Sydenham High Street. Suddenly Beth remembered she had been specifically warned not to come here, and her foot went down on the accelerator.

'Got to watch out now, babe, there's a little turning off here for the first house, but we mustn't miss it or we'll have to go miles... there, there, *there!*' Nina shrieked suddenly, all but wrenching the wheel round herself as Beth nearly sailed past the turning. They did a little circuit in the one-way maze of streets and ended up parked outside a terrace of redbrick homes. It was horribly familiar.

'But this isn't it, is it? The one you meant?' Beth turned to Nina.

'Yeah, yeah, babes. Come on, let's have a look,' her friend's hand was already on the door.

'You can't be serious, Nina. This is the one I've already been to... the one where I, you know...' Beth said faintly.

'Oh, yeah? Is it? Oops, sorry, babe,' said Nina, not sounding all that repentant. 'Just remind me what the address is again?'

Beth tutted to herself. 'Thirteen, Calthorpe Road,' she parroted obligingly.

'That's right. Well, we're here now. Worth a quick look?' Nina was as chirpy and irrepressible as ever.

Beth looked at her with irritation. 'You do know what I found in there, don't you?'

'Wasn't you, was it, though? It was that poor agent girl,' Nina put her head on one side. 'You said so.'

'All right, it was her. But it was still really...' Beth broke off and shuddered.

She didn't know whether she could actually physically get out of the car and go back into that house. She'd looked at it online, but that was different. She certainly wouldn't venture in willingly. Maybe murderers liked revisiting the scene of their crimes. But she was having enough trouble suppressing images of that limp and bloodless arm, the tragic vulnerability of that wrist, thin for a man... weighed down by death and a surprisingly chunky wristwatch. Wait a minute, she hadn't remembered that bit before. She stored it away for later. Now, she contented herself with giving Nina a very hard glare indeed.

'OK, let's go to the next, then,' said Nina impatiently, shrugging and tutting as though Beth was holding them up out of some bizarre whim, instead of an understandable wish not to give herself an even worse case of the heebie-jeebies.

Beth sniffed. She knew that Nina would much prefer it if she got over her foibles, gave in and went over the house again, but she wasn't up to it. Maybe when a bit of time had passed. Like fifty years. Possibly more.

She signalled to move out, and soon they were on their way again, puttering through the streets. In daylight, Beth could see how much they differed from Dulwich. They had a more serious, less luxurious feel, the houses packed in tightly. But they were solidly built Victorian homes, and full of the sort of gracious details that were eschewed by modern architects – whether on aesthetic grounds or just to cut costs to the bone, Beth didn't know.

Nina was silent, still exuding disapproval of Beth's wimpiness, which Beth felt was harsh. By now she was not expecting great things of their surveillance trip.

It was only a five-minute drive to the next stop on Nina's itinerary. 'Here, pull over,' she yelled out suddenly. Beth was beginning to pity any taxi driver who ever picked up her friend.

Luckily, this street was very quiet, and Beth had no trouble sliding into a parking spot. This time, the house was blessedly unfamiliar, the *For Sale* sign in neon yellow marking it out from its neighbours. They got out and surveyed the property.

It looked as though there had been a belated attempt to spruce the place up. The wheelie bin nearest the gate could hardly close on its payload of old paint tins and decrepit brooms, while the path bore signs of having been very recently weeded. Unfortunately, no one had removed the debris, maybe because they'd already thrown their brooms away. Yellowing clumps of defunct dandelions and curled-up couch grass were strewn over the red and cream chequered paving slabs – by the look of things, original Victorian.

The windows were dusty and blank, and the front door was a nice shade of turquoise, but was also covered with a film of dust. Was this neglect, or the daily pollution from the nearby high street? Beth wasn't sure.

The neighbouring houses on either side looked more

welcoming and were in a better state of repair. Beth tried to see the terrace with unjaundiced eyes. If she didn't already own the snuggest house in Pickwick Road, and therefore the best little home in the world, would she be attracted to this place? It was clearly bigger than hers, which was a very good thing. And, with a bit of love, it could be really nice. She thought back to her own attempt at sprucing up their exterior, the window box which now bore such clear signs of being Magpie's new favourite four-poster bed. If – when – they put the house on the market, people would be judging her and her efforts to make the place presentable. She ought to be a lot more charitable to people facing the same struggle.

'Looks... very nice,' she said to Nina, who raised her eyebrows.

'That's as may be, babe. Notice anything about it, though?'

'The old mops? Or the fact that they're not great gardeners?'

'Nah. Think more... structurally.'

Beth was silent for a beat. The house didn't look as though it was listing to one side or the other. No visible cracks. Nothing broken, as far as she could see. She was at a loss. 'Um, doesn't look like it's got subsidence?'

'Nah, babe.'

'Erm, Japanese knotweed?' she asked, kicking a little clump of dead dandelion with her foot. She'd recently discovered that Japanese knotweed was a very bad thing indeed, although she still wasn't entirely sure she'd be able to spot it in a line-up of garden pests. She'd delegated getting rid of her mother's crop to her feckless older brother, Josh. And, as far as she knew, he'd been successful. She certainly wasn't going to venture into her mother's garden to find out more. After all, if there was a recurring problem, she now knew her mother's next-door neighbour would definitely tell them all about it.

Nina was looking at Beth as though she was failing her

spelling test for the third time. 'All right then, if you're not getting it, I'll give you a clue. Look at the *number*.'

Number? Beth looked wildly at the front of the house. What on earth was Nina on about? And what was this stupid guessing game anyway? As if she didn't have enough to do, Nina was wasting her precious time on a wild goose chase... Then she saw it, on the wrought-iron gate, and on the entrance itself, just above the doorbell. It was the number thirteen.

SEVENTEEN

The next day, Beth made a superhuman effort to get herself together early and be ready when Jake left for school. Not to walk with him; those days were over, and she had more or less accepted that. Most of the time. But today she would, instead, tail him from a safe distance.

She told herself she was not a superstitious person. She was rational, at heart. But she had spent a surprising amount of time last night googling the number thirteen. 'Triskaidekaphobia', it was called, the irrational terror which those two digits provoked in some people. Was it possible, was it even credible, that this estate agent murderer was a sufferer, provoked to kill by a mania brought on by a simple set of numbers? Or was it all just a coincidence?

She dreaded even broaching the subject with Harry. He'd definitely think she'd lost the plot this time. And he might even be right. She also wouldn't be mentioning any texts to him. Another one had come late last night, the message even terser than the last: *Don't try your luck. Stay away from Sydenham.* Did the mysterious texter know she'd been back there with Nina? It was a scary thought.

She was walking along Calton Avenue, head down and with the troubles of the world on her shoulders, when she spotted a pair of shoes that were so new, shiny and expensive they could only belong to one person. Her burdens suddenly seemed to increase. It was Belinda McKenzie.

'Morning, Beth. Just going to ignore me, were you? Very polite,' the woman snapped.

'Hi Belinda. Sorry, I'm a bit preoccupied...'

'Oh yes, busy, busy, busy these days, aren't you? Meddling in matters that don't concern you.'

This was exactly the slap in the face that Beth needed. Belinda had been pumping her for details on these very matters only the other day. 'I thought you wanted me to keep my eyes and ears open?' Beth said, her social smile stretched paper-thin.

'Well, you're hardly going to spot anything with your eyes glued to the ground like that, are you? Walking along like a sulky teenager.' Belinda harrumphed, sounding not unlike one herself.

'You're off to school, too, are you?' Beth asked, hoping against hope that Belinda would say no, and veer away towards the parade of swanky shops. She, of all people in Dulwich, must have a lampshade frill that needed urgent and very expensive pimping. But Beth was doomed to disappointment.

'Just having a chat with the head. Don't get me wrong, Dr Grover's doing a great job understanding my Billy, but there are one or two points where he just needs, let's say, a bit of clarification.'

Frantically reading between the lines of this statement like a Bletchley Park operative on a deadline, Beth contented herself with a non-committal, 'Oh?' It was all Belinda needed.

'Of course, I was always willing to lend a hand at the Village Primary' – Beth suppressed a shudder as she remembered the poor deputy head's recurrent psoriasis – 'and I'm more than happy to do the same for Dr Grover. Well, *Tommy*.'

At this flagrant use of Dr Grover's first name, Beth blanched. She'd been a member of Dr Grover's team (a very junior cog, but still part of the super-efficient Wyatt's machinery) for years now (ahem, a couple anyway) and she wouldn't dream of addressing him thus. Part of her couldn't help admiring Belinda's gall. The other part very much wanted to have a ringside seat when Janice heard Belinda bandying the name *Tommy* around.

'Riiiight. So, you're popping in to see him?'

'Didn't I say exactly that, Beth? Do pay attention,' Belinda said dismissively, upping her pace all of a sudden. 'Mustn't be late.'

'I'll leave you to it,' said Beth, already panting a bit. Belinda's stride was nearly the length of Beth's whole body. She didn't want to arrive at her desk scarlet and sweaty for no reason. 'Have a great meeting.'

Immediately, Beth reassessed her agenda for the morning. Top of her priorities was going to be winkling out of Janice what was going on with Billy – two meetings with a parent was a very unusual occurrence. One was normally more than ample to iron out whatever the problem had been and set the child back on the right path or, very occasionally, to start to pave the way towards the Wyatt's exit.

But that couldn't be happening with Billy, could it? Not so soon after the start of Year 7. And Jake still hadn't mentioned anything at all to his mother. Mind you, he hadn't really spoken much for what seemed like weeks, beyond the odd grunt when she asked if he was hungry/tired/ready for bed. Although they did finally seem to be on better terms now, which was a relief.

One thing was for sure, Katie was going to be agog at this development. Charlie had come off a very poor second in some bruising encounters with Billy. If Charlie was still bearing the brunt of Billy's bluff, hectoring manner, then his mum would want to know everything the school was trying to do to control the situation.

Unlocking her office, Beth squinted through half-closed eyes at her in-tray to see if that would make the pile of filing that had accumulated there since her last clear-out look smaller, then sidled round it and sat in her beloved swivel chair. A quick whirl on this usually made her feel tons better about life, and today proved to be no exception. Soon she was picking up the phone to Janice and rather tentatively making enquiries about one Mrs McKenzie and her appointment with the head.

'Hmm, Beth, before I give out any information to you, do *you* have anything to tell me?'

Beth realised that she'd done nothing, so far, to make good on her reckless promise to check on Dr Grover's behaviour. She still didn't believe for one minute that the guy was up to anything. But a deal was a deal.

'I'm going on a recce this evening, tailing him,' said Beth, hoping a bit of private eye jargon would make Janice feel she was definitely putting in the effort. It seemed to pay off.

'In that case, although I am the soul of discretion, I'll just leave you with the thought that Billy and Wyatt's may not be enjoying a long association. Unless things change.'

Beth's mouth opened in a wide O. Although Janice couldn't see her expression, she seemed to understand the shock value of her statement all too well. 'But, Beth, this is most definitely confidential. If Mrs McKenzie achieves an improvement in Billy's behaviour, then this will all go away. And we don't want any of the boys to know what's going on, for obvious reasons.'

Beth wasn't so sure about this. Surely a very good and organic way to ameliorate the behaviour of the class bully was to let the boys know the situation wasn't going to be allowed to continue? But she realised that she didn't have experience in the field – apart from bringing up a non-bully, that was.

'I completely understand. Don't worry,' said Beth. 'And I'll let you know the moment I find something out on the, well, on the other matter.'

Once she'd put the phone down, she realised the awful dilemma she was faced with. One word from her would have the power to assuage all her best friend Katie's concerns, put her mind at rest, reduce tension at home, soothe Charlie, who was after all Beth's son's soul mate, and help to normalise a difficult predicament. But she'd just given a solemn promise to Janice.

It was the kind of thing she hated to be stuck with. Beth had a very pronounced sense of right and wrong – it was the reason she was always getting involved with the dramas of Dulwich in the first place. But there were two different sets of rights here – Charlie's right to a quiet life, safe from bullying (and hence his mother's right to a good night's sleep), and Janice's right to confidentiality. Crossing the line would put Beth firmly in the wrong – a place she hated to be.

She stewed over the situation, nervously biting at her fingernails, a habit she'd thought she'd kicked years ago. *If only Colin were here.* She realised she missed his quiet, soothing presence and, what was more, his secure moral compass. Colin wasn't one for grey areas. Even when he did something naughty – he'd recently scoffed an entire chicken which Beth had been about to roast – he'd done it for the right reasons. Sort of.

Well, he'd been very hungry. And just like Oscar Wilde, he wasn't great with temptation. The fault had really been Beth's for leaving the bird unattended, though she'd absolutely no idea until that moment how much contraband a determined Labrador could stuff away, nor how quickly. And the outcome had been good, in that Beth had been spared the effort and misery of cooking for her judgemental mother. It hadn't been so great for Colin himself, who had spent several days rueing his decision all over the pavements and front gardens of Dulwich, while Beth had stood by with double her usual quantity of little plastic bags, doing her level best to pretend he was nothing to do with her. He still couldn't quite look poultry in the eye. Probably just as well.

Was there a way that Beth could have her chicken and eat it, as it were? She looked at her mobile phone. There was no doubt that recent texts from Katie had lacked their usual sunny bounce. Beth knew how it was to put your whole life and soul into one other being. She had done the very same thing with Jake, until recently. Then her life had expanded. Harry had come along, and her interest in mysteries had burgeoned at the same time. Was this one of the reasons why Jake's nose was so out of joint at the moment? Beth put that little thought to one side for now, to mull over later. Her friend and her own dilemma had to be her focus for now.

The whole matter of Billy was weighing on Katie's family so heavily. Beth composed a text to her friend, but just before pressing send, she thought again and deleted it. Could she make her message more oblique, a bit vaguer? No, she knew Katie would demand instant clarification. Any mother would. Just as she was trying another form of words, the phone rang, making her jump out of her skin. It was Nina.

'Babe, just got a new instruction. You're going to love this.'

Beth sat forward, relief and interest all over her face. 'Tell me.'

'It's in Sydenham, it's three bedrooms, it's got a garden, original Edwardian features, it's near the pleasant local amenities—'

'Nina!' Beth broke in. 'I can read the details on the website. I thought you were saying it would get us somewhere with the investigation. I didn't realise it's just something that might suit me house-wise.'

'You're missing the point, hon. It's both. It's got its original fireplaces with tiled surrounds—' 'Nina!'

'*And...* it's number thirteen.'

EIGHTEEN

There was a distinct nip in the air as Nina and Beth drove along the quiet Sydenham streets that night. Due to the one-way system, the residential areas were beautifully clear of traffic, though you did occasionally come across a car doing a tired three-point turn when it came upon a dead end and realised it had gone wrong somewhere in the maze. As they worked their way round to the correct road, a thin drizzle started to fall.

Suddenly, Sydenham started to look decidedly glamorous. The car headlights bounced off the sheen of moisture on the road, which lit up like thousands of diamonds strewn in their path. The trees along the pavements drooped down, darkly mysterious, and even the gentle hiss of the rain was hypnotic, a backing track to the soothing swish-swash of Beth's windscreen wipers. The streets were deserted, though whether that was terror induced by the recent murders or the more prosaic allure of Netflix, it was hard to know. Certainly, there was an unearthly blue glow from many of the front rooms, suggesting people were glued to their tellies – but were they binge-watching box sets, or concentrating on the local news?

'After we've cased this joint, I might have another job for

us,' said Beth, trying to make the prospect sound as enticing as possible, without giving away too many hard and fast details. She knew that Nina had left Wilf with a babysitter and that, on her income, time was definitely money. But she was dying for a bit of company, if she really had to make good on her promise to tail poor old Dr Grover. Janice had breathlessly told her she would text the moment he set foot out of the front door. Beth was hoping against hope he would stay true to his uxorious public image and remain in the bosom of his family tonight.

'Yeah, hon?' Nina said distractedly, squinting at the house numbers through the rain. 'Aha, that looks like our mark,' she said, and they parked opposite one of the familiar redbrick homes that seemed to crop up all over Sydenham. Yes, sure enough, there were the figures on the gatepost – a thirteen rendered in nice curly wrought iron, but then painted a rusty red that toned too well with the wall and was almost invisible. Did this mean the owners were phobic, too? Did they share the superstition that gripped a good percentage of the nation? Even Beth herself was a little more cautious if the thirteenth fell on a Friday, though she knew it was silly. Nothing major, but she might not walk under a ladder. She knew people who were much worse on this front – her mother, for example, would look balefully at a black cat on any date in the calendar at all, and wasn't too fond of Magpie either. But there could be other reasons for that.

Notwithstanding its discreet door number, this three-storey building seemed to scream respectability, if that quality would ever raise its voice. It was the type of house that Beth could easily imagine a character like Charles Pooter going into rhapsodies over.

It was subtly different from its neighbours in terms of the detailing on its little quasi-porch, a wooden structure that had pretentions to spread like a magnificent pergola, but in fact hovered a bare couple of inches over the front door and on a day like this would provide only the briefest respite from the rain. Maybe it also afforded enough space to stash a Wellington boot or two. Nowadays people often pressed these niches into service to leave out their recycling boxes, but only if they didn't mind people counting their empty wine bottles. Beth was by no means a heavy drinker – the last few nights excepting, she thought with a brief remembered wince – but she wasn't at all sure if she would brazenly put out her usual screw-top Chardonnays for the neighbours to gawp at. But maybe Sydenhamites were less snobby.

The house had quite a few little extras that made it look special. It had stained-glass panels in its front door, with a pretty floral design, and a little frieze of coloured glass in the front room bay, too. Its neighbours opposite had something similar, but crucially with subtly differentiated patterns.

Was it the kind of place where Beth could see herself? She sighed a little. Yes, but no, was always going to be her answer. Life at the moment was so easy. Both she and Jake could walk to Wyatt's – in many ways the centre of their lives. If they moved here, Beth would condemn herself to becoming one of those mothers who spent hours each day inching up and down the roads in and out of Dulwich, and no doubt killing herself and her son by tiny stages thanks to pollution, stress and boredom. Then there was the question of where to park when you actually arrived in Dulwich. There was no room at the school; only a few of the most exalted got a pass. Beth would be scurrying around the back streets hunting for a space as frantically as a squirrel searching for acorns in the autumn.

She sighed. On the other hand, she certainly couldn't stand the current situation much longer. Pickwick Road, which had been just right for so long, now felt as close to collapse as Little Bear's chair in the fairy tale, while she was Goldilocks, on the verge of doing a runner. She felt as though she was drowning half the time – not in porridge, but in books. Something had to give. But if she was serious about making a go of it with Harry, then she had to accept he came with his own baggage. There didn't seem to be much of the psychological variety, thank goodness, apart from his pronounced tendency towards high-handedness. But yes, he did have plenty of the physical type. Honestly, she was making a terrible fuss about a few thrillers, she decided. She closed her eyes to the thought that it was much easier to decide this when she was out of Pickwick Road and not tripping over the dratted things at every turn.

What options did they really have? They needed to find somewhere that was big enough for them all, and that was not going to be in the centre of Dulwich. She looked out as the rain continued to patter down, growing in strength now. After a minute or two, she put her arm up to wipe the condensation from the window. Soon they wouldn't be able to see a thing. Though there really was nothing going on anyway. She turned to Nina.

'So, what's the idea? Do you have keys to the place?'

'Nah, babe,' said Nina with a theatrical shudder. 'I'm not going into any of them houses, things being what they are. That's for the front-end bods. And the lookers, I s'pose. People who don't know any better. We're just going to sit it out, see if anyone turns up.'

Beth reflected. She had a feeling she had just been classified as a 'looker' – the type of person who seemed to be, in Nina's estimation at least, just cannon fodder for a maniac. She immediately resolved that she wouldn't be making any more late-night or even afternoon bookings, now that it got dark so early. The memory of the light in that house... At the time, she'd just thought it was a bust bulb, which was common enough. But now she wondered.

The rain started to fall in sheets. Sydenham, which she had considered quite enchanting in the mist only a few minutes ago, was now hardly visible. And the house? Lovely though it might be, she could just as easily be looking at it on her laptop at home.

'What do you think? Will anyone actually turn up?'

Nina blew out her cheeks, the exhalation making her curly strawberry blonde fringe dance for a moment. She checked her watch. 'I'm thinking nah, it's getting late, innit? The girl agents will be well nervous about coming out at this time. And even the lads... well, in the current climate change...'

Beth closed her eyes for a moment. 'So, we're here for nothing?'

'Nah, babe. You never know, do you? Worth checking it out. Have a Twix,' Nina said, brandishing a multipack.

Beth, much mollified, chomped down on the snack and reflected it was actually quite nice to be sitting here, warm and dry, hearing the rain tapping on the tinny roof of the Fiat and chatting to a friend. Mind you, it said a lot about her current view of her own home that she'd rather be sitting in the dark in a car than be snuggled up at home with Jake or Harry.

''Nother one?' Nina shook the gold packet at her.

Beth eyed the bars covetously but shook her head after a longish pause. 'I shouldn't.'

'Nah, go on. It's not a proper stake-out, is it, if we're not eating? Look at the NYPD and their doughnuts.'

'Yeah, but in those films the bad guys show up and then the cops have to chase them. If I eat many more of these, I'll die of a stroke even trying to get out of the car,' Beth said sadly.

'Suit yourself, babe. I'm not going to say no, though. We can throw the spare ones out of the window at the killer,' said Nina, rustling away. After a few moments of chomping, she spoke up again indistinctly. 'Oops, too late, babe, all gone. Well, we can chuck the empty wrappers, anyway.'

'That'll stop them in their tracks,' said Beth, grudgingly impressed that Nina had got on the outside of so many Twix bars so fast, and slightly regretting her own decision to be virtuous. Too late to reconsider now. 'Maybe we should get going.'

'Yeah, I need to pick Wilf up and get him to bed. Oh well, we gave it a try, didn't we, babe?'

Beth didn't want to say that the whole thing had been a bit of a waste of time. What had been the chances that the killer would be irresistibly drawn to another number thirteen? Very, very slim, she decided. Never mind. Just then, her phone beeped. She looked down at it, expecting Janet. But no, it was another message from the withheld number. She felt a clutch of dread. *You don't listen, do you? Now you'll pay.*

Beth shuddered. Whoever it was seemed to be getting crosser. And were they actually watching her? She glanced over her shoulder, stared through the windscreen, but could see nothing. She started the car up as quickly as she could, and soon they were shooting down the hill back to Dulwich.

As they paused at the village traffic lights, Beth sat up a bit straighter. Had that been another ping from her phone? God, what now? She looked down at the mobile, sitting on her lap, knowing she shouldn't check it. The lights went green so she pulled in quickly at one of the diagonal parking spots close to the art-shop-cum-toy-store – a place she'd been dragged to many a time by Jake when he'd been small.

'Sorry, Nina, just got to read this. It could be that thing I mentioned earlier,' Beth said, squinting in the half-light at the screen.

'No probs, hon, but I'm going to get out here. Nearly home, and I've got to get back to get Wilf, don't mind, do you?'

Distracted, Beth looked up only to see Nina whisking out of the car and closing the door firmly behind her. She waved frantically at her, but Nina just blew her an airy kiss, put up the hood on her white puffball coat and marched off down the road, nimbly dodging the puddles. Beth tutted but bent again to her phone. Thank heavens, it was only a text from Janice. But it wasn't good news either – Dr Grover was on the move.

Beth read it through, then looked up to think. As she did so, she caught sight of a car swishing past in her rear-view mirror. Hang on a sec, wasn't that Dr Grover's silver Volvo? Now it was sitting at the intersection just in front of her, waiting to turn left into Court Lane.

Beth fumbled for her keys, wrestled with the gear stick, then finally got the Fiat into reverse and chugged out into the road.

She wasn't sure whether to hang back or not, but it was a moot point. By the time she'd managed to manoeuvre the car into position, Dr Grover had purred forward, and swung in a graceful arc. Then the lights inexorably changed to red again, and Beth was stuck where she was. Had he gone up Calton Avenue, towards the school? Or had he actually turned off and gone down Court Lane? Beth knew she'd be marooned at this interchange for ages. It was a Dulwich bugbear, the glacial slowness of this set of traffic lights. It caused tailbacks of angry mummies every morning.

Not for the first time, Beth wondered whether she'd get caught if she just turned anyway. There was hardly anyone around. But it wasn't worth it. If anything else, with a policeman boyfriend, she was willing to bet good money she'd be caught on camera and then she'd either have to explain herself to Harry or he would be hauled over the coals because of her by some higher-up. She couldn't do it. Her fingers tapped an impatient rhythm on the steering wheel, and she found the car's biting point and held her foot there, poised to go but resigned to stay.

She craned her neck forward. Could she spot the Volvo? There were red tail lights disappearing up Court Lane, yes, but at this distance and in the now pelting rain she couldn't be sure whether they were Grover's or not.

Beth tried to think about it logically. It was pretty likely that

Dr Grover would be going to Wyatt's. He must have umpteen jolly good reasons to check on something, even in the middle of the evening. Agenda for a meeting tomorrow, that he badly needed to look at right now? Report left on his desk and needing work right now? These were perfectly possible scenarios – except that, in Janice, Dr Grover had the most organised wife and helpmeet any busy head could require. All right, Janice was only working part-time these days, but still, Beth couldn't imagine a situation where Dr Grover wouldn't have every bit of documentation he needed at his fingertips, any time, even at night. No, Beth had a very bad feeling that Dr Grover was bound for Court Lane.

And what would he be doing there, at this hour, without his beloved wife and child? He wouldn't be going to see Katie, of that Beth was certain. What about one of the other families in the street with children at Wyatt's? There were umpteen people living there, of course, that he might well know and could possibly be visiting, but still, there was only one face that kept leaping to Beth's mind. One woman she was seeing. With immaculately ironed white jeans, perfectly straightened blonde hair and a creaseless face to match. Surely he couldn't be, could he? He wasn't... seeing Belinda McKenzie?

If so, was that the reason he'd had her in his office twice already this term? Was there even some glimmer of truth in Belinda's hints that her relationship with 'Tommy' was rather more cordial than you'd expect from the mother of a bully brought in to be told off about her child's behaviour?

A thousand possibilities flicked through Beth's mind as the light finally went green. She turned the car past the strange little burial site on the corner – where rumour had it that some of the last plague victims in London were buried in unmarked graves – and went up the long, long road. Both Katie's and Belinda's houses were on the right-hand side, going towards Lordship Lane. This was the 'posh' side, of course, as it backed onto the beautiful green acres of Dulwich Park, though arguably the houses on the left had the better view – and frankly no one in Court Lane was exactly slumming it.

Beth drove as slowly as she could, helped by Southwark Council's liberal use of sleeping policemen. These huge hillocks in the road meant she was hard pushed to get out of second gear. The poor little Fiat grumbled its way up the road like a donkey at a gymkhana doing its best to clamber over obstacle after obstacle. She turned her head from left to right, scanning for a silver Volvo, but after the first ten houses she realised it was hopeless.

The whole of Dulwich seemed to own a sleek silver car, and to have parked it in the shimmering rain. The cars were crammed in so close together that she had no chance of reading the number plates, even if she'd thought to ask Janice what Dr Grover's actually was. She'd seen it enough times, parked in pride of place outside his office at Wyatt's, but she didn't have the first clue what the registration was. When she was at the top of the road, she did a U-turn and bumped all the way back down again. But it was to no avail. The road was deserted. She seemed to be the only person silly enough to be driving around in the rain.

There was no way to tell where Dr Grover and his silver Volvo were now.

NINETEEN

After a weekend spent worrying about her lack of progress on all fronts, and a Sunday night of sleepless tossing and turning – and not in a good way – Beth was less than chirpy on Monday morning over breakfast. Harry was no better. He got out the milk, and Beth, on autopilot, immediately put it away in the fridge again. Harry tutted and slammed it back down on the table with enough emphasis to get Beth's coffee cup to jump. Jake, watching silently from over the rim of his bowl of Coco Pops, eyes going from one adult to the other, screwed in his headphones and turned his music up.

Normally, Beth would have insisted on an unplugged meal. But today she rather sympathised with his desire to zone them both out. And they'd had a recent chat, so Beth knew they were on a reasonably good footing. She didn't push it. Meanwhile, she and Harry spooned up their own cereal silently. Beth knew she should mention the threatening texts, but she just couldn't face it. She'd tried chatting to him, when she'd finally got in after squishing the Fiat sideways into the last parking space in Dulwich Village on Friday night, and he had not played ball.

Admittedly, all her conversational gambits had involved

trying to dredge information about the Sydenham slayer out of
her one police source – a game Harry seemed to see through
distressingly quickly. And she might not have been at her most
charming, she conceded, as she had got soaked on the way from
car to house, and a quick glance in the mirror by the front door
showed a reflection that was more drowned rodent than Mata
Hari. But one couldn't blame a girl for trying, surely? Or so
Beth thought, anyway.

It looked as though Harry felt very differently about the
matter. Now, with the most perfunctory of air kisses somewhere
in the region of her fringe, he was off to work. Jake merely
grunted in response to his 'See you later, mate', even though, as
far as Beth could see, the boy was lucky to have got actual words
out of Harry.

Today Colin had set up camp right on the doormat after
Harry's departure, determined that no one else was going to
leave the house without him, so Beth clipped on his lead and
they followed Jake up the road to school. Beth didn't even
bother to remonstrate with her boy about how much nicer it
might be if they walked in parallel. She needed the time alone
with her thoughts.

Colin turned to give her an encouraging lick on the hand
every time they stopped to cross a road, and Beth realised the
poor old boy was anxious. How awful. The unsettling situation
between herself and Harry was causing everyone in the house
to suffer. Everyone except Magpie, of course. If the strange
glitter in her eye this morning had been anything to go by, as
Beth had closed the front door, the naughty moggy was just
waiting for the day when they all stormed off and didn't bother
coming back, leaving her and her kind to take over Pickwick
Road. And the jaunty cat-that-got-the-cream twitch of her tail
suggested she thought that moment was pretty near.

Once Beth had got herself settled at her desk, and Colin
was stationed over in the conference corner as usual with his

beloved blanket, she did her best to turn her mind to work. She opened up the document containing her outline of Sir Thomas Wyatt's biography, trying not to notice the number of days which had passed since she'd last done this. She was just leaning forward, willing herself to add a sentence or two to something that currently looked, to her jaundiced eye, more slimline than outline, when she became conscious of a heavy weight on her feet. Colin had sidled over from his usual work-station and was now lying right over her ankles.

She looked down and met two trusting pools of brown, looking rather beseechingly up at her. 'All right, boy,' she said, smoothing his soft, dark head. She didn't have the heart to dislodge him, even though she was already losing sensation in her legs. Poor old thing. He was definitely having a needy moment. She'd adopted Colin in difficult circumstances. Some-times, it seemed he remembered that too.

Despite the pins and needles, Beth was managing to tinker quite successfully with her synopsis, when her phone rang. Cursing mildly, she reached for it.

'Hello?'

'Beth?' There was a deep voice in her ear. 'It's Dr Grover here. Wondered if you could pop along to my office?'

'Sure,' squeaked Beth, fumbling with the phone in suddenly damp fingers and nearly cutting the great man off in shock. Usually any messages from on high would be relayed to her via the lovely Janice.

She had been summoned by the head once before, but that had been to explain her findings after she had solved the little business of a murder on school premises. Since then, and certainly since the departure of her nemesis the bursar, the top brass had more or less left her to bumble along as she saw fit.

Good grief. Could this mean Dr Grover had finally noticed that her much-vaunted biography of evil swashbuckler Sir Thomas Wyatt had not magically appeared on his desk, as she'd occasionally (in her more optimistic moments) assured him it would? Did he want to cross-question her about deadlines? And if so, did she have anything she could actually say on the subject?

'Um, when were you thinking of?' she flannelled, flipping through the crisp pages of her work diary which served an almost entirely ornamental purpose on her desktop. There seemed to be precious few interdisciplinary staff meetings which required urgent input from her on the best indexing methods to be deployed with pre-war cricket records. 'After lunch next Tuesday could be good...' And would just about give her enough time to get her story straight.

'Right now, please, Beth. See you in a moment.'

'Oh,' Beth found herself replying to empty air.

She reluctantly moved her legs from beneath the warm and sleepy Labrador, rubbing them briskly to get the circulation going again, and swung her bag onto her shoulder. Colin got to his haunches, looking drowsy but showing every sign that his urgent duty was to give her a guard of honour on her way to this troubling appointment, but Beth persuaded him to stay put. She was pretty sure that, whatever the head had to say, he wouldn't want to be confiding it to an ancient dog.

TWENTY

It was immediately apparent that the Dr Grover in front of her this morning was not the Winnie the Pooh figure in a Hermès tie that she was so used to. Gone was the avuncular, unflappable man who steered the school so effortlessly to ever greater heights of academic success every year. Also absent was the charm that had helped him triumphantly circumnavigate the slavery scandal Beth had inadvertently mired them all in.

Instead, he was glaring at Beth from behind the yards of gleaming mahogany desk. Even the luscious red roses in the vase, constantly replenished by Janice, were showing wickedly sharp thorns today.

'So, Beth,' he began sternly, looking over the rims of his half-moon glasses at her.

These were a new affectation, and did serve to make him look tremendously intellectual. Today, his eyes were as icily blue as the glaciers in the Scandi noir thrillers to which he was addicted. Beth felt even shorter than her five-feet-mumble, and bowed her head to contemplate her scuffed pixie boots like a naughty schoolgirl.

'I saw you on Friday night.'

Beth's head shot up. 'Erm, you *saw* me?'

'Yes,' he said tersely. 'You were following me.'

'I was?'

'You were, and now you are echoing me. Both are tiresome, frankly. What is this about, Beth?'

Beth tried to avoid those gimlet eyes, now boring into hers, but it was impossible. As many a misbehaving pupil had found out in this room, there was no swerving Dr Grover. He really had the cross headmaster schtick down pat.

'Um, just, you know, trying to find out a few things about the killings, erm, over in Sydenham...' Beth said, trying for airy and casual, and realising she was probably achieving terrified and vague. 'How did you know it was me?'

'This may surprise you, Beth, but not that many people in Dulwich drive an ancient rusty green Fiat 500. They can probably hear your gear changes in Peckham.'

Beth was rather stung by this. She preferred to think of her Fiat as trusty, not rusty. True, she could rarely afford to trouble a garage to fine-tune it, let alone chisel off the layers of corrosion. And true, it wasn't a six-figure thoroughbred of a vehicle like most of the others in Dulwich, but her Fiat had done her proud over the years. And also, wasn't it a bit beneath Dr Grover to be so sniffy? He must know all too well that on her salary she could scarcely afford to upgrade to something swisher, even if she cared that much about appearances. As far as she was concerned, the car went when she put her foot on the accelerator, and at the moment it was proving a handy place for Nina to leave empty crisp packets, and that was all she really required of it.

'I wasn't following you, exactly, Dr Grover, I was just...'

'Just what, Beth?' Dr Grover gave her an exasperated look, though amusement seemed to lurk around the corners of his eyes.

'Well, er, I was just driving up Court Lane, really...'

'Hunched over the wheel? And peering into the distance, and from side to side, like some kind of Sherpa? Driving up and down the road for good measure?'

At this, Beth subsided. Wherever Dr Grover had secreted his car, it had obviously been an excellent vantage point from which to observe her antics.

'Well, this thing in Sydenham is getting serious. Someone needs to keep an eye on it...'

'Yes, but I wasn't in Sydenham. As we both well know. Beth, I have some sympathy for your, well, for want of a better word, investigations. And heaven knows, you've had some success in the past. But I am not a killer, as I think even you must realise. So, I suggest we decide that, as far as you are concerned, my activities are entirely off-limits for you, in perpetuity. I hope I make myself clear?'

'Yes, yes, of course,' Beth stammered. *As crystal clear as Janice's lovely vase.*

She opened her mouth to try and point out, rather belatedly, that she did have a friend who lived in Court Lane, so that surely counted as a legitimate reason for being in the area... but it was too late. Dr Grover had switched his attention pointedly to his laptop and was busily keying in something deeply urgent.

'Um...' she ventured, but he didn't even look up.

The interview was over. He tapped away busily for a few moments longer, then finally switched his searing glance to her, seeming astonished, and quite put out, that she was still there. She didn't need telling twice.

But even as she scurried out of the room, all but curtseying in her haste to be gone, Beth was turning over in her mind that strange phrase Dr Grover had just used. *'My activities.'* Activities, indeed. What, exactly, did he mean by that?

It wasn't the same at all as explaining he'd been on an urgent errand that night. He could so easily have said he'd been off to the Tesco garage near the Horniman. It was close to the top end of Court Lane, and it would have been a legitimate reason for him to have been out driving late at night. Janice could have sent him on a crucial nappy run. Or maybe they'd needed baby wipes? That would have been something Beth could immediately have understood and accepted. There were so few normal shops in the centre of Dulwich that people had to drive around for ages before chancing on a humble carton of milk or a pack of butter.

But no. He hadn't said that. He'd said, '*my activities*'. And what innocent, happily married man had nocturnal *activities* that he didn't like to discuss? And that, at all costs, he didn't want observed?

Beth's mind raced as she trudged away from the grandeur of the main school building, across the acres of tarmac to her own little archives office. Colin gave her a hero's welcome, which she realised she didn't deserve at all. The encounter with Dr Grover had made her feel rather shabby, like a down-at-heel private eye tailing some sleazebag of an adulterer.

She settled back at her own desk and Colin flopped onto her feet again with a sigh. He only had time to give her a very quick reproachful glance, covering her perfidy in going for walkies without him as well as a ticking-off for removing his nice comfy pillow, before sleep reclaimed him. But Beth had rarely felt more awake – or more puzzled.

Prior to her little chat with Dr Grover, she had been willing to put money on the fact that Janice was suffering from an over-active imagination. Stuck at home for much of the time with a small, demanding baby, facing the inevitable sleep deprivation even a joy like little Elizabeth brought in her wake, and having to recalibrate her relationship with her husband, who had previously meant everything to her and was now, like so many new fathers, struggling not to feel irrelevant, Janice could have been excused an outbreak of paranoia.

Now, as Beth twirled a pencil between her fingers and

gazed, unseeing, at her screen, the words of her book proposal were registering even less than usual. She realised she wasn't so sure any more that it was all in Janice's head.

Dr Grover, despite his steely manner, had definitely had the defensive air of someone who was hiding something. He had been as firm but fair as he always was; he hadn't been bullying or unpleasant at all – apart from that sideswipe at Beth's car, but that was probably what ninety-nine per cent of Dulwich residents felt about it. Yet Beth had definitely felt very small – even smaller than usual – in front of his desk. She hated to say it, or even think it, but had there nevertheless been a tinge of her old enemy there?

Tom Seasons, the late and extremely unlamented bursar of Wyatt's, had been a master of bluster and obfuscation, never shy of using threatening behaviour to distract from his own or his associates' activities. When he had parted company with the school, she'd been delighted. The news that he was suing over his dismissal seemed entirely in keeping with his aggressive ways. Yet maybe his tactics had rubbed off on Dr Grover. The two men had worked together for many years, very successfully. It had always seemed that Seasons had been the bad cop to Dr Grover's good one. But maybe Dr Grover could swap roles when he felt like it.

Janice suspected an affair. Could Beth really see Dr Grover embarking on a clandestine fling? And if so, could Belinda McKenzie *really* be the object of his affections? It didn't bear thinking about. Not only would the happiness of one of Beth's dearest friends be dragged down in flames, but Belinda would surely become even more insufferable, if that could be imagined.

Beth shut her eyes briefly as she thought about the soirées Belinda would throw, the patronage she would hint at – or actually wield – if she had any say at all over entrances to Wyatt's. Move over Louis XIV, Belinda McKenzie would be the new

Sun Queen of Dulwich. That was assuming, of course, that she managed to convert an affair into a marriage. Was it possible that Belinda could actually dethrone Janice and become the third Mrs Grover? It was a horrible thought. But Beth wouldn't put it past the woman. No, not at all.

This ought not to be a consideration to be measured against Janice's misery, but Beth had suffered enough of the slings and arrows of Belinda's outrageous behaviour to dread the outcome if the woman ever achieved her dream of controlling Wyatt's. For, though Dr Grover might be distracted for the moment by lust (and she sincerely hoped he wasn't), Belinda would definitely be in it for power rather than sex. She was all about status, and Wyatt's was the pinnacle of so much in Dulwich. Via Dr Grover, she would be pulling all the strings.

Would Belinda swap Barty, and his banking millions, for Dr Grover and all that the school could offer? Beth didn't have to think about that one for more than a few seconds. Janice would hardly have time to shove baby Elizabeth's tiny onesies into a suitcase before Belinda would be battering down the door with her silicone-inflated bosoms, her troupe of 'prodigiously gifted' children in tow. Bobby, the youngest of the brood, was probably the reason she was aiming so high – word had it at the Village Primary that the teachers were still having to guide him when forming the 'tricky' letters, even though he was now in Year 6 and about to enter the secondary transfer fray.

Belinda would be Mrs G mark three before anyone could say *before death do us part*, for sure. And Barty, her poor old current meal ticket, would be consigned to the dustbin of her story before anyone could say the dread words 'family law'.

It was a ghastly scenario, so chilling that for a moment Beth forgot the real mystery she was probing. Murder. Two deaths, of innocent people. She chastised herself for putting Belinda's bossiness above, or even on a par with, such genuine evil. There was no contest. Belinda might be a colossal pain, but she wasn't a homicidal maniac. If the worst came to the worst, all Beth would have to do would be to carry on with her present strategy, and keep well out of her way. That would be more difficult if Belinda suddenly became the mistress of Wyatt's, as well as the rest of Dulwich. She'd be lurking in Dr Grover's office, directing proceedings as much as she could. And she was bound to decide that one of her own cronies was far better suited to a nice little sinecure in the archives office than Beth herself.

Beth realised she was supposing that Dr Grover had no say in the matter. But to those who knew Belinda, this was a given. Anything the woman really set her heart on, she tended to get. This stretched from chattels to people. Dr Grover might be quite stern when he wanted to be – as he had just proved – but was he any match for Dulwich's uber-mummy when she really had the wind in her sails? Beth rather thought not. She was deeply disappointed in the man, she had to say. He was more observant than she'd given him credit for if he'd spotted her so easily last night, but if he was really tangling with Belinda, he was still not nearly as far-sighted as he needed to be. Swapping Janice for Belinda was going from goddess to gorgon.

But Beth was letting this nightmare scenario run away with her. She needed to concentrate on what was really happening – solving the estate agent business. Yet she also had to think of what on earth she was going to say to Janice. Her friend was definitely going to be ringing her for an update – and pretty soon, if Beth knew her. She had to get her story sorted out.

Beth peered at her screen with tremendous concentration, as though it was a crystal ball which was going to reveal the best form of words to use when breaking bad news, very gently, to someone who definitely didn't want to hear their worst suspicions confirmed.

TWENTY-ONE

A few hours of solid concentration on crucial matters like where to put the latest play programmes, and whether to rustle up a quick montage on Wyatt's Christmas Fairs through the ages, allowed Beth to calm down a little. Dr Grover loved to show parents her archive displays, and knocking out a few now might really help get her back into his good books. The fact that Janice had strangely not yet rung helped a lot.

Perhaps Janice didn't want to know the truth? As a pronounced ostrich when it came to bad news, Beth could appreciate the feeling. She'd always tended to hide from unpleasantness – and much else – for as long as she possibly could. She knew there was an Egyptian river named after this tendency (*denial*, a joke Harry made loudly and often), but she felt a healthy period of resistance to novelty, particularly things that didn't necessarily bode well, allowed her subconscious to get used to ideas even while she was busily rejecting them on the surface. Janice must be more like her than she'd thought. Or maybe she'd finally had it out with her husband, he'd come up with a plausible explanation, and they were all loved-up again?

Anyway, Beth very much hoped the dreaded spectre of Mrs

Belinda Grover was purely a product of her own imagination. She needed to stop giving it headroom. Even her fevered thought earlier that she must put everything into solving these murders had abated slightly. After all, Harry was on the case. There was always the possibility he could do this on his own, though her experience definitely suggested that he needed nudging to concede a solution was really necessary in every scenario. He was much too happy to let things plop into the quicksand of unsolved crime that lurked at the centre of the capital's policing strategy.

She felt quite abashed. Her son and her lover, and even her dog, were all disgruntled and unsettled in their various ways. The anonymous texter was furious with her. Now her boss was pissed off, too. This was serious. Without her income from Wyatt's, she didn't have even the slenderest hope of paying the school fees. Perhaps it would be better for everyone if she concentrated on something different for a change. She'd done a good morning's work on stuff she was actually paid to do. And this evening, she could consider producing an edible meal for her family, for instance. That would be an exciting novelty for them all.

By the time Beth slotted her key into the front door, she was swinging a bag of pricey ingredients from her arm and had a much happier Colin on the end of the lead. A breezy (not to say cold) walk through the park had livened him up no end, and he seemed to have forgotten his earlier neuroticism in that wonderfully doggy way. No burning resentments and nursed grievances with a Lab. What you got was what you saw: an old dog with a waggy tail and a heart the size of Dulwich itself.

No sooner had Beth let them into the hall than she stubbed her toe on another box, which had mysteriously appeared since this morning, blocking the entrance to the sitting room. She felt all her hard-won equilibrium disappearing in a whoosh of anger, which blazed up from her tiny boots to her suddenly sticky fringe with the pace of a forest fire.

Suddenly she was kicking at the dratted box with an enthusiasm she'd never once shown in all her Saturday morning football sessions with Jake. Once it was satisfactorily dented, to the point of splitting at one corner, she looked up to find herself being stared at by two sets of eyes. One was chocolate brown and endlessly forgiving. The other, denim blue and scorching a hole through to the back of her skull, did not look nearly as kindly.

Beth tried a tremulous smile. There was no response, not for a long, endlessly stretching moment. Then Harry turned on his heel and stalked off to the kitchen.

The flimsy plastic of the bag round her wrist chose this moment to suddenly give up the ghost, and Beth found herself ankle-deep in the doings of a spaghetti carbonara; double cream, bacon and a packet of pasta spreading themselves nice and evenly over the tiled floor. She would have wept, but she didn't have the energy.

TWENTY-TWO

Today could hardly be worse than yesterday, Beth thought, with what passed for optimism these days. She sat at the kitchen table, not feeling bright but definitely on the early side, waiting for Jake to sidle down for breakfast. When he did, and immediately stuffed in his earbuds, she reached over and yanked them out, and insisted on a bit of conversation instead.

It was definitely nice to catch up with her boy, but neither of them was exactly at their best in the mornings. A few stilted exchanges later, and she was rather wishing she hadn't bothered. They both rushed through their cereal to get the moment of quality time together over as soon as humanly possible. But at least Harry wasn't there to curdle the atmosphere still further. He'd slammed out of her bed and the house at the crack of dawn.

Once she was installed at her desk again, and worrying whether she'd really jeopardised her Wyatt's career with her foolhardy surveillance on Dr Grover the other day, the phone shrilled. Colin put his head up and gave her a look, then subsided again. He was staying over in the conference corner today, and Beth felt obscurely cold-shouldered, though on the plus side she could still feel her toes.

Beth picked up the receiver carefully, dreading hearing Janice's voice. Or even Dr Grover's deep tones. Lord, surely he couldn't be dragging her in for another carpeting? She'd spent a blameless, if bleak, evening within her own four walls yesterday, being ignored by everyone except Magpie the cat, who'd shed fur all over her with what seemed suspiciously like glee. Grover couldn't accuse her of following him again.

But to her relief, it was Nina on the other end. 'Babe, you'll never guess…'

Beth struggled to understand her friend through what was clearly a very large and deliciously crunchy mouthful of something. Quavers? Hobnobs? It couldn't be an apple, could it? Nina's five a day usually consisted of bags of crisps, not fruit… Beth wasn't sure what the answer was, but immediately her stomach started to rumble inappropriately. It was barely eleven o'clock, but it suddenly seemed an awfully long time since her rushed breakfast with Jake.

'What's happened?'

'Nuvver one's been attacked, innit? But the thing is…' There was another pause and, when Nina spoke again, Beth was glad to hear that she seemed to have swallowed down the last of her family bag of Wotsits or whatever today's snack of choice was. 'It was twenty-seven.'

'What? Twenty-seven people were attacked? That's a massacre!'

'Nah, babe, nah. Listen. Someone was attacked, at number twenty-seven.'

Beth took a moment to scale down her horror from a full-blown bloodbath to a single act of violence. 'Oh, OK then,' she said.

Then she realised that, even though this was less epic in scale, it was really no better. Someone was out there having a pop at people, and nobody was doing anything to stop it. Again, she quickly corrected herself. Maybe the reason Harry had been in such a rush this morning was not his haste to remove himself from her side but an urgent call to sort out this latest atrocity. Despite herself, she felt a little bit relieved.

'You're not getting it, hon. Twenty-seven? D'you see? It wasn't a number thirteen, that's what I'm telling you.'

'Aha, now I'm with you. So, the only connection we thought we had between these incidents—'

'Has gone. Yeah, right. Sorry about that, babe,' Nina said, mumbling again now. 'Oops, gotta go. Client,' she said, slamming down the phone.

Beth was left in the sudden silence. Then Colin whined gently in his sleep and scrabbled with his front paws. Whichever rabbit he'd been chasing in his dreams had temporarily disappeared down a hole. Beth knew how he felt.

They were right back at square one again. Everyone she knew disliked estate agents; that was a fact of life. They were seen as a necessary evil, but an evil just the same, making money like parasites out of what was well known to be a chart-topping form of stress, one of the most gruelling experiences a person could face. Moving home was right up there with death and divorce, and estate agents sat there, rubbing their hands and counting their money, as it all happened.

She knew it was probably not rational the way people projected their horror at moving house onto these hapless folk with their talk of 'mature gardens laid to lawn', a phrase no normal person ever came out with, and their mien of barely suppressed pushiness. But there it was. Of all the groups to be preyed on by a killer, estate agents were probably going to elicit the least sympathy. Take nurses, for example. If a serial killer started picking them off, she was willing to bet the good folk of Dulwich would be out on the streets with their pitchforks, determined to root out the culprit. Even hedge fund managers and accountants, she was willing to bet, would get a better press. All right, only slightly, even though the place was teeming with them. But estate agents? Not so much.

Yes, the issue was being discussed by everyone she knew, but as a vague curiosity rather than a menace that had to be stopped. Mind you, it was all going on in Sydenham, which people in SE21 did consider a world far, far away, if not a different galaxy.

Everyone who had ever moved house probably had a motive. She hadn't met a single person who'd loved the experience of buying a new place, and who didn't consider they'd been royally fleeced at some stage of the proceedings. Stamp duty, commission, the whole process of exchanging contracts and then completing weeks later. Sometimes it all seemed expressly designed to fall through, encourage the perfidious practice of gazumping, waste money and leave people bruised and saddened.

But was there someone around who seemed to have more than the usual resentment to play with? Beth hadn't come across anybody yet, and Nina's Twilight Barking of the profession hadn't turned anything up either. And who was her mysterious texter? Harry was bound to know more than she did, but would do his usual uncanny impression of all three wise monkeys if she asked him any questions.

No, it was futile, thought Beth crossly. Another person attacked, now – though she didn't yet know the fate of this latest victim. She immediately flipped open her laptop, dodging the school's firewalls with a skill that would have made Jake proud, and had a quick surf. But there was nothing to be gleaned out there yet. There were news stories aplenty, but they were heavy on lurid speculation and very light on facts. A couple of papers had already dredged up the Suzy Lamplugh case that Beth had sadly recalled. It was inevitable, she supposed, that journalists would make the connection. Estate agents, murders – put those terms into any search engine and you'd come up with the same indistinct snap of a pretty blonde girl in her twenties. The grisly truth that her body had never been found meant that she was forever cast as the mysterious missing beauty in a horrible twist on every Disney Princess movie. Would her Prince Charming ever come, and release her from limbo? Beth hoped so.

Maybe, if Beth could get to the bottom of this case, it would even link up to the other one so long ago. But that might well be stretching things. After all, skilled detectives had been trying to solve Suzy Lamplugh's disappearance for years. And Beth didn't kid herself that she was always on top of the mysteries she kept tumbling into. More often than not, it wasn't reasoned deduction that got her to a solution. Yes, she sat around thinking, trying her best to be like Hercule Poirot, cudgelling her little grey cells. But sometimes things only got sorted out because people were coming at her with blunt instruments. Once they'd attempted to murder her, it was a lot harder to pretend they hadn't bumped off others.

She shook her head. Better to stick with what she had on her plate right now, or on her laptop at any rate. She scanned another article. There, trotted out again, were the few facts that she already knew. Nothing fresh. Not even very much on the second murder. Odd that there was still no name. That must mean the police hadn't identified the person yet, which was sad in itself.

She cursed Harry. He was sitting on so much information. Why couldn't he just give her a couple of pointers? It was no skin off his rather fine nose. Yes, he needed to avoid copycat killings. If he chucked the facts around willy-nilly then anything might happen. But she, of all people, was surely no risk? He just didn't trust her, she tutted. But then she supposed there were regulations and things. Damn him for being so law-abiding, she thought, then snorted a little to herself. Even she couldn't be cross about a law man sticking to the rules, could she?

But the trouble was that, without proper information, Beth always ended up having to cast around for herself, stirring up who knew what kind of trouble. Perhaps it wasn't always the wisest course of action, but what choice did she have? She owed it to the poor man in the cupboard... and to whoever had come next.

Maybe, just maybe, the killings were unconnected. But Beth dismissed that idea straight away. It had to be too much of a coincidence. Two estate agents, both in Sydenham, meeting sticky ends in under a fortnight? And now another attack. No, there was a connection all right, and she just had to find it.

She clicked on the next article. The same weary facts, though shuffled a little in terms of order. But she could more or less recite them now. She gazed on, and found something new – a quick, only the mean-spirited would say very quick, guide to the charms of Sydenham. Beth was intrigued to discover the area had originally been called Shippenham. It said a lot about the shifting sands of the Sarf Lunnen accent that this had eventually morphed to Sydenham. In the 1700s, it had boasted medicinal springs which had brought people flocking. Then in 1854, Sydenham became the magnificent, glittering Crystal Palace's second home. Built for the Great Exhibition in Kensington in 1851, it was too big to stay in central London, but there was plenty of space for it out in Sydenham and it brought tourists flocking.

No wonder the redbrick houses that Beth had seen were on such a lavish scale. Granted, not an awful lot had happened since 1854, apart from the burning down of the Crystal Palace in 1936. This seemed to signal the end of Sydenham's glory days. With the medicinal waters drunk dry and the Palace reduced to ashes, Sydenham still boasted very solid Victorian housing stock, but was otherwise having a quiet time of it now.

Beth sighed. Would she ever be ready to part company with her current surroundings and consent to be shifted up the hill, as the Crystal Palace had been? And was it a bad omen it had burnt down? No, that was silly. That had happened nearly a century ago. If she was looking for signs and portents, two deaths and an attempted murder were surely more alarming.

She scanned on. Next on the website there came a few pictures of the redbrick houses – hmm, there was no denying it, they were very nice. A couple of shots were now garnished with the crime scene tape that always seemed to trim such sad tales, the grimmest sort of urban bunting. One frame was of that first house. She stopped for the obligatory quick shudder at the memory. But this next one... Wait a minute, could she see from this picture exactly where the second house was, which road it was in?

She squinted a bit. She knew it was a number thirteen. Was there anything to be gained by driving round there? Maybe she could see if she knew any of the police who would inevitably be stationed outside. One advantage of having Harry about the place was that all the other officers tended to treat her as though she was some sort of regal consort. Meghan Markle, perhaps, to Harry's prince? In her dreams, maybe. She caught sight of her own reflection in the laptop. No, more like the Queen Mother, minus the flowery hat. The venerable old lady had been about the same height.

She turned her face determinedly from her screen. There was nothing else to be gleaned here. No, she needed to get out there and find some new connections, fast.

Once the resolve was made, Beth found she was able to concentrate a lot more easily on more immediate concerns – the ton of filing which always seemed to accumulate when her back was turned, and which needed to be gently massaged into her huge collection of Wyatt's detritus. Though she was constantly having purges of the more arcane contents of her shelves, the school did insist on keeping copies of all current publications, no matter how trivial they might be. And it would keep on staging plays, organising special assemblies, having meetings and arranging sporting fixtures, all of which generated a blizzard of programmes, pamphlets and reports. Finding a spot for them was very much Beth's problem.

Still, on a day like today, when pausing to think of any of her personal conundrums – or even her extracurricular ones – brought her up against a well-built redbrick wall, there was something very therapeutic about the mindlessness of stashing things away. She always loved restoring order, whether it was on the mundane level of tucking a Year 8 Rugby B-team report onto the right shelf, or the slightly more highfalutin concept of balancing the scales of justice. It did a lot to soothe her soul.

Beth felt an unwarranted glow of virtue as she left Wyatt's that afternoon. Colin, walking alongside his mistress, seemed to detect her lighter mood and every now and then would break into a merry trot, wagging his tail and smiling up at her. They were both bowling along contentedly towards home, and a chew toy and a nice cup of tea respectively, when Beth was hailed by a voice that could cut lead crystal at fifty paces. Oh no. Not Belinda McKenzie again.

She willed herself to carry on and ignore the shout. But that just meant Belinda ratcheted up her voice to new levels of foghorn loudness. 'Beth! *Hey!*'

She exchanged resigned glances with Colin, and both turned slightly. Immediately, Belinda was pounding up the pavement towards them, that extraordinary stride making short work of the distance.

'Beth. You should really get your hearing checked,' Belinda said with a mirthless laugh, her bag swinging round and catching Beth on the shoulder, pushing her slightly into the Wyatt's railings. Colin surprised both himself and his mistress by baring his teeth and emitting a low growl.

Belinda took a step away. 'You really need to keep that mutt under control,' she muttered. Her own matching set of expensive and enormous Irish wolfhounds were currently towing their latest dog-walker round the park. For someone who was always saying how much they adored animals, Beth had noticed that Belinda had remarkably little to do with her own.

'Shh, Colin,' said Beth, patting his head soothingly and getting drooled on for her pains. 'What's up, Belinda?' she asked, wiping her fingers on her jacket and not bothering to disguise the hostility of her tone. Belinda had made it clear in a thousand ways recently that she considered Beth to be the scum on the pond of life in Dulwich, while she herself was a flashing, dashing Siamese fighting fish.

'Oh, I just wondered if it might be nice to go swimming again with the boys, you know, like we did that time.'

Beth swivelled her neck upwards to get a better look at Belinda's face. It was even blanker than usual. The woman couldn't be suggesting this seriously, could she? Their encounter at the swimming pool in Greenwich a while ago had been entirely accidental. Beth had had an unfortunate wardrobe malfunction, which Belinda had found utterly hilarious. Of course, Belinda herself had been decked out in a costume so spectacular that it would have made any aspiring Bond girl in the area give up and go home immediately. Add in Beth nearly getting drowned, and altogether it was not an experience she was planning to repeat this side of Judgement Day.

Beth's silence must have hinted as much, because Belinda suddenly burst into speech. 'To be honest, Beth, I need your help with something. Billy seems to have got off on the wrong foot at Wyatt's. I was wondering if you, with your insider knowledge of the school, could give us a few pointers?'

Beth reeled. This was not what she'd been expecting, to put it mildly. A telling-off, an imperious bit of unwanted advice, a put-down; she'd been braced for all of those. Even another slap into the railings with that dratted bag as Belinda pushed past, though Colin might have cleverly put a stop to those. But a naked appeal to her better nature? No, this was nothing short of astonishing. And very hard to compute.

She spent some moments wrestling with different trains of thought. Belinda was potentially, even quite possibly, the woman who was wrecking her friend Janice's life. Could Beth, in good conscience, give Belinda any help at all, knowing this? This had to be some sort of ruse. Belinda must want to find out how much Beth, and therefore Janice, knew about what was going on with Dr Grover.

Or, wait a minute, was Beth just letting Janice's paranoia affect her? There was not a scintilla of proof yet that connected Dr Grover, Belinda and sex – apart from Janice's gut feeling and a bit of circumstantial evidence. And, of course, Beth's rather odd interview with Dr Grover himself, and the mention of 'activities' which had so stuck in her craw.

Could Belinda genuinely be asking for advice? Although that would be a world first, it wasn't entirely impossible. Her meetings with Dr Grover might well have been only concerned with trying to get Billy's behaviour sorted out. And that would certainly be a reason for the two to be in contact. Belinda was not a woman who liked to hear the word 'no', and brooking any criticism of one of her brood would be very difficult. It might well take Dr Grover more than one attempt to get Belinda to listen to him.

But that didn't answer the real question: why the subterfuge? Why the nocturnal visits? True, Barty McKenzie could have been at home when Dr Grover glided up Court Lane in his Volvo. Maybe it had been a meeting with both parents? But why on earth would it have been conducted at the McKenzies' home? Wyatt's was known for going that extra step for its pupils, yes, but home visits? After hours? Surely that was pushing it a bit. If other parents found out about the special service Billy seemed to be getting, then everyone would want the same for their kids. Dr Grover would be hurtling up and down Dulwich Village twenty-four hours a day, with no time for running the actual school. It was all very odd.

Or was it simpler than all that? Had Belinda managed to tempt Dr Grover into a fling? He might be at his most suscepti-ble, a bit sleep-deprived (Beth knew he wasn't getting up to do the night feeds, but he wouldn't be able to blot out all sounds of a crying baby), a bit disgruntled maybe about his wife's new focus. He definitely wouldn't be the first man to stray in such circumstances.

But would Belinda actually seduce the head as a sort of bribe to keep her son at the school? Beth didn't even need an answer to this last question; Belinda's knickers would be halfway down Calton Avenue before you could say 'scholarship'.

Yet if Belinda really did have Dr Grover and his libido in her pocket, why on earth would she be bothering with Beth? She was under no illusions about where she stood with the woman: lower than knee-high to a snail; lower even than she actually stood in real life. Belinda couldn't bear her. Yes, she'd given Jake one of her coveted tutoring places when an opening had cropped up in Year 6, but Beth had failed signally to show the sort of slavish gratitude that Belinda expected and relied on.

Then, through a series of unconnected and bizarre events, various friends and acquaintances of hers had fallen foul of Beth's little investigations, and Belinda was definitely angry about that. Leaving Beth out of her recent 'welcome' get-togethers was, in the petty mummy-world Belinda inhabited, tantamount to an open declaration of war. And now, to come cap-in-hand, or massive bag on shoulder, and ask for help? It was as though the Pope had abandoned the woods and chosen instead his gleaming throne in the heart of the Vatican for the purposes of defecation.

Even the thought that she could be witnessing the biggest climbdown Belinda had ever made did not tempt Beth, however. She was left wondering how on earth she could frame a 'no' without making the situation between them even more toxic, when Belinda spoke again.

'I've heard on the grapevine that you may be looking to move house. Of course, Barty is *like that* with John from Coombes and Badger. Not to mention Piers Frampton, like I said before. They get first dibs on all the best places, you know.' It was quite a sweetener.

Beth shuddered inwardly. Although she'd got her current home in Pickwick Road via a behind-the-scenes tip-off, that had been years ago, through her dear dead father. Somehow that made it above board, and not the sort of sneaky jiggery-pokery she might otherwise have disapproved of.

Her father had never managed to become the business whizz that her mother had yearned for, but he'd been an easy-going, friendly man, and had been well liked. He'd had plenty of contacts in and around Dulwich. He'd taken to golf in a big way before he died – almost certainly as a way of evading Beth's mother – and one of his partners, Jeff Bletchford, had been a leading light in an estate agency in the village. Although her father had departed for the big clubhouse in the sky when Beth had been still at school, his chum Jeff had never forgotten him, and when she and her late husband James had first been looking for a place, he'd taken her aside.

Beth remembered it clearly. In those pre-Jake days, she had been doing reasonably well at her job as a freelance journalist. Without the distraction of motherhood, she had been willing and able to put in the ridiculous hours the profession demanded, and was always available to cover the stories none of the staffers wanted to touch. Nevertheless, her salary had remained in the handful-of-beans category, rather than the literal bean-feast that the newspaper executives were so palpably enjoying, with their share options, expense account lunches at the Savoy, and chauffeur-driven cars. And although James had had a good job, he too was at the start of his career. Neither of them then knew how tragically short it was going to be.

They'd started off renting, but one day she'd trooped into the estate agents, through curiosity as much as anything. She hadn't expected to find anything at all even approaching a corner of her budget. But she had promptly been whisked into a private office by the courtly Bletchford, then in late middle age, whom she remembered from the occasional Sunday lunch, her parents' Christmas sherry gatherings, and, of course, from her father's funeral.

'Word in your ear, Elizabeth dear. Pickwick Road. Funny little houses, they don't sit so well with our more, shall we say, well-heeled clients? But perfect wee starter home for you. I know for a fact the buyer is keen to shift it, pronto. Go round, have a word. Say I told you.' Here, Jeff Bletchford tapped the side of his nose and twinkled at her like a benevolent uncle.

Beth remembered her wary feeling. Was this really the right thing to do? But on the other hand, how else would she get a toehold in the market? And, when she'd decided to go round and have a look at the house – from the outside, at least – of course she'd fallen in love with its quirks. Although it was so very Dulwich, and in the heart of the village itself, the house and the entire street seemed to have a dash of non-conformity to it which spoke to her soul straight away. She'd been down this road before, but never paid much attention. It was always like that, wasn't it? Unless you were truly looking, you didn't see what was right in front of your face.

They always said it was not what you knew, but who you knew, and in Dulwich possibly you could even extend that to *why* you knew them. She'd found herself having that little word, dropping the heavy name of her benefactor, Jeff, with the owner. And hey presto, before she knew it, she and James were moving in. The house hadn't even been on the market for a day. That was the way it worked in Dulwich. Beth wasn't really proud of having finessed the system – but she hadn't had a lot of choice back then.

And now? Did she really have more options open to her? Yes, in theory, she had Harry's salary to add to her own paltry wages, but she also had the lead weight of the school fees round her neck. And was her relationship with Harry rock-solid enough to convert into the shackles of a mortgage? That was a serious commitment. His current tight-lipped stance wasn't making her feel that a lifetime with him was going to be enormous fun. One of the reasons they were having to shift was to find room for his stupid books, even though she was now secretly enjoying zipping through them when he wasn't looking. But freeing up a bit of capital to fling at Wyatt's was another very pressing motive. She had to face it. Even if she didn't move with Harry, she'd still have to move.

Accepting a favour from Belinda was a much bigger deal than graciously allowing a friend of her father's to smooth her way. There would be strings attached and, knowing Belinda, they'd wrap themselves around Beth like particularly affectionate boa constrictors. She'd never be free of the woman if she took this step. Belinda would expect total loyalty from the moment Beth took up her offer – at least until death, and probably way beyond that. Did Beth want that kind of complication? But did she really want to move out of SE21, either?

Beth sighed inwardly. Being a grown-up often seemed to consist of juggling between options which were way short of ideal. It was a good job no one told you this when you were little, she reasoned. Otherwise nobody would want to leave childhood behind. Of course, some people never stopped being small. She looked down at the pavement to give herself a minute more thinking time. Inadvertently, her eyes lighted on her tiny shoes. She compared them with Belinda's size seven boots, in the sort of glossy chestnut leather that Cossacks would hurl at their servants to polish for hours. The high sheen must have blinded their opponents when they rode into battle. Beth averted her gaze.

This was how things worked in Dulwich, but did she want to be beholden to Belinda? On the other hand, she was getting nowhere fast with her own search for the perfect new home for her little family... Meanwhile, Belinda was growing petulant.

'Think it over, why don't you?' Belinda said, in tones which suggested that she wanted Beth to do the direct opposite, and collapse in a heap of grovelling thankfulness at her shiny feet. 'Just don't keep me hanging around too long. Opportunities like this don't grow on trees, you know. Especially not round here.' She didn't add, *and particularly not for people like you*, but Beth could feel the words heavy in the air. 'Barty's got plenty of friends we could be helping out. So many people in Dulwich are interested in property at the moment.'

With that, Belinda turned on her smart heels and strode away, her bag ricocheting off a small bush and into a nanny with a pushchair as she went.

'Sorry,' mumbled the nanny, but she was talking to thin air. Belinda was soon a dot on the horizon, striding back to her massive pad in Court Lane, where no doubt she would be masterminding the homework of her brood in a bid to ensure they could take over the centres of power in a bloodless coup as fast as humanly possible. They might not achieve this until they'd reached their early twenties, but that certainly wouldn't be Belinda's fault.

Beth looked after her for a moment, offered a consolatory smile at the poor nanny, and slowly began stumping homewards herself. Her mind was buzzing with this strange offer, the memories it had unwittingly stirred up, and the ramifications of saying yes to a woman like Belinda McKenzie.

At the same time, she dimly recognised that Belinda, pushy and annoying as ever, had definitely not come over as a woman in love. Surely that was the panacea that smoothed away all edges, imparted the rosiest of glows, and caused those fathoms-deep in it to show their most benign faces to the world? Whereas Belinda had been straightforwardly offering Beth a deal – the possibility of a house (or at least a stab at one) in exchange for help with Billy. It wasn't proof that nothing was happening with Dr Grover – but as far as Beth and Janice were concerned, it had to be a good sign. Definitely food for thought.

And while Beth was mulling the whole tangled matter over, right in the middle of the street, not far from the gates of Wyatt's School itself... a rather large penny dropped.

TWENTY-THREE

It was twilight, and Beth and Nina were hiding out in her Fiat 500 again. Beth tutted inwardly as Nina shaped her crisp packet into an impromptu funnel, tilted her head back and shook the last few morsels directly into her mouth, then dropped the empty bag onto the floor as naturally as a tree shedding leaves in autumn. There was a definite price to be paid for having Nina as her sidekick, Beth decided. She'd only just managed to clear out the detritus from their last stake-out. She shuffled uneasily in her seat.

'What, babe?' Nina turned to her, mouth ringed with toxic-looking orange dust. Her cheeks were contorted with their heavy burden of Wotsits.

'Nothing. Just wondering how long we'll be waiting, I suppose. And whether it'll be like last time.'

Suddenly Beth's phone shrilled. She turned round to fish it out of her bag, which she'd stowed on the back seat to give Nina more elbow room as she attacked her huge array of essential snacks. She just had time to press 'accept' before the call went to voicemail – then her heart sank. Oh no, it was Janice. The conversation she'd been dreading for days. Now she'd only gone and answered it, at the most inconvenient moment possible.

'Hi lovely, just wanted a quick word,' Janice said a little breathlessly. There was a snuffling sound in the background.

'Are you OK?' asked Beth, her eyebrows steepling, glancing quickly over to her passenger and hoping Nina wouldn't be able to overhear Janice's half of the conversation. But her friend was almost invisible, face inserted deeply into her second family pack of Wotsits. Even so, Beth really hoped Janice didn't have more suspicions to share. Or, worse, any concrete proof to offer. This certainly wasn't the moment. And Beth could hardly give Janice a full run-down on her carpeting by Dr Grover while Nina was in the car. But, thank goodness, Janice was all sweetness and light.

'Do you know what, Beth? I think I got it all wrong the other day. Tommy has been, well, going the extra mile with a couple of the parents. But it's nothing at all like... er, what I was fearing. Definitely not,' she said, while the snuffling got louder in the background. 'I'm going to have to go in a second, Elizabeth's just waking up, but I just wanted to let you know. I think I've been letting the lack of sleep get to me, I started imagining things... I've not been myself. And Tommy didn't want to tell me what he was doing. The silly man actually felt guilty that he was having to go out and leave me to sort out these awful parents. Honestly, some of the people at Wyatt's...'

Beth was a bit alarmed, hearing the unusual level of anger in her friend's voice, but Janice pulled herself together and it disappeared.

'I think I underestimated how tricky it would be, having a little baby and trying to come back to work... Poor Tommy. He's been doing his best, but it's been hard on him too.'

'Well, I'm glad you've got things sorted,' said Beth, trying to sound as convinced as she could. But, despite herself, a niggle of doubt remained.

Was she being ridiculous, though? It did seem like a reasonable explanation for Dr Grover's *'activities'*, though he could have been more open with Beth about it. But if it satisfied his wife, then that was the important thing. As long as Janice was happy...

In the background, the gentle snuffles ratcheted up to mewling cries, then Elizabeth started a full-on roar. With a very quick farewell, Janice was off to do what she did best – soothe and sort and smooth the way. Back to business as usual.

Suddenly Beth's phone beeped. Beth squinted at it. Was there something Janice had forgotten to tell her? No, it was her anonymous friend again. Well, hardly a friend. *You don't listen, do you? While you're out, what's happening at home?*

Beth stowed her phone with a shiver. She didn't even want to think about what that could mean. They didn't know where she lived, did they? No, she was being paranoid. It was just a random idiot, trying to scare her. Nina piped up, wiping off her orange moustache with the back of her hand. 'I've got a good feeling, you know. Think we're going to crack it tonight,' she said, swilling the last of the Wotsits down with a two-litre bottle of Lucozade.

'I hope you won't need the loo,' said Beth distantly, still worrying about the text and aware that she sounded ridiculously prim.

'Don't worry, once I've finished the bottle, there'll be plenty of room to go,' Nina said, shaking the drink with a lavish wink. The liquid fizzed ominously.

Beth was almost certain that her friend was winding her up. Even if the plastic bottle was capacious enough, she really wasn't sure that the Fiat was. It was quite tricky reaching anything on the back seat, or getting stuff out of the glove compartment, for that matter. Any more gymnastic manoeuvres involving clothing removal, careful positioning and gravity would be a nightmare, especially with a very unwilling audi-

ence. She really hoped something would happen long before
the Lucozade had a chance to work its way through Nina's
system. She hated to think how much orange stuff was swilling
around in her friend's stomach now that the Wotsits were
forcibly making the acquaintance of the drink.

Luckily, there was a distraction. Beth heard the distinctive
tip-tap of a woman's shoes on the pavement. Quite high heels,
by the sound of it. Should she turn round and gawp, or would
that give the game away? She wasn't sure if it was dark enough
to see what they were up to in the car, from the outside. She
decided it was safest to carry on facing the front, and hope
whoever it was wouldn't notice two women lurking in a Fiat for
no good reason on a suburban street in the increasingly gloomy
evening.

Sure enough, the tip-tap continued steadily; the woman
didn't seem to be pausing at all. The sound of her progress was
rather lovely, like a metronome tapping out a beat on the
autumnal street. Beth envied her ease in the high heels, especially on the uneven slabs of the pavement. She definitely
would have fallen headlong if she'd attempted to trot along so
fast. Some women were just brilliant in heels, and others, like
her, were destined always to stick very close to the ground with
their footwear, even when they could sorely do with the extra
inches.

Beth hardly dared breathe as the woman came abreast of
the car. Would she see them? Would she say something? Tap on
the window, even, as Belinda had done? But, unfortunately, she
carried on right up the road and out of their field of vision, the
tapping fading away as she went. After all that! She wasn't the
one, then.

Well, it had been unlikely anyway, Beth reasoned. They
were almost certainly looking for a man, someone strong enough
to have strangled the first estate agent and shoved him into that
cupboard. That would have taken a good bit of force, plus large

hands and a nice firm grip, she supposed. Goodness knew what had happened to the second victim; Harry was not divulging a thing, and there still seemed to be a news blackout, too.

Beth knew she couldn't have done either task – the strangling or the stuffing – even if for some incredibly bizarre reason she'd been motivated to kill in the first place. The ramming of the corpse into the larder must have been particularly difficult. She knew that she struggled every week – well, probably every fortnight if she were strictly honest – with her own vacuum cleaner. The long and bendy neck of the contraption and the inflexible body didn't seem to get on well together at the best of times. Certainly, they never seemed to want to return peacefully to the understairs cupboard when she'd finished her labours. There was usually a lot of pushing and shoving involved, which didn't add a jot to the joy of the task.

She shuddered to imagine how much more difficult it must have been to manhandle four lifeless limbs and a lolling head. And bodies were, quite literally, dead weights, weren't they? Even someone young and in reasonable shape like that poor lad would be heavier than several sacks of potatoes. No, it would have to have been a man. Or an unusually strapping woman.

'Who's looking after Jake tonight?' said Nina, now unwrapping a KitKat, snapping it crisply in two and offering half to Beth. Beth considered resisting for a nanosecond, to signal her disapproval of junk food to her friend, and then realised that was utterly pointless. Nina would continue on her merry way whatever Beth did. And who was Beth to talk, anyway? The Haribo wrappers infesting her handbag told their own story. She might as well enjoy a bit of chocolate while it was on offer.

She accepted the bar gratefully, sinking her teeth through the chocolate into the crispy wafer. Yum.

'He's at Charlie's tonight. Harry will be home... but not for a while,' Beth said with some relief. The texter couldn't get his – or her – hands on her boys. She'd been in two minds about Jake going to Katie's, and hadn't really wanted to overburden her friend, who was grappling with Charlie's 'massive' homework load. She had also felt Jake was fine to be left on his own for short periods – but now she was very glad he was in Court Lane.

Harry might well be extremely late back indeed. He was now running a double murder investigation. All leave would have been cancelled, and as he was inevitably running the show, he'd be leading from the top, modelling the kind of dedication and focus that he desperately wanted – and needed – his team to emulate. The constant pressure on resources meant he'd be lucky if he managed to pinch a couple of extra bodies from another department to help out with all the enquiries they'd have to be making.

Being a policeman at Harry's level, nowadays, seemed to Beth to be pretty much akin to being a glorified office manager, sandwiched between the high-ups controlling the purse strings and the lowly uniformed officers who'd be trying to sneak off for the odd hour of sleep. It was no wonder he was so keen to close every case down.

Beth wondered if she'd be like that, if she had to face his choices. But no, she was still filled with the zeal that came of being determined to get justice, or at the very least a result. Harry might tell her she was naïve, but she'd managed it before. And she was going to do it this time, too, she told herself, crunching the last bits of KitKat with relish.

But she didn't want to leave Jake at Charlie's for too long. He'd be having a great time, of course, but it wasn't really fair on Katie, who wanted to keep Charlie at his own personal grindstone. Beth sighed. If only she could get it together to be a proper tiger mother. But she couldn't even muster enough cat energy to give Magpie a run for her money. Jake would just have to muddle through, without the constant pushing that would no doubt see Charlie hurtling through all his exams with flying colours.

Secretly, Beth couldn't help wondering what happened to these kids who were pushed so hard by their parents. One day it wouldn't be appropriate for Katie to be supervising Charlie's every move. When he was finally an investment banker, say. What would happen then? Would he suddenly regress and sit at home all day in his pants with his PlayStation? She was hoping that Jake, by contrast, would have had time to grow out of such childish things gradually and develop into a beautifully mature, sensible adult.

'Can't wait until Wilf is old enough to be left on his tod,' admitted Nina, munching away on what Beth suspected might well be KitKat number two. 'He's back with the neighbour. Same one what had him the other night. He wasn't best pleased, though he likes her telly. It's bigger than ours.'

Beth digested this silently. If the television was larger than Nina's, then it might well be the biggest in the entire world. Nina's flatscreen, state-of-the-art model took up almost one whole wall of her living room. Beth had been a bit shocked when she'd first seen it, which she realised was a silly, and typically Dulwich, reaction. The telly was marvellous. Watching it immersed you in whichever programme you were watching. It was like being at the movies every night, only better.

There was a curious reverse snobbery about tellies operating in SE21. Everybody had one, but everyone also pretended never to watch anything on it. And if they did admit to catching a glimpse of the odd David Attenborough nature show, which seemed to be the only respectable option, they had to insist that their set was small and old. Heaven forfend that you could actually enjoy something so lowbrow as televisual entertainment.

She'd once overheard one of Belinda's cronies boasting that she'd swept into the electrics department at Peter Jones and demanded their smallest, cheapest telly. Another had immediately trumped this by revealing that her own infinitesimal, antique set was actually crammed into a cupboard with the doors tightly locked shut, unless said nature programme was on. Beth inwardly resolved to get a giant telly – as soon as they finally moved house and no one in Dulwich could judge them.

But wait, hadn't Katie said that Belinda had been considering setting up a movie screening room in her basement? That was off-putting. 'Digging out' had suddenly become the new loft conversion, as far as Dulwich was concerned. A few years ago, all the poshest houses had worn plastic sheeting rainhats, as their upper storeys were converted into swish new bedroom suites. Now everything had been turned on its head, and there were skips and monstrous JCB diggers everywhere as underground pools and gyms were embedded beneath the pavements. It wouldn't be long before the entire district fell into an enormous and entirely self-inflicted infinity sink hole.

Maybe if Belinda was determined to recruit her as her new best friend, or at least drag Jake round for playdates with Billy, Beth would have the opportunity to scrutinise the movie room plans for herself. She hadn't been in Belinda's house for ages, and had probably missed at least two complete cycles of interior décor fads. She knew it was silly, but if Belinda was going big on the screen front, Beth now suddenly wanted to go small.

'How much are you paying your neighbour?' Beth asked Nina idly, to fill the time as much as anything.

For surveillance, you had to have endless patience, and if you were working with Nina, a very weak sense of smell. Beth wrinkled her nose as Nina ripped open another crisp packet. The reek of something that a white-coated technician in a lab had blithely thought might approximate cheddar cheese and red onion was filling the car. It was actually a lot closer to the stench of Jake's ancient football boots.

Beth quickly wound down the window a little way, and fat droplets of rain splattered on her hand and leg and, more ominously, on the panel of window control buttons. Dr Grover's comments about the rustiness of her little Fiat might have been mean, but that didn't mean to say they weren't accurate. She didn't need any water in her electrics, that was for sure. She closed the window regretfully, decided to take very shallow breaths for a while, and looked out into the gathering darkness instead.

'Not paying her,' Nina said, from deep inside the bag. 'Just doing stuff in kind, you know.'

'Oh, does she have kids, too?' Beth asked.

'Rottweilers,' Nina mumbled.

Hmm. Beth was now imagining poor little Wilf, sitting in front of a telly much bigger than he was, surrounded by slavering dogs. It was really quite worrying. 'Did she say how long she'd have him for?'

'Nah, she's chillaxed, isn't she?'

Beth was silent. She couldn't imagine anything less calming than owning multiple Rottweilers. She still knew so little about dogs, despite her surprising stewardship of Colin. But Colin was more of a person than a real dog, she reasoned, with his innate ability to be so much more considerate than most of the humans that she shared her life with. An irresistible vision of Harry's boxes popped into her mind, towering over her and her house. And she'd already mused on Jake's rancid boots.

Yes, Colin was a gent, all right. Even his horrible habit of goosing her friends was something he seemed to persist with out of an obscure sense of obligation, like an eighteenth-century dandy who'd been misinformed that the ladies required that little special attention. But a pack of Rottweilers? She hoped that their owner was feeding them properly. Tiny Wilf might well appear quite a tasty morsel.

'Do you take them for walks, then?' Beth couldn't help smiling at the idea of little round Nina being towed along by a number of big strong dogs, like a water-skier in her white puffa jacket.

'Nah. Wilf does.'

Beth saw Wilf in a new light, and with a great deal of respect. He was obviously a dog whisperer. Jake, by contrast, would be having a very easy time of it. Despite his built-in resistance, Katie would have forced him and Charlie through at least some of the homework he was bound to have, like a sergeant-major knocking a bunch of squaddies into line. But by now they would have been released into their natural habitat – Charlie's fabulous playroom. Its shelves of expensive toys were now untouched, and the only thing that got much use was the sofa opposite the (by Dulwich standards, not by Nina's) large TV, which was permanently hooked up to the latest PlayStation must-have.

Beth had spent so much of her life worrying about the effects of these games, their addictive consequences and the wider problems that would occur if Jake applied their mores to the world at large. It was a huge relief that tonight, he was round at lovely Katie's and her friend would have to do the wrestling with her conscience. The trouble was that it now did seem quite hard to occupy boys if they weren't plugged into a device and trying to kill things.

At that age, Beth's brother, Josh, had started to become interested in photography – admittedly probably so he could pester girls to pose for him. But at least that had involved human interaction, and with the opposite sex to boot. Jake was still too young for that, Beth thought quickly, but the time would come... Yet would he ever even meet a girl, attending a boys' school and spending the rest of his time attacking pretend aliens?

All the old hobbies, making model airplanes, collecting stamps, even getting interested in train sets, now seemed unspeakably slow. And, to be honest, she wouldn't be that thrilled if her beloved boy shrugged on an anorak and spent his weekends noting down train chassis numbers at North Dulwich Station. But there must be something in between old-school geekery and internet destruction. Something Jake would be able to look back on when he was a man, and remember doing with pride. Surely all the computer gaming would just morph into one big Super-Mario-Fortnite-Call-of-Grand-Theft-Tetris? His whole childhood was going to be a blur, with maybe a catchy little earworm of a soundtrack, if he was lucky.

Luckily, Nina jolted her out of her thoughts.

'Look, over there. What's that?'

Instantly, Beth was upright and peering. Unfortunately, it didn't get her far. The car had inexorably misted up, whether through Nina's pungent ersatz cheese fumes or just the results of a bit of chit-chat in a confined space. Beth rubbed at the window with her sleeve, but the pattern of raindrops on the outside blurred everything as effectively as Vaseline on a lens.

'I can't see a thing. What's going on? What are you looking at?'

'Can't you see him? There, there,' said Nina urgently, stabbing with a finger.

But Beth could see nothing but darkness in front of her, and pitch blackness to the side. True, there were some blurry shapes over by Nina, but they could have been a gang of killers, or equally they could have been wheelie bins, marshalled on the pavement for collection day. Rubbing a circle in the condensation had failed. There was nothing for it but to crank the window down a tiny bit and hope that whoever – or whatever – was outside didn't hear. She'd just have to ignore the rain if it pattered in on her, and hope it wouldn't blow any fuses either. There were worse things than a wet arm and a stalled car. Like a dead estate agent, for instance.

Through the tiny gap in the misty window, Beth saw to her horror that there was, indeed, a dark figure in a hoody strolling past them. His gait – she was pretty sure it was a he – was silent, thanks to his springy-looking trainers, and was unhurried, confident, his stride swinging out in a business-like way. He knew where he was going, and he would get there fast. Just when she was thinking that someone so purposeful couldn't possibly be up to anything nefarious, he paused, darted a quick look in both directions, and seemed to zoom in on the car.

Both Beth and Nina instinctively ducked down, then Beth realised this was probably the biggest giveaway of their presence they could have offered, short of sending up a flare or tooting on the horn. They should have just stayed stock-still. She'd have to hope that the interior was so steamed up he hadn't seen them moving. But wouldn't that, in itself, be suspicious? What could cause windows to fog up so much, except for people lurking inside, spying away? Beth could only hope the man wasn't that much into logic.

The figure stayed still for a long, long moment, and Beth felt the pulse beat in her head. It was as though all the blood in her body had suddenly become loud. Much too loud. Without moving, she glanced over at Nina, and found her friend was staring right back at her. Their terrified gazes locked. Nina's cherubic little mouth opened in a perfect O; it looked very much as though she was on the verge of a good old bout of shrieking. Very slowly, Beth put her finger up to her lips. Nina nodded infinitesimally, eyes still wide, the whites shining out in the darkness.

Then whoever it was moved seamlessly forward again, and loped right through the garden gate of the house the women were waiting outside.

Nina and Beth stared at each other, nonplussed. Beth had never really thought, for one single solitary moment, that something would actually happen while they were sitting here. Now she was wasting time, while murder might be being done inside. Did she want another pale corpse on her conscience? She took out her phone with a shaking hand, and dialled Harry. Of course, it went straight to voicemail. Then she threw the phone to Nina and scrabbled with the door handle.

'Call 999 – or whatever the hell it is these days,' she yelled, before wrenching the car open at last and dashing down the path into looming darkness.

Nina, grabbing the phone and pressing its buttons randomly, gasped as a text message flashed up on the screen: *I warned you not to meddle. Now you'll never see that stinking old furball of a cat again.*

TWENTY-FOUR

Beth sat in her kitchen, her hand still shaking, and thought over the events of the past twenty-four hours. If it hadn't been for that chance encounter with Belinda, she would never have pieced together the connection between the murders and Barty's Dulwich estate agent friend. Imagine being so desperate to drive up house prices that you would stoop to murder, Beth shuddered. When had people round here grown so amoral? What was the matter with them all?

The house was quiet; the way she liked it. Both the men in her life were out. Harry was dealing with the aftermath of the case; Jake had trooped off to school ages ago. Beth, however, was giving herself a day off. A duvet day, though she hadn't quite managed to stay in bed. There was too much going round and round in her head. Now she sat at the kitchen table, with Colin on her feet. His presence was such a comfort. She reached down and stroked him while he looked round the room, stared at Magpie's empty bowl and whined briefly. 'I know, boy,' she said quietly. 'I know.'

She sighed, shook her head and picked up the newspaper, scanning the headlines. The journalist seemed to have put together all the facts in record time. Facts that had taken Beth much too long to assemble herself. *Local Businessman Charged with Killings*. She wondered if Harry had just told them what to write. Well, top marks for getting it in the paper so quickly.

She read the story avidly, though she knew it inside out by now. Piers Frampton's plan had been a simple but terrible one: to shore up prices in SE21 by wrecking the market in outlying areas. Every nought that dropped off the end of a price in Dulwich meant a hammer blow to the heart of the poor old investment bankers and brokers who lived here. Not that they were poor in monetary terms, but they definitely felt under threat, from the fuel crisis and the fear that London's housing market was finally crashing, and the general mood of anxiety in the country. They were people who spent their lives striving. Mostly striving for more, but sometimes striving only to stay exactly where they already were.

Beth did have a sneaking sympathy. Everyone wanted to protect what they had; it was an ancient instinct, which ensured the race's survival. And she knew she possessed it strongly herself. But you could definitely take it too far.

For Barty's friend, Piers, the evil scheme had been working like a charm. The deaths in Sydenham had meant the property market there had more or less collapsed. He'd paid hitmen to bump off the poor hapless estate agents. For someone with his wealth, it had only taken a whisper or two in the dodgy pubs on the other side of the Thames, and the deeds had been done.

Beth had virtually been the only person still looking around in Sydenham, and that was only because she was interested in the murderer, not the properties. He'd found out about her enquiries, thanks to bloody Belinda McKenzie, and had started texting her to frighten her off. Well, it hadn't worked, she tutted, then felt the weight of guilt as Colin shifted restlessly at her feet again.

Beth turned back to the paper. You couldn't currently give

away one of the grand houses around Sydenham with a packet of cornflakes. Meanwhile, Dulwich prices had zoomed up: the area was perceived more than ever to be a tiny safe harbour in the swirling mayhem that was south-east London. People would pay a premium to feel safe.

This reinforced Beth's own problem, and made a bigger place in the village all the more unobtainable. Yes, her own house was worth more as a consequence of this man's terrible actions, but then so were all the others that she'd like to move to. It was like reaching for the top shelf, only to find you were always one rung of the ladder too low. A problem that Beth was all too familiar with.

When she was younger, she would never have thought that places in Herne Hill or Honor Oak would be changing hands for millions of pounds. She, of all people, knew the pangs of being priced out of her childhood home, forced further afield. But it went without saying that she wouldn't hurt the tiniest sparrow to change the situation; let alone murder the innocent to keep her bank balance healthy. Unlike Belinda and Barty's close friend, Piers, Beth was no monster.

Her hands reached out to clasp her mug of tea, partly to stop the tremors, partly to suck up some warmth. They were well into autumn and the house was chilly during the day. The central heating now worked perfectly, thank goodness, but was timed only to click on once Jake was back.

There was a sort of irony in it all, she thought. She'd been to what seemed like a thousand dinner parties where the topic on everyone's lips had been the stresses of buying a house. Of course, these people meant it entirely in a First World problem sort of way. They could all afford not only removal men but packers and unpackers too, so up- or downsizing was just a question of driving to the new place and waiting while someone else brought your stuff in. That was discombobulating enough,

Beth didn't want to downplay the strain at all. Moving could be murder; everybody said so.

But trust a cold-hearted Dulwich businessman to make that statement literally true.

Beth shivered. Confronting that boy in his hoody had not been the bravest thing she'd ever done. It was one of the stupidest, though; right up there with some of the other hare-brained notions she'd developed over the past couple of years. This time, however, it had been exactly the right thing to do.

She replayed it in her head: her mad dash up the path, her pixie boots squeaking and slipping on the slick surface. The way she had pretty much fallen headlong into the back of the hooded figure. So much for stealth, she chided herself. But in the event, it hadn't turned out too badly. Though no one could deny she was very, very small, Beth was no willow wand. The young lad, being rushed from behind by the equivalent of a Shetland pony with the bit between its teeth, and standing as he was on slippery terracotta tiles (an attractive original Edwardian chequerboard feature, as the property details no doubt proclaimed), went over like a very obliging ninepin, whacking his head on the little porch balustrade as he did so.

Nina, sitting in the car, having dropped Beth's phone on the floor in shock and then fumbled to dial the right number, had sighed with relief as the man lay still, then she'd clambered out to comfort her friend and keep an eye on the inert body in front of her.

It hadn't been long until the distinctive wail of sirens had caused neighbouring curtains to twitch. Beth saw the cold blue lights advancing towards her. As usual, she tensed, expecting a very cross Harry to stride up and yell at her. But this time, it was the comforting yellow and white stripes of an ambulance instead. The youth in the hoody was soon strapped up and shipped away, and Beth and Nina clambered back into the car, exhausted.

Nina had turned to look at her. 'Home?' she had said expectantly. 'Listen, babe, I don't know how to tell you, but you need to get back...'

But Beth had shaken her head and flatly refused to listen. She had something here she badly needed to do. She'd extended her hand, and then opened up her fingers. The street light had been just enough to show a silvery gleam. In her outstretched palm lay a front door key.

TWENTY-FIVE

Beth wasn't proud of what she'd done next. Nina was an irrepressible character, a bender of rules, a person who organised things to suit herself – but crucially, she wasn't a lawbreaker. Beth, by contrast, knew that she believed very firmly in abstract notions like justice, and right and wrong. But she was perfectly happy to transgress petty regulations sometimes, if she felt the situation demanded it.

Nina, already late for Wilf, and showing much less interest in the case than Beth had expected, had been extremely reluctant to set foot in the house.

'But we've got to see what's been going on. See who's behind all this,' Beth had said.

'It was that guy in the hoody, and he's off to A&E now. Hope he's having to wait three hours to get seen,' said Nina truculently. 'Anyways, I need to get back for Wilfie, and you've got to—'

'Oh, come on, Nina. Let's just have a tiny look,' said Beth.

And it was too late to turn back. She was already back up the path, sliding the key into the lock, opening up the door and beckoning Nina to follow her. She knew it wouldn't be long before the police showed up. An unexplained serious injury outside a house in Sydenham? That was going to be called in pronto, and it wouldn't take Harry long to join the dots. She wanted to be in and out before that happened.

In the end, Beth remembered, it had been just as she expected. The downstairs had been the usual tired sort of décor that movers would want to leave behind, and buyers would want to rip out. As she had thought, though, it was a bit of a different story in the bedrooms.

Nina had been literally clinging onto Beth's jacket, begging her to turn round and go home, as they'd wound their way up the creaking stairs. Beth had held out her phone on torch mode and they'd followed the wavering beam of light. The first two bedrooms had been empty and blameless, though Beth had distantly admired their high ceilings, through habit alone. The family bathroom was a bit tired but otherwise fine. It was the third bedroom which had seen all the action. Here, there were unmistakable signs of very recent occupation: the duvet was rumpled; there were clothes strewn around the room; there was a whiffy old takeaway on the bedside table; and, bingo, an open laptop on a desk by the curtained windows.

It was just as Beth had deduced. The hoody boy, now probably suffering a concussion, had not been living here. He must have been sent by Frampton to bump off another estate agent – or to put the frighteners on Beth herself, she realised. His clothes, from what Beth had seen as he lay full-length on the ground, had been the cheapest chain-store buys, well-worn and not that clean. The pile of discarded belongings here, on the other hand, bore all the latest labels and were brand new. The laptop was a top-of-the-range MacBook, and lying in a corner there were even some noise-cancelling headphones that would have cost the best part of three hundred quid. Yet whoever had been living here had actually just been one more homeless person – warmer and drier than the poor souls who clustered outside central London's stations, but just as itinerant.

Back in her own kitchen, in her beloved Pickwick Road home, with her lonely dog, Beth put her head in her hands, thinking the whole scene over. It was such a tough world now, even for the children of Dulwich. She knew her heart shouldn't bleed for such lucky and privileged kids, but it wasn't all plain sailing being brought up like this.

Nurtured so carefully, educated so expensively, in many ways these kids seemed to have a charmed life, especially from the outside. But there was always a price to pay. The type of parents who had spent a fortune from playschool onwards expected a return on their investment. They were doctors, bankers, lawyers and, in exchange for their hard-earned cash, they wanted a troupe of mini-doctors, bankers and lawyers following in their wake. If this outcome didn't arrive right on schedule, they were disappointed.

Beth, of all people, knew from her mother's sidelong glances and sighs what a body-blow it could be when a parent felt their flesh and blood had not come up to scratch. And she had so often felt the needle-sharp jabs that were Wendy's surreptitious revenge. God, she hoped she'd never feel that sense of let-down and resentment towards Jake. At the moment, she assumed she'd just be thrilled if he got a job, any job, at some point down the line. But then, realistically, she was making so many compromises and sacrifices to keep him at Wyatt's, not least the move away from her beloved Dulwich. Wouldn't she, too, end up bitter if her boy didn't make the most of the chances she'd given him, at such cost to herself? If he ended up as a squatter in an empty house, wouldn't she be gutted? Or would leaving the hothouse of SE21 actually improve all their chances of remaining sane? The jury was out.

That thought brought her inexorably back to the property issue, which lay at the heart of these murders. The children of

Dulwich, however well or badly they'd fared in the exam system, were inevitably pushed out of the nest in the end, though that was happening later and later these days. And then no sooner had they gone than they now seemed to boomerang right back. It wasn't so unusual to find that what had once been the au pair's attic room had been hastily recolonised by a twenty-something who'd graduated but then failed to snare a job, or had a so-called internship instead. These were supposed to be a means of garnering experience, and the prospect of a legitimate job was always dangling somewhere on the horizon, but really they meant long stints of unpaid labour. Only those with well-off parents need apply. Who, in less wealthy circles, could go on supporting an adult child for year after year? And internships meant these kidults couldn't pay their parents any rent, much less scrape together the sizeable chunks of cash necessary for a deposit on their own homes.

Getting a foot on the housing ladder had never been easy. Now it was like jumping onto a moving high-speed train. No wonder the little network of illegal squatters had grown up – gently-born Dulwich boys and girls, just trying to enjoy some sort of independence, however illusory it really was. They must have been swapping addresses together on social media, and moving on when sales were eventually brokered. All they'd needed was one contact in an estate agency to tip them off when the type of chain-free, empty property they needed was available. Beth thought irresistibly of the chunky wristwatch that had encircled Richard Pettit's pale wrist.

In the current stagnant market, hardly any sales were being made, so Pettit's legitimate commission must have dried up. In this state of stasis, those who could go elsewhere to rent outside London, where things were cheaper, did so. They left their properties empty – and, as Beth had seen, such houses were ripe for exploitation. A hundred here and there meant a bed for a month, while legitimate London rents were eight to ten times as high. For the Dulwich dispossessed, it was the perfect way to find a temporary roost. And the money had meant a Rolex for young Richard Pettit – not that he'd had much time to enjoy it.

It was just unfortunate – and here Beth shook her head, and selected another, much more appropriate adjective: *tragic* – that an evil businessman had decided to make this sad situation worse. He wasn't preying on these wandering twenty-somethings, though. Even here, Piers Frampton had remained true to Dulwich snobbery. Perhaps he hadn't even known about the squatting racket. Beth was pretty sure he wouldn't have wanted to put his neighbours' children at risk. No, the ones he'd paid to have bumped off were the expendable young estate agents. Poor Richard Pettit fell into that category, and so too did Trevor Pinker – the second lad to die. In a way, Beth was glad to read his name in the paper – at last, he'd been identified and acknowledged. Somewhere, there would be a family deep in mourning. But not in Dulwich.

These boys had never been part of life in SE21, so – in Frampton's view – Pettit and Pinker been expendable. Killing them had been a way of perpetuating the Dulwich property bubble, a system that was bringing in money for him, and by extension excluding so many from the next step on the road to adult independence.

It was a truly horrible crime. And, Beth thought in disgust, it was probably the most snobby of all those she'd come across so far. The fact that the Trustafarian, nomadic kids had been spared, that only the worker bees had been so cruelly picked off, was bad enough. But the whole idea had been designed to shore up something that was iniquitous in the first place – the bonkers state of the London housing market. All these elements combined to make the murders so full of evil intent, on every level, that Beth reeled from them. Give her good old-fashioned lust and anger as motives any time. Greed made for the coldest of crimes.

And Piers Frampton had hardly even got his own hands dirty; he'd hired people to do his foul work for him. Harry had been right to tie the deaths to drug culture, to that extent anyway. The criminal gangs running parts of London meant there was no shortage of lowlifes willing to do a bit of freelance work when required – if the price was right. But the texts to Beth's phone did tie Frampton securely to his dastardly plot. Though he'd withheld the number, his subterfuge was no match for the Met's digital forensics.

Beth eyed the cat flap in the kitchen door. London sometimes seemed like no place for poor innocent pets. Or children. Or grown women for that matter.

Yet London was still the place where all the plum jobs were. Young people had no choice but to cling on here, as close to the centre as they could manage, fleeced by landlords, paying hand over fist for the rubbishy rail service, and working for free to crown it all.

The youth of today, thought Beth. Once upon a time, people had shaken their heads saying those words, decrying the lax morals and declining standards they encapsulated. Yet now the young seemed to have such a raw deal – state education was struggling; universities charged a fortune; jobs were scarce and insecure. Beth's own job often seemed hand-to-mouth and wasn't going to cover all her outgoings, now that Jake's Wyatt's bills would be thumping in once a term. But at least she had one. And there was a roof over her family's head. They had possibilities – they could relocate and reduce the school fee crunch.

And she also had another option, one that she had been resisting for a long time. She could touch her mother, Wendy, for some money. As Wendy had crowed loudly and often, her husband had left her very comfortably off when he'd died so suddenly. Wendy had precious few outgoings, save the fees at her beloved Bridge club. Would she begrudge her only grandson? Given the way that Josh flitted from woman to woman, Jake was probably the only grandchild she was going to get. Presumably he'd inherit something from her in the end. Would it be so wrong if Beth asked her mother to pre-empt any arrangements she might be considering making in her will?

Beth's skin crawled at the very thought. She hated asking for favours and loathed being beholden to people. She was never keen on admitting she needed help, whether it be heavy lifting or, in this case, the loan of thousands of pounds. But beggars couldn't be choosers. Or couldn't be if they wanted to stay put, anyway.

So, she had alternatives to consider, even if some weren't attractive. She was much better off than most people, who didn't have the luxury of any sort of choice, she knew that.

Beth blew out her breath. The case was closed, much to her relief; never had anything made her feel so grubby. She was glad, so glad, that the awful Piers Frampton would be locked up, even if it offered Belinda McKenzie yet another reason to hate her. But it wasn't Beth's fault if another of the woman's friends had turned out to be certifiable.

Nor had there been a link with the Suzy Lamplugh case from long ago. That now seemed to be a different sort of crime altogether. Beth was sad she couldn't find anything that might assuage that family's dreadful pain, but maybe she'd been deluded in thinking everything would tie up neatly with a nice bow. Life wasn't always like that, as she kept being shown.

She always hoped and strived for resolutions, but there was another mystery still to be solved – Belinda's connection with Dr Grover, and Dr Grover's curious mention of '*activities*'. The more Beth thought about that, the more she came to believe that Janice's fears had been, thank goodness, groundless. Like Janice herself, she had to conclude that the head's explanation passed muster. He must have been helping Belinda and Barty McKenzie with Billy. Although that meant he was hanging out with Belinda far more than was really necessary, it wasn't for the pleasure of her company.

Thank goodness Janice had decided to draw a line under the whole business. Endless broken nights could give rise to a lot of odd thoughts, as Beth remembered. As soon as her beautiful daughter Elizabeth was sleeping better, Janice's fears would no doubt seem as far-fetched as a July frost over the school playing fields.

And, courtesy of all the hoo-ha, Harry seemed to have cooled in his enthusiasm for moving. No one wanted to think they were buying into a system leading to misery and murder. When Beth had caught sight of his phone this morning before he shot off, she was pretty sure he'd even deleted the Rightmove app from his home screen.

Perhaps that was because, when she finally made it home from the police station last night after making her interminable statement and after ascertaining that the boy in the hoody was going to be fine, Colin had gnawed his way right through several of the policeman's big boxes of books. True to form, Colin had been extremely thorough. The volumes that hadn't been chewed to a pulp had been very comprehensively slobbered over. It was almost as though the old dog thought there was something edible in there, mused Beth, eyeing an empty box of dog treats poking out of the bin. That reminded her, she really must take the rubbish out.

Without so many books to shelve, they'd actually have just about enough space right where they were.

And seeing Harry's woebegone face at the terrible state of his books had meant that Beth had been flooded with a sudden surge of love, affection and possibly guilt, which had led to an enthusiastic celebration of their relationship. She half-smiled. He'd certainly gone off to work that morning with a bit more of a spring in his step. And, despite everything, she was feeling a lot more optimistic about the future, too.

Staying put wouldn't solve the Wyatt's fees problem, that was still pressing... but she'd put off that phone call to Wendy for now. She ambled over to the kettle, flicked the switch and shoved a fresh teabag into her mug. As the kettle chugged into noisy, steamy life, Beth told herself she just had to take one thing at a time.

She walked over to the French doors, looking into the scrubby, cold garden beyond. There, right outside the door, was Magpie's favourite tree, its branches standing bare and empty.

Beth relived her return home, full of dread, and her frantic search through the house, with a heart growing heavier and heavier at every step, the words of the evil text echoing in her mind.

It had been a relief beyond all others when she'd eventually thought to look outside, and spotted the verdant gleam of highly disapproving feline eyes.

Magpie was still looking distinctly militant, so far refusing all blandishments to come back in. She must have had quite a run-in with Piers' lackey. It was no real surprise when Harry discovered at the hospital that the boy in the hoody from the Sydenham house had several rows of bright red parallel lines scored into his arms on both sides. He must have been too cowardly to confess his failure to Frampton.

Magpie wasn't going to forgive and forget in a hurry, that was for sure. Beth felt another stab of guilt, at putting her beloved pet in danger. But suddenly that phrase, 'Sufficient unto the day is the evil thereof,' popped into her head again. It was so very Dulwich. And so very true. Magpie was fine, her boys were good, and Colin was just lovely. Things were a lot brighter this morning than they had been for ages.

Beth looked round her pristine kitchen, in her beloved house in the heart of SE21, and broke into the sunniest of smiles.

A LETTER FROM ALICE

Thank you so much for choosing to read my book. I love writing about Beth Haldane and I hope you've enjoyed finding out what she got up to this time. If you'd like to know what happens to Beth next, please sign up at the email link below. Your email address will never be shared and you can unsubscribe at any time.

www.bookouture.com/alice-castle

If you enjoyed the story, I would be very grateful if you could write a review. I'd love to hear what you think. I always read reviews and I take careful account of what people say. My aim is always to make the books a better read! Leaving a review also helps new readers to discover my books for the first time.

I'm also on Twitter, Facebook and Goodreads, often sharing pictures of cats that look like Magpie. Do get in touch if that's your sort of thing. Thanks so much again, and I really hope to see you soon for Beth's next adventure. Happy reading!

Alice Castle

Alicecastleauthor.com